THE HEADLESS ARCHER

THE LELANDIS ADVENTURES
BOOK ONE

THE

HEADLESS

ARCHER

THOMAS BERRY

This story is dedicated to you.

Thank you for picking up my book. I am an independent author, and this is my first novel. I would love to write for a living, so if you enjoy this story, please recommend it to friends and family.

Contents

CHAPTER ONE

The Story of the Headless Archer

Long before humans built cities and learned to write, when we dwelled in caves and hunted with spears, we looked at the night sky in wonder. The thousands of visible stars are part of our swirling galaxy. Beyond these stars, there are countless more in countless other galaxies spanning distances that baffle the mind. The sun is our star, and every other star in the Universe could be orbited by planets like Earth, where life thrives. Is there somewhere that lies beyond our Universe? Our ancestors knew very little about the specks of light in the night sky, but they created stories inspired by them. As we have understood more, we have learned that we know so little. There are mysteries all around us, waiting to be revealed, but only to those with curious minds.

Beneath a clear night sky, in a clearing on the grounds of Bridgeward Estate, a semi-circle of tents surrounded a crackling campfire. It was a warm night, and the Milky Way could be seen arching overhead. A half-moon gently illuminated the campsite, but the surrounding woods were dark. An owl sat perched on the branch of an ancient oak tree, watching as three adults prepared for the night's stargazing. There was not a breath of wind, but the tents still fluttered with the activity of excitable students within. It was the final night of a school activity weekend, and the students had been told to rest in their tents as night fell and the stars emerged. Unsurprisingly, there was very little resting.

The inside of Sam, Colin and Joe's tent looked like a meteorite had hit it. Damp socks, mucky trainers, sweet wrappers and sleeping bags were spread everywhere. The three friends sat scoffing their last reserves of sweets.

"Does anyone know any good ghost stories?" asked Joe, a small boy with big glasses and floppy hair.

"You're definitely in the right tent," answered Sam with his mouth full of chewy toffee. "I reckon Colin has been waiting all weekend for someone to ask."

"Oh yes!" replied Colin with his eyes widening. "What do you want to hear about? The Plague Town goblins? Or the haunted tunnels beneath the Old Fort? Or maybe—"

"Come on, Colin, you big bookworm," interrupted Sam, "tell us about the Headless Archer! After all, we are camping in his woods!" Sam was a lean and sporty boy who always wore colourful football shirts. In contrast, Colin was stocky, clumsy and always wore black. He was also a proud bookworm.

Colin rummaged in his rucksack and pulled out a small, crimson book with elaborate gold writing adorning its cover. A musty smell filled the tent as Colin flicked through the book's pages.

"I picked this beauty up at a car-boot sale a few weeks ago," Colin exclaimed. "It's almost a hundred years old. Aha! The Story of the Headless Archer."

Colin took his torch and placed it beneath his chin to light the underside of his round face. He paused to build up tension and then began to read the story.

"Many years ago, before the Old Town was abandoned after the Black Death, the people of Bridgeward endured a year of terrible pestilence and famine. The winter was bitterly cold, the spring was terribly wet, and the summer was unbearably hot. Crops failed, livestock died, and the people of Bridgeward starved. The Lord and his family hoarded what food was grown and feasted on venison, pheasant and other game hunted on their estate. As their waistlines grew, so did the resentment of the people of Bridgeward.

"That summer, a young archer returned home from the

battlefields of France where he had been fighting for the King of England. He strode through the town to his family home with his longbow slung over his shoulder, his quiver around his waist and a worn canvas satchel by his side. His mother, father and sister were delighted to see him. Beaming smiles appeared on their gaunt faces, and happiness filled their hearts even though their stomachs were empty.

"The archer's parents had no food to offer their son after his long journey, and he quickly learned of the greed of the Lord and the suffering of the people of Bridgeward. Angered by the injustice, the archer set off for the Lord's estate with his longbow and quiver. Before the sun set that evening, he returned to Bridgeward with a deer over his shoulders. That night his family feasted like the Lord in his manor. It had been a long time since they had gone to bed with their stomachs full.

"Early the following day, the archer was awoken by angry shouts and loud banging on the door. The Lord had heard about the hunting of his deer, and his men had been ordered to make an example of the archer. The archer was seized from his bed and dragged to the town centre with his shirt loose, his belt swinging from his waist and no shoes on his feet. The Lord's men rang the town bell, and a large crowd gathered. The archer was wrestled into the town stocks. His head and arms protruded uncomfortably from the rough holes in the heavy oak clamp. The people of Bridgeward were ordered to throw their rotten food at him, but no one did.

"The archer lifted his head as high as he could and spoke to the Lord's men, 'You fools! Do you think these people have any rotten food to throw? They don't have enough to eat! There is no waste here. If you want rotten food, go to the Lord's manor. You'll find unfinished dishes from last night's feast, although you'll be lucky if anyone is stupid enough to throw what can be eaten.' As the archer spoke, the Lord appeared on horseback, his face bloated with rage. The crowd remained impassive. They admired the bravery of the archer, but they feared the Lord and his men.

"The Lord dismounted, unsheathed his sword and marched towards the archer. 'I do not care if you horrible creatures starve,' he shouted, gesturing angrily with his sword. 'You are of no concern to me, until that is, one of you hunts on my estate. If no one will throw their food, I will take matters into my own hands!'

"With these words, the Lord raised his sword high above his head and brought it down upon the neck of the archer. The archer's severed head fell to the ground. There were gasps and screams from the crowd at the unexpected cruelty. The Lord ordered that no one should touch the head and body of the archer. The crowd dispersed, night fell, and the town of Bridgeward was filled with sadness.

"The next morning, birds sang as the sun rose. The people of Bridgeward awoke to find that the body and head of the archer had disappeared, and the stocks had been smashed to pieces. Brightly coloured dragonflies darted around the splintered oak shards; flashes of electric blue, neon yellow and bright red.

"On Bridgeward Estate, the Lord was preparing for a hunt. Black clouds were forming in the sky. The Lord rode towards the woods as the rain began to fall. By the time he reached the woods, the rain was pouring, and the wind was howling through the trees. Branches and acorns were thrown to the ground, and brightly coloured dragonflies appeared mysteriously. The Lord's horse stopped suddenly, rose on its hind legs and released a blood-curdling bray. Among the trees stood the archer. His right arm was raised aloft, holding the bedraggled, wet hair of his dangling head. 'You shall not be returning to the manor for a feast today, Lord!' the archer shouted. 'These woods are now mine, and anyone who sets foot in them is mine to hunt, beginning with you!'

"With these words, the Headless Archer placed his head in his old canvas satchel and threw it over his shoulder. He nocked an arrow in his longbow, pulled the string back and shot the arrow straight through the Lord's cold heart. The Lord staggered backwards and fell against the glistening wet trunk of a wild apple tree. In the Lord's dying moments, he saw the Headless Archer turn and disappear through the falling rain, followed by the bright and brilliant dragonflies.

"From that day, the Archer became a soulless spectre haunting the woods of Bridgeward Estate. He who was once a brave and honest man became a shadow, trapped between our world and the next. He exists in the shadows of the trees, on gusts of wild winds and in the storm's thunder. With the dragonflies by his side, he hunts anyone who enters his woods."

There was a moment of silence when Colin finished the story. The silence was broken by Joe, whose voice was muffled by the sleeping bag he was hiding under, "I'm not sure I want to go stargazing anymore…"

"Awesome story, Colin!" exclaimed Sam. "It's not real, Joe. Don't be such a softie. Besides, how could someone aim an arrow with their head in a satchel? Oh, wait a minute, maybe he has telescopic nipples?" Sam lifted his football shirt over his head to reveal his torso. "I see you, Joe!" He said in a mock scary voice.

"Yeah, I suppose you're right," Joe said, laughing. "Besides, we've got Mr Montero to protect us. We all know he was in the SAS, right?"

"Absolutely!" replied Colin sarcastically. "And he's a black belt in Tor Kin Non Sens."

Mr Montero was a P.E. teacher. He was shaped like a big oak cupboard, and he moved with about as much fluidity. His broad shoulders were perfect for carrying the large chip he chose to burden himself with. In contrast, Miss Wilson was a very modest and sensible geography teacher. She was the youngest teacher at school and also the smallest. She wore old-fashioned clothes she bought in charity shops, and her hair was always tied up. There was a rumour that she had been a talented sportswoman before becoming a teacher, but Miss Wilson never spoke about this.

Mr Montero had never been a talented sportsman. However, if making up stories about sporting achievements was a sport, he would have been a world champion. Everyone at school had heard about how he 'once had a trial for Manchester United', 'once knocked out a heavyweight boxer' and 'once turned down a chance to play rugby for England'.

The two teachers sat on logs next to the campfire, talking casually to the Head Instructor of the activity weekend. The sun had set less than an hour before, with its rays penetrating the clouds that sat on the horizon. It had been a beautiful summer day.

"How do you feel this weekend has gone?" asked the Head Instructor. "It's the first time we've run a camp on the grounds of Bridgeward Estate."

"I've enjoyed most of it," replied Mr Montero, not considering that the Head Instructor might be more interested in the students and not the teachers. "The orienteering reminded me of my time in the SAS."

"Yes, the students did enjoy the orienteering," added Miss Wilson, who chose to ignore Mr Montero's spurious claim to have been in the SAS (an elite unit of the British Army). "There is so much space on the estate. A number of the children have said they enjoyed the high ropes course too, although some of the less adventurous children found it quite a challenge".

"They need to toughen up," exclaimed Mr Montero. "Some of these kids are right little softies."

Miss Wilson found Mr Montero exceptionally annoying, particularly when he talked over her and tried to take control of situations she had under perfect control. However, she chose to hide her annoyance because she felt this was the polite thing to do. She also hid how much she enjoyed watching the students mock Mr Montero.

"I'm glad to hear that the students have had fun," continued the Head Instructor. "This place has so much potential. Rumour has it there's a cave complex somewhere beyond the old orchard. I'm going to ask a colleague to investigate it. We might also be able to take over some of the outbuildings. The estate's administrators are very keen to start paying off the Lord's debts."

"There have been a lot of rumours about Bridgeward Estate recently," Miss Wilson replied. "Do you know what has been happening?"

"I know probably as much as you and anyone else who lives in Bridgeward. People have always said that the Lord is an honest and pleasant man, so the criminal investigation came as a great surprise. The police still haven't got to the bottom of it. There are rumours of massive financial irregularities and widespread money laundering. A board of administrators is now looking after the estate."

"I'd love to look inside the manor," said Miss Wilson. She looked beyond the campfire and along an avenue of trees to where the manor stood proudly in front of a half-moon. "It's beautiful but spooky. Have you seen the headless statues standing in the archways of the manor's veranda? And the gargoyle sculptures on the roof? No wonder this place has that ghost story about the Headless Archer."

"Nonsense!" exclaimed Mr Montero, spotting an opportunity to be brave. "There's no such thing as the Headless Archer."

Miss Wilson and the Head Instructor did not need this pointed out to them. The Head Instructor ventured an explanation, "The Story of the Headless Archer started after the English Reformation when some people knocked the heads off the statues on Bridgeward Estate because they disliked idols."

Mr Montero knew nothing about the English Reformation, and he had no idea what idols were, but unlike a smart person, who would enjoy the opportunity to learn something new, Mr Montero just ignored the Head Instructor and began daydreaming about being a wrestler.

Meanwhile, Sam, Colin and Joe were still gobbling sweets in their tent. Sam proposed an idea; they should sneak out of their tent, pretend to be the Headless Archer, and scare some other students. This was, of course, a very silly idea, but boys are good at coming up with silly ideas when their spirits are high and their blood sugar levels are even higher. It was unanimously agreed that this was an excellent plan. The boys picked up their torches and snuck out of their tent.

Miss Wilson, Mr Montero and the Head Instructor were still quietly preparing for stargazing beside the campfire. Beyond the tents, the woods of Bridgeward Estate remained quiet and still. The friends crept around the back of the tents, carefully stepping over roots and guy ropes with the occasional furtive smirk at each other. Sam was the chief mischief-maker and led the trio. Joe was at the back, and the further away from their tent the boys crept, the more he peered into the dark woods, thinking about the story of the Headless Archer. When the friends reached the other side of the campsite, they crouched down.

"I think Mia, Jay and Ingrid are in that tent over there,"

whispered Sam. "They deserve a good scare for beating us in the orienteering!"

The friends crept out of the shelter of the oak trees. Just as they were about to reach their target, a torch was switched on inside the tent.

"I don't feel very well!" exclaimed Ingrid. Two more torches were turned on quickly. "I think... I think... I'm going to be sick!"

Nothing animates people in a small space quite like the threat of vomit. Mia and Jay quickly abandoned the tent, partly to seek help for their ill friend but mostly to avoid being covered in half-digested marshmallows, spaghetti hoops and toast. They sprinted to the campfire seeking Miss Wilson's help. The boys turned and ran into the woods to seek refuge behind a tree.

"That was a near miss!" whispered Sam, revelling in the risk and adventure.

"Do you think they can see us among these trees?" replied Colin, who had been jolted out of thinking this adventure was a good idea. "Could we sneak back to our tent without anyone noticing?"

"What?" exclaimed Sam, "and miss Ingrid vomiting all over Miss Wilson? Or even better, Mr Montero! This could be brilliant. I'm not going anywhere."

Sam and Colin continued watching events unfold. Behind them, Joe looked into the dark woods where the silhouettes of oak trees were just visible in the moonlight. Despite the drama around the campfire, everything remained quiet and calm in the woods. Joe's mind turned again to the story of the Headless Archer. Suddenly, a flash of electric blue caught his attention. He turned to see where it went. Then a streak of neon yellow caused him to spin back the other way. A dash of bright red whizzed past his left ear. Joe stood captivated by the beautiful, darting colours. There were dragonflies everywhere.

The dragonflies began zig-zagging into the darkness of the woods. They lit everything they passed with their vibrant glow. Joe was entranced. He forgot about Sam, Colin and the story of the Headless Archer as he followed the ribbons of light into the woods. A crumbling brick wall covered with vines appeared in the distance. In this wall, there stood an oak door with rusty hinges that clung to its rotting timbers. The door was ajar, and the dragonflies coalesced to dart through into a walled orchard.

Ducking under the branches of ancient fruit trees, Joe followed the bright insects towards the middle of the orchard where an apple tree stood. Its branches were gnarled and twisted, but it bore perfect fruit. Joe examined the apple tree by the pale white light of the moon and the kaleidoscopic glow of the dragonflies. On its ancient trunk, half-covered by ivy and moss, Joe spotted a simple figure carved harshly into the raw bark. It was about the size of his hand.

The dragonflies disappeared the moment Joe spotted the carving. Joe was suddenly aware that he was alone in the dark woods. He fumbled for the torch in his pocket, and his heart began to race. An urge to sprint back to the camp flooded Joe's body, but curiosity made him turn back to the tree for one last look. With his torch in one hand, he brushed aside the clambering ivy to reveal a carving of the Headless Archer.

Joe screamed as the ground beneath his feet began to shudder. He tried to run back to the campsite, but he floundered on collapsing earth. Dust and soil rose all around him as the ground gave way completely. Joe found himself sliding down between the deep roots of the apple tree towards the sound of rushing water.

CHAPTER TWO

Dragonflies

Colin and Sam heard the scream and turned to discover that Joe had disappeared. Without hesitation, they switched on their torches and ran into the woods. Sam sprinted along the recently trodden path through the undergrowth, and Colin followed with far less athleticism, stumbling over logs and crashing through low branches. The beams of torchlight bounced through the woods as they ran. Sam reached the orchard first. He spotted Joe's torch on the floor and headed towards it, unaware it was perched on the edge of a hole. Sam spotted the hole just in time, and with flailing arms and a panicked grimace, he came to a skidding halt right at the chasm's edge.

Before Sam could catch his breath, Colin blundered ungracefully past him towards the hole. Instinctively, Sam reached out and caught Colin's arm as he began to tumble. Colin was swung in an arc across the chasm, crashing into a tangle of muddy roots and loose soil. From the waist upwards, Colin was pressed against sloping earth, but his legs dangled in the void below. One hand held a thick root, and the other was firmly held by Sam.

"Hold on, Colin!" Sam shouted. "When I count to three, I'll pull, and you try to climb out!"

"Quickly! I'm slipping!"

"1... 2... 3... Pull! Swing your left leg up... and push hard... against that root."

As Sam and Colin heaved and struggled, clumps of soil fell

into the chasm. Eventually, Colin was wrestled onto the firm ground, where he collapsed breathless and exhausted. He was completely covered in mud, and there were scratches all over his arms and legs.

"Joe!" shouted Sam from the perimeter of the hole. "Are you down there? Can you hear me?"

"Sam! Is t-that you?" replied Joe, his distant voice echoing in the dark chasm. "I c-can't hear very c-clearly. There's rushing water somewhere n-nearby. I'm okay, but it's d-dark, and I'm s-scared! The Headless Archer! You n-need to g-get me out of here!"

By now, Colin had caught his breath. He returned to the edge of the hole when he heard his friend's anguish. "Take it easy, Joe! The Headless Archer is just a silly story. Think about it, how could someone with no head shoot an arrow? The Story of the Headless Archer started after the English Reformation when people knocked the heads off the—"

"What on Earth are you talking about?" interrupted Sam. "Now's not the time for being a swot!"

"Sorry, yes, you're probably right, another time maybe. Just keep calm, Joe! We're going to get you out!"

Sam and Colin knew they needed to get help quickly. They agreed that Colin would run back to the campsite while Sam would remain with Joe.

Everything was calm and quiet at the campsite. Miss Wilson was sitting on a log with Ingrid, who moments earlier had almost decorated the inside of her tent with the contents of her stomach. Mia and Jay were there too, watching the campfire flicker. They were greatly relieved that no tent redecorating had taken place. The tranquillity was shattered when Colin bungled into the clearing, filthy and bruised.

"HELP! Miss Wilson! Joe has fallen into a huge hole in the woods!"

"Colin! What have you been doing? You were told to remain in your tents!" Miss Wilson was concerned and cross, but she remained composed.

"I'm sorry, Miss. It's a long story, and I know we'll be in big trouble, but Joe has fallen into a deep hole. He's okay, but it's a really big hole."

"I am very disappointed that you've been out of your tents," Miss Wilson replied. "Such silly behaviour. What were you thinking? Mia and Jay, please find Mr Montero and let him know what's happened. Tell him to bring the first aid kit, a rope, and anything else that might be useful."

Mia and Jay were pleased to have been given such an important task, particularly by their favourite teacher. They set off to find Mr Montero.

Miss Wilson then spoke to Colin and Ingrid, "I'd like you both to get the other teachers from their tents. Explain what has happened and ask them to take over the watch. Students should remain in their tents. Colin, this does not mean you are off the hook."

The other students were now peeking out of their tents to see why there was so much noise. They watched as Miss Wilson ran into the woods towards the orchard.

Mia and Jay had been very close friends for a long time. Jay had a friendly, caring face and a mop of very curly hair, and Mia was elf-like, tough and smart. The two friends found Mr Montero sitting in the dining tent, hunched over his phone like a caveman.

"Mr Montero," Jay began, "Miss Wilson has asked us to tell you that Colin told her that someone fell in a hole."

Mr Montero was engrossed in a game on his phone. He furrowed his brow and poked out his tongue in concentration. "Hold on… almost there… difficult level," he replied.

Jay and Mia looked at each other. They felt more urgency was required. Mia took a step closer to Mr Montero and spoke more firmly, "Sir, someone has fallen down a big hole and is hurt. Help is needed."

"Hold on… almost defeated giant caterpillar… one more pumpkin!"

"Sir, are you listening to us?" Jay asked.

There was no response.

"Mr Montero," Mia began, "five children have been dragged into a hole by a purple alligator. The camp is under attack from midget Vikings, and you appear to be wearing old lady's underwear."

Mr Montero's focus remained on his phone. "I know... I know... I'll be right with you."

Jay and Mia looked at each other again. Normally, mocking Mr Montero was great fun, but now was not the time. Mia grabbed the phone out of Mr Montero's hands like she was grabbing a toy from an overgrown baby. "Sir!" she declared, "Joe has fallen into a big hole and is in danger. Miss Wilson has gone to his aid, and she needs your help."

With his concentration broken, Mr Montero's first instinct was to be angry, but he quickly processed what he had been told and realised there was an opportunity for heroism. "Where are they? Where's the hole? Tell me more about these Vikings and alligators."

"What are you talking about?" responded Mia innocently. "Someone has fallen into a hole! We need rope, a first aid kit and anything else you think might be useful."

"Yes, quite right," Mr Montero said. "Now, where did we put the ropes?"

"They're behind you," replied Mia. "Beside the first aid kit."

"Ah yes! Excellent. Okay, now for the first aid kit."

"It's behind you," replied Jay. "Beside the ropes."

"Exactly!" whispered Mr Montero in hushed tones as if he were passing on top-secret information. "That's where we always used to keep them on secret missions." He grabbed a coil of rope in one hand and the first aid kit in his other. "So, where is this purple Viking then?"

"HOLE!" Mia and Jay shouted in unison.

"A student has fallen into a hole!" Jay continued. "There are no Vikings, no alligators and no old lady's underwear."

Mr Montero paused and looked very sheepish. "Who's been talking to you about old lady's underwear? How did you find out about that?"

Mia rolled her eyes. "Too much information – forget about it. Follow us, and we'll take you to the hole."

Mia and Jay led Mr Montero quickly across the campsite and into the woods. The other teachers were emerging from their tents to take over the watch.

Mr Montero was someone who desperately wanted to be admired and respected. This was why he made up so many ridiculous stories, like the one about being in the SAS. Now he was in a position to be a hero. The problem was he had never been in the Cub Scouts, let alone the SAS, so he possessed none of the skills that might come in useful in this situation.

Mr Montero struggled to keep up with Mia and Jay as he bungled through the woods. The rope over his shoulder started to drag along the floor. Mia and Jay soon spotted Miss Wilson beside the hole, reassuring Joe. Sam had been told to sit by a tree a short distance away.

"Stay back, girls!" Miss Wilson said when she spotted them. "Why did you come into the woods? I told you to get Mr Montero!"

"He's just behind us, Miss," replied Jay. "We didn't think he'd be able to find the way by himself. He doesn't have a torch."

Miss Wilson and the two students looked back along the path that led to the campsite, and there was no sign of Mr Montero.

"So you led Mr Montero into the woods," began Miss Wilson, "which is something I didn't tell you to do, then you ran away, leaving Mr Montero with no means of seeing where he is going. Sit over there with Sam and keep away from the hole. Don't do anything until I return." Miss Wilson then ran back towards the campsite.

"The hole is so massive!" Sam said excitedly as Mia and Jay sat down next to him. "Me and Colin almost fell in too, but I caught Colin and swung him right round, and then I managed to pull him clear, and then he went back to the camp, and the hole is HUGE! Do you want to take a look?"

"Don't be silly, Sam," replied Jay, who was naturally cautious and sensible. "It looks very dangerous."

"And Miss Wilson did tell us to stay here," said Mia, lifting herself and craning her neck to see down the hole.

"Well, aren't you a pair of goody-goodies!" exclaimed Sam. He stood up and crept to the hole. "I'm going to have another look! How are you getting on down there, Joe?"

Jay was unimpressed. "Sam! I don't think you should be—"

"When are y-you going to g-get me out? It's c-cold and d-dark, and I just want to g-go home!"

Jay immediately felt Joe's loneliness and vulnerability. Feeling compelled to comfort him, she moved carefully to the hole's edge and called out, "Don't worry; we'll get you out soon. Mr Montero has a long rope and… and… we'll tie it to the tree… and you'll be able to climb out."

Joe's voice also made his desperate situation very real to Mia, and this was the excuse she needed to see how big the hole was. Mia joined Jay and Sam beside the chasm. At that moment, a beam of torchlight lit up the apple tree in front of them.

"I told you three to stay clear of the hole! Goodness me! Is no one doing what they are told tonight?" Miss Wilson had returned with Mr Montero stumbling along a few strides behind her. "Right, Mr Montero, here's the hole. I've phoned the police and—"

"It's quite alright… Penny, my dear… I've got this… all under control!" Mr Montero was blundering towards the hole, breathing heavily, but not heavily enough to stop him from being patronising. Somehow, Mr Montero had managed to turn the neatly coiled rope into a tangled mess that snaked chaotically around his limbs and dragged along the floor. "Calm down, everyone… and don't panic… this is a situation… that requires specialist training… and a cool head!"

As Mr Montero spoke the words 'cool head', he tripped on the rope and stumbled forward. He reached out with his arms to break his fall and accidentally threw a portion of the rope around Mia, Jay and Sam. Miss Wilson had the misfortune of standing directly in front of Mr Montero, and she turned just in time to see him crash into her stomach. She was folded in half like cardboard and flew backwards into the chasm. Mr Montero's momentum took him flying across the top of the hole. His head smashed into the carving of the Headless Archer on the trunk of the apple tree. He then fell into the hole like a basketball rebounding off a backboard and dropping into a hoop.

Mia, Jay and Sam had just enough time to gasp in shock before the rope, which was looped around them, tightened due to the rapidly descending Mr Montero. Mia, Jay and Sam followed Mr Montero, Miss Wilson, and Joe into the chasm with a sudden yank. Below them, the sound of rushing water could be heard. Above them, the roots of the apple tree began to creep, weave and ravel like snakes in a pit. The hole disappeared in this tangle of roots, and the teachers and students fell in complete darkness. Then suddenly, the void was filled with flashes of electric blue, neon yellow and bright red.

CHAPTER THREE

Auntie Dot and Mistletoe

"This train will shortly be arriving at Bridgeward Station," announced the train driver over the sounds of air-conditioning humming and wheels clacking. His voice was so dull it could have been used to sedate people at the dentist. Lily and Oliver were pleased to hear the announcement. It had been a long journey, and they were both starting to think about lunch.

Lily and Oliver were twins. Freckles were scattered over their faces, and their hair was generally quite wild. They looked similar but different, and they got along well, largely because they did not interact much. Oliver spent most of his time playing computer games, and Lily spent most of her time messaging friends on her phone. They lived in a busy area of London in a small flat with their mum. It was not easy being a single parent, so Auntie Dot had asked the twins' mum if she would like Lily and Oliver to stay with her in Bridgeward for a few weeks at the start of the summer holidays. Auntie Dot could not wait to see her niece and nephew.

"Did mum say Auntie Dot was going to meet us at the station?" said Oliver, looking up from his phone.

"I think so," replied Lily, who had been listening to music. "It would be much easier if she owned a mobile phone like everyone else, and then we could just message her."

"She'd better have a TV at this new house," said Oliver. He gazed out the window of the train as he spoke. "Remember when we visited her a few years ago, and she didn't even have the internet? Surely she has the internet now? It will be a boring start to the summer holiday if she hasn't."

The views from the train had changed greatly since the twins left London. At first, the train had journeyed through a landscape of tall apartment blocks, dense housing estates and busy high streets. The urban landscape was slowly replaced with open fields, woodlands and quiet towns where cricket games were being played. Not far from Bridgeward, the railway began to hug the coastline. The train wound through tunnels, and passed dunes and alongside beaches where colourful beach huts faced the blue sea. Every town they passed was bustling with people visiting for the summer holidays.

"I really hope Auntie Dot doesn't turn up in that horrible car," said Oliver.

"Oh! It was horrible," agreed Lily, looking up sharply from her phone. "It looked like one of those coin-operated cars toddlers sit on in shopping centres."

"I'm still recovering from that incident in London."

"I can still see the look on the Queen's face," said Lily, cringing as she spoke. "As for that weird dog, he was having the time of his life. He looked so pleased with all the mayhem. I've never liked that dog; there's just *something* about him."

The last time the twins had seen Auntie Dot was when she visited them in London in her green and white Citroen Dolly (an old and peculiar little car). It was the Queen's birthday, so central London was prepared for parades, processions and celebrations. There were road closures, large crowds and police everywhere. On the drive home from the supermarket, with the twins in the car, Auntie Dot had managed to drive onto The Mall and past the Queen's carriage as it made its way through St James Park. Things ended dramatically with armed police and the Queen's Household Cavalry surrounding the car. Auntie Dot panicked and offered them all gluten-free cheesecake in the hope of calming the situation. Remarkably it worked. Even the Queen's corgis had some. It was all over the news.

The train pulled into Bridgeward Station and came to a halt. Lily and Oliver grabbed their bags and stepped out of the cool carriage onto a baking hot platform. Auntie Dot spotted the twins immediately. She was standing on the platform waving excitedly while her dog, Mistletoe, sniffed around.

Auntie Dot was a rather large woman who always wore fabulously bright dresses and gaudy jewellery. Her hair was messy and held back with large, colourful headbands. Mistletoe was a beagle with patches of white, brown and caramel fur. He had big floppy ears and a sullen look in his eyes.

"Oh, it's jolly good to see you! Auntie Dot exclaimed. "Come and say hello to Mistletoe, and give me a big hug!" Before Auntie Dot had finished her sentence, she had grabbed the twins and squeezed them so hard they could feel their ears inflating.

"Hi, Auntie Dot," said Oliver, "it's nice to see you. Thanks for coming to pick us up."

"Yeah, thank you," added Lily. "We're looking forward to seeing your new house."

This was not strictly true. The twins were rather unenthusiastic about the holiday, but they were good-natured and polite.

Lily touched her stomach. "Do you mind if I quickly buy a sandwich? I'm so hungry—"

"Oh no, no, no!" interrupted Auntie Dot. "Why would you eat one of those horrible sandwiches? Full of nasty chemicals and gluten – terrible for the bowels. You'll be parping like a brass band. I've been baking all morning! Let's get home, and we'll have a proper feast."

The thought of a feast was very appealing to the twins, far more appealing than parping like a brass band.

"Do you still drive that little car, Auntie Dot?" Oliver asked.

"Oh no! She's long gone. I've got something much more exciting now! An Italian racer – very fast – handles beautifully." Mistletoe barked excitedly.

Lily and Oliver felt relieved, and they followed Auntie Dot off the platform with a sense of excitement. Perhaps she had bought an old Ferrari, or maybe a Lamborghini. Maybe this holiday was not going to be so bad after all.

"Here it is, darlings!" announced Auntie Dot with the pizazz of a gameshow host revealing a star prize. "A sporty racer from the 1970s with brand new tyres!"

Lily and Oliver were very unimpressed. Auntie Dot was standing beside a bright-red tandem bicycle. It stood next to an old butchers' bike with a small front wheel and a big basket. Mistletoe hopped into the basket and settled himself down. Lily could swear he was smirking at them.

"So, we're not driving to your house then?" Oliver asked. "We've never ridden one of these before. I can't even remember the last time I rode a normal bike."

"Yeah, I'm not sure this is such a good idea," said Lily. "I'm starving, and I haven't got very good balance."

"Oh, you're such a pair of boring Bertys!" exclaimed Auntie Dot. "If I were you, I'd be fighting to be at the front. The person at the front steers and doesn't have to face the other person's bottom."

Lily quickly jumped onto the front seat.

"That's the attitude! Now, Oliver, when you're facing Lily's bottom, count yourself lucky she didn't have one of those horrible sandwiches."

With that, Auntie Dot hopped on her butcher's bike and led the way out of the car park onto the streets of Bridgeward. Behind her, Lily and Oliver weaved around erratically as they tried to coordinate their efforts on the tandem bicycle with its skinny wheels. The twins focused so hard on staying upright that they did not notice the vehicles queueing up behind them, waiting to pass. After a while, Lily and Oliver found a rhythm.

"That's it! Your dad and I used to ride one of those. Such jolly good fun! We're almost there. Just another couple of kilometres up a small hill." Auntie Dot was sitting perfectly upright with her large bottom enveloping the saddle, and she was barely breaking a sweat. Meanwhile, Lily and Oliver were hunched over their handlebars, breathing heavily and rocking from side to side with the effort of pedalling.

"Can… you change… the gears," puffed Oliver. His thighs were burning.

"No… I don't know… how. We'll just… have to… ride faster… or… we'll fall off."

The twins picked up the pace for one last push to the top of the hill. They caught up with Auntie Dot and then overtook her.

Mistletoe barked. He was clearly upset with being beaten.

"That's the spirit!" shouted Auntie Dot. "Jolly good fun! The last one to the top is a boring Berty!"

The two bikes finally arrived at the top of the hill, where Auntie Dot, Lily and Oliver dismounted to catch their breath. Auntie Dot was having a great time. Lily and Oliver felt exhausted and very hungry but also rather pleased with themselves. From this spot, the trio had a wonderful view of Bridgeward. In the distance, waves were gently lapping on the town's sandy beaches, and in the foreground, yachts dotted Bridgeward Estuary.

"There's so much to do in the area," began Auntie Dot. "We're not far from home now, so you can easily ride or walk into town. In the far distance is the Old Fort." Auntie Dot pointed to a prominent headland dominated by a huge fortress. The fortress was so big that cricket was being played on the grass inside the curtain wall. "There are miles of haunted tunnels beneath that fort. The first fort was built there by the Romans. Talking of the Romans, there's a Roman amphitheatre near the fort too. You can also visit the remains of the Old Town. It was abandoned after the Great Plague. There are stories of goblins coming out from the ruins at night. That bridge over the Estuary is Saint Wandalgan's Bridge. Legend has it this is where Saint Wandalgan defeated a Troll. There are so many fun stories in Bridgeward! It's steeped in history!"

"What's that big church over there?" asked Oliver. He pointed to a building that was dominating the skyline.

"That's not a church; that's a cathedral! One of the largest in Europe too. You must go there. Inside, you can see the Great Map, the Spell Book of the Woodland Folk and the Bridgeward Clock. Jolly good fun! I'll tell you more when we get home. Come on, let's get going. It's all downhill now past Bridgeward Estate to my lovely new house: the Old Rectory."

The Old Rectory was on the edge of town, and it was separated from Bridgeward Estate by its large and messy garden. The house was built with cream-coloured bricks that were weathered and worn with age. Limestone blocks surrounded its windows and doors, and it had four tall chimney stacks protruding from an irregular roof that looked like it was in desperate need of repair. Second-floor windows jutted out from the steep roof, and the guttering was being pulled down by clambering honeysuckle that covered a large portion of the building.

"I wasn't expecting your new house to look like this," said Lily.

"It looks very old and... erm... *rustic*," added Oliver.

"It's a work in progress! I haven't had it for long. The roof leaks in places and some of the windows have been boarded up until I can repair them. There's no hot water either. There's quite a long list of things to do, but it's all jolly good fun!

"No hot water?" Oliver questioned. "Does it have electricity? Internet? TV?"

"Yes, we have electricity, but it's old and unreliable. I do not need the internet or TV. Look around you! There's more than enough to keep me and Mistletoe busy. Right, come on in. Let's have lunch!"

"No internet or TV?" Oliver whispered to Lily. "This is going to be so boring! Do you think Mum knew about this?"

"I'm too hungry to think about it right now," Lily replied. "Let's just have lunch. It was Auntie Dot's talk of home baking that kept me going up that hill."

CHAPTER FOUR

The Spell Book of
the Woodland Folk

The twins followed Auntie Dot through a small front door beneath a pointed limestone arch. They stepped into a dark hallway with a patterned floor of black, white, claret and blue tiles. The colours of the tiles had dulled with age. There was a staircase with a threadbare carpet and a chunky oak bannister. The wallpaper was peeling from the walls, the ceiling was stained with yellow patches and there were cobwebs in the high corners.

Auntie Dot led the twins from the dark hallway into the kitchen. "This is the first room I finished," she announced proudly. "It took some elbow grease, I tell you! Jolly good fun!"

The kitchen was amazing. A black oven sat in an old fireplace with bunches of herbs and cast iron pots hanging from a rail above it. The cabinets and worktops were beautifully crafted from wood, and the floor was the same as in the hallway, just brighter, cleaner and without any broken tiles. It was quite a change from the cramped kitchen in the twins' flat in London.

Auntie Dot opened a small window. The smell of the clambering honeysuckle drifted in on a wave of cool air that mingled with the smell of fresh baking. Lily and Oliver's eyes almost popped out of their heads when they spotted the dining table. It was laden with bread, cheeses, homemade pickles, sliced ham, fresh salad and orange juice. There were also two vases filled with meadow flowers.

"Don't hang around, darlings," exclaimed Auntie Dot with a smile. "Wash your hands, sit down and fill your boots!"

The twins did not need a second invitation.

"This is brilliant!" said Oliver with a mouthful of cheese sandwich.

"Amazing!" agreed Lily, as she slapped ham between two slices of bread.

"So this is the Old Rectory," said Auntie Dot. "I've finished restoring the kitchen, but that's about it so far. I've put you in the nicest bedroom. Don't expect anything as nice as this though. There are two bathrooms, both of them are very old, but they're clean and will do for now. Remember, there's no hot water at the moment, and the electricity isn't too great either. Count yourselves lucky you didn't visit in the winter! That was jolly good fun! You can go anywhere you like in the house and garden. Just be careful of broken floorboards and crumbling plaster. There are also some gigantic spiders, and I'm sure there is a family of bats in the loft."

"Are you going to have some food too, Auntie Dot?" asked Lily. Her cheeks were bulging with a half-chewed ham sandwich.

"No, not for me, thank you!" Auntie Dot replied.

"That's a shame," responded Oliver as he mentally divided the food in two and not three.

"My stomach is far too delicate for all that gluten," continued Auntie Dot. "It's awful for my bowels. It would make me very windy, and nobody wants that." Mistletoe shook his head very seriously. "I've started to eat like a caveman, you know, *Paleo*."

"What? Like woolly mammoths?" exclaimed Oliver.

"They're extinct apparently," replied Auntie Dot, "the lady at the supermarket told me. The supermarkets don't even stock elephant, something to do with *dwindling numbers*. So instead, I add protein powder to almost everything."

"Did cavemen really have protein powder?" asked Lily.

"I suppose they must have done," Auntie Dot replied. "It must come from a berry or something. Anyway, I'll be having a kale and cauliflower smoothie for lunch today. Mmm... delicious!"

The smoothie sounded revolting to the twins, and Auntie Dot

seemed to be trying very hard to convince herself otherwise.

"Now, I'm sure you're both wondering if it's safe to explore Bridgeward Estate."

Lily and Oliver kept eating.

"You know, after the school group incident."

Lily and Oliver looked blank.

"You've heard about the missing school group, haven't you?"

Lily and Oliver still looked blank, and Mistletoe gave an uncharacteristic howl.

"I thought you two spent all of your time in front of a television? Do you not watch the news?"

"I'm sorry," Lily said, "we don't know what you mean. Has a school group gone missing?"

"It's been all over the news!" Auntie Dot exclaimed. "The rescue team has been working day and night trying to find them. A cave complex has been discovered near the estate's old orchard. A couple of weeks ago, four students and two teachers went missing on a camping trip. I feel very sorry for the young geography teacher. I bet she's struggling – such a delicate little thing. Luckily for the students, the other teacher is Flex Montero." Auntie Dot began to blush slightly. "He used to be in the SAS, you know. I'm confident he'll have kept them all alive. He used to be my personal trainer. He's so knowledgeable! He's the one who taught me to eat like a caveman: kale and cauliflower smoothies, with added protein powder, every 3 hours."

Oliver wondered where cavemen plugged in their blenders whilst Lily imagined a group of cavemen stopping their hunt because their alarms had gone off and they needed their smoothies. Mistletoe just rolled his eyes and turned over in his basket.

After the twins had finished their lunch, they took their bags to their bedroom. Both beds were metal-framed, sagging in the middle and had faded floral sheets. The room also had two bedside tables and a tall wardrobe that stood awkwardly due to the wonky floor. The room did not look like it had been decorated for a very long time.

"Oh no!" Oliver exclaimed as he sat down on the side of his

bed. "There's no signal. That lunch was amazing, and Auntie Dot is wonderfully barmy, but this place has no TV, no internet and no signal. What are we supposed to do for two weeks?"

"And I have to share a bedroom with you," added Lily. "I'm definitely not getting back on that bike again."

"I'm going to phone mum to let her know we've arrived safely. Do you think she could fit a TV in her car? And maybe my games console?"

"Even if she could, she's not going to be here until next week," Lily pointed out.

"This is going to be so boring!" exclaimed Oliver as he flopped back onto his bed. The bedsprings creaked and pinged unpleasantly. For a moment, Oliver thought he was going to hit the floor.

"Let's look around," said Lily, "and see if we can find anything interesting to do."

The twins spent the rest of the afternoon exploring the house and passing time playing games on their phones. Auntie Dot served a delicious roast dinner and persuaded the twins to sit outside with her to enjoy the warm summer evening. She was her usual talkative self, and the twins were polite but noticeably uninspired by their new environment. The electricity cut out shortly after sunset, so the twins went to bed.

The following day, the twins woke up to the smell of fresh banana bread drifting through the house. They descended the stairs gingerly, drawn by the smell.

"Good morning, darlings!" welcomed Auntie Dot. "I thought you'd never get up! Banana bread? And did you have a good sleep?"

"Yes and yes," replied Oliver, wincing as he sat down. "The banana bread smells amazing."

"I'd love some, please," said Lily, who also winced as she lowered herself down onto her seat. "I slept very well, thank you, although Mistletoe woke me up in the middle of the night. He was barking outside."

"He's been doing that a lot recently, and I have no idea why. There must be something in the woods on the estate he doesn't like, possibly deer. He always comes back after 10 minutes or so." Auntie Dot handed Mistletoe a crust of banana bread and started speaking childishly, "Isn't that right, Mistletoe? You're just telling those silly deer to go away." Mistletoe looked surly as he took the crust.

"We're thinking of wandering into town today to look around," said Oliver. "My phone has run out of battery, and I might be able to charge it in a café. I suspect we'll get signal in town too."

"Oh, good idea! You can take the bicycle too if you want. You were getting the hang of it yesterday."

"That's very kind of you," Lily replied, "but I think we'll give it a miss. I could barely get down the stairs because my thighs hurt so much."

"Me too. It must have been that hill," added Oliver, rubbing his legs under the table.

"I know just the thing!" exclaimed Auntie Dot. She lurched forward abruptly with her hands on her hips and started counting loudly in time with her lunges. "Flex Montero told me cottage-cheese smoothies and lunges get rid of sore muscles! Would you like a cottage cheese smoothie?"

The thought of a cottage cheese smoothie made Lily and Oliver feel slightly unwell, so they politely declined the offer. The twins finished their breakfast and got themselves ready to walk into town. Auntie Dot gave them lunchboxes as they left.

"Please promise me you will not spend all of your time sitting in a café on your phones," Auntie Dot asked. "At least visit the cathedral. I'll be very disappointed if you don't. You'll love the Spell Book and the Great Map. You won't be able to call me because I don't have a phone. If you get in trouble, congratulate yourself because you're having an adventure. Then use your initiative and sort it out yourselves, just like your father and I did when we were your age. Please be back for dinner."

Auntie Dot was giving the twins lots of freedom. Their mum had only recently started letting them walk to school on their own. That said, they did not ask to go out much anyway. They preferred to stay at home playing on computers or their phones. This meant the walk into Bridgeward, with the freedom to do what they liked for most of the day, felt very exciting. The twins were also a little nervous, although they were trying not to show this to each other.

By the time the twins had reached the centre of Bridgeward, their thighs had loosened up, and it was a hot day. They went into the first café they spotted, ordered some milkshakes and found some seats next to a power point to charge their phones.

"Should we actually go to the cathedral?" Oliver asked. "Or shall we pretend we went to make Auntie Dot happy?"

"I don't think that would be very nice," replied Lily. "She's made such an effort to welcome us, and I don't want to let her down."

"Fine," replied Oliver, "but let's keep it quick. It'll probably be very boring – just like a church but bigger and with more gravestones. We could have lunch afterwards."

The twins walked to the cathedral in the early afternoon. The cathedral entrance was beneath a large, pointed archway made out of blocks of limestone. There were two smaller doorways on either side of this entrance surrounded by ornate stonework. Above the main entrance, there was an enormous stained glass window crowned with three large turrets. There was a busy lawn in front of the cathedral with two war memorials, tree-lined paths and park benches.

Lily and Oliver joined the queue to enter the cathedral. In front of them, foreign visitors chatted excitedly in various languages. When the twins eventually stepped into the cathedral, they were immediately struck by the enormity of the inside space. The long nave stretched ahead of them down the centre of the cathedral. It was flanked on either side by rows of large columns forming high arches. It was refreshingly cool, but the sun still made an impression by gloriously illuminating the vibrantly coloured stained glass window above the entrance. Softly coloured light rays patterned the cathedral floor where Lily and Oliver stood admiring the window.

"Did Auntie Dot say something yesterday about a Troll being defeated on a bridge?" asked Oliver.

"I think so. It was Saint Wandle-something."

"I reckon that's him up there. Can you see? He's the dude on the horse wearing a suit of armour, and it looks like he's killed the Troll with his spear."

"You might be right," said Lily. She then pointed at a different part of the window where two regal figures sat on thrones. "They look like a king and que—"

"Check out the weird monsters at the bottom!" interrupted Oliver excitedly. "That dude has a face in his chest and no head, they look like Goblins, and that man looks like a frog. See? He's got a small, round body and really long arms and legs! This is brilliant! There's a group of knights fighting a Giant down there. The Giant is about to whack them with a big club. WALLOP!" Oliver pretended to swing a big club, and he almost hit an elderly tourist around the head. He quickly apologised. "Auntie Dot was right about this cathedral – it's pretty cool!"

"Shall we check out that big map?" asked Lily. She thought this was very interesting, but she was not as excited as Oliver. "Or shall we look at the clock, or maybe the Spell Book? I'm quite hungry, so let's look at one and then head outside to eat lunch."

"I reckon the Spell Book," replied Oliver. "Maybe it has some spells for turning people into frogmen. I reckon you'd look good with slimy skin, long legs and a body like a beach ball. Oh, wait, you already do!"

"Shut up!" replied Lily with a smile on her face. "This frog girl got you up that hill yesterday. You were about as much use as Mistletoe. Let's go. I want to find a spell that turns your sandwich into a cottage cheese smoothie."

The twins continued to chat as they walked through the cathedral, following the signs to the Spell Book of the Woodland Folk. The signs took them down the nave, into one of the transepts and up a tight spiral staircase. They emerged in a long and narrow library with dark, wooden floorboards and floor-to-ceiling shelves filled with leather-bound books. In the middle of the library, there stood two large globes and three small desks made from the same dark wood. The Spell Book of the Woodland Folk was in a display cabinet beneath the only window at the far end of the library.

An old man with grey hair, a short beard and spectacles stood beside the Spell Book. He was talking in a posh accent to a group of tourists, "This item is very mysterious indeed. There's nothing else like it in the world as far as we know. It's written in a strange, unknown language. It's beautifully illustrated with fascinating images similar to those on the Great Map and elsewhere in the cathedral. So why is this manuscript called *The Spell Book of the Woodland Folk*? Well, you see, in the early 1500s, hysteria spread throughout southern England. Witchcraft was being blamed for everything unfortunate that happened. When a child died, someone fell ill, or crops failed, people blamed witchcraft. And where there is witchcraft, there are witches! So people began hunting for them.

"The people of Bridgeward had always been suspicious of those living in the surrounding woods, so this is where they went looking for witches. Many innocent people were imprisoned, tortured and burnt at the stake. Around this time, the Spell Book of the Woodland Folk found its way to the cathedral. It was thought to be a book of spells used by the witches in the woods because of the strange language and mysterious drawings of fantastic creatures. Sadly we know very little about this document because no one has ever been able to decipher the mysterious writing. Many fine scholars have tried."

Lily and Oliver moved towards the display cabinet as the man spoke. The Spell Book was far larger than a regular book and lay open on a stand. Its cream-coloured paper had wrinkled and discoloured with age, but the illustrations and elaborate gold script were still vibrant. The writing was peculiar, without any recognisable letters. Nestled among the characters and symbols was an image of a gnarled apple tree and a headless figure carrying a satchel, a quiver, and a longbow. Most striking of all were the three brightly-coloured dragonflies; they were electric blue, neon yellow and bright red.

CHAPTER FIVE

Boom-Box Bert

The lawn outside the cathedral was a popular place to have lunch on a sunny day. There were workers in high visibility jackets, parents with children, professionals in smart suits and groups of teenagers. Lily and Oliver left the cathedral and scanned the lawn for a spot to sit down. There was a space in the middle of the grass, and the twins weaved through the crowd towards it.

"Is it me, or are people looking at us?" Oliver asked.

"Yeah, I thought that," Lily replied. "People probably just like to watch each other while they're eating. It's a bit uncomfortable though. I'll get out the sandwiches."

Music could be heard in the distance as Lily rummaged in her bag. The music got louder as the twins started eating. It was the sort of music parents play in the car.

"I don't understand why people play their music loudly," said Oliver. "Just because someone likes a song, it doesn't mean everyone else wants to listen to it. It's like those numpties who play loud music in their cars outside our London flat or those people on the Tube. Why don't they just wear headphones?"

Oliver looked over his shoulder and saw an old man walking across the crowded lawn towards where the twins were sitting. The man had long, grey hair beneath a scruffy woolly hat. His skin was wrinkly and very suntanned. A patchy beard was growing on his chin, and he wore a baggy, tie-dye shirt that looked like it had not been washed for half a century. The man wore denim shorts that revealed his skinny legs and knobbly knees. Over his shoulder, he was carrying a retro boom-box. It was blasting out a song so cheesy you could grate it over a pizza. The song was not the only cheesy thing; a rather ripe smell was beginning to put Lily and Oliver off their ham sandwiches.

"Are you joining me today?" the man said to the twins with a gummy grin.

"Err... what do you mean?" responded Lily, who could feel the cold sweat of embarrassment forming on her skin. It felt like everyone on the lawn was staring at them.

"We're... just happy eating our lunch," added Oliver.

The man was not interested in a reply to his question. He had placed his boom-box on the ground and was busy dancing in a bizarre manner. There were rhythmic kicks, lots of hip wiggling, pointy fingers and the occasional pelvic thrust. His face was screwed up as he became utterly entranced by the pop classic coming from his boom-box.

Lily and Oliver were very confused by what was going on, and they looked around and saw that they were not the only ones. Some people found the whole thing very amusing, others were just baffled, and many people were carrying on like this happened all the time.

"Okay, this is weird," Oliver said quietly to Lily. "Let's get away from this nutcase."

"Agreed," replied Lily, "and quickly, before one of us gets whacked by a misplaced high-kick."

Lily and Oliver hurriedly packed their bag and walked away from the strange man. A few people gave them sympathetic smiles as they passed. They found a bench on the edge of the lawn and sat down.

A boy of a similar age to the twins sat down next to them and spoke, "You're not from Bridgeward, are you? Everyone in town knows about Boom-Box Bert. People think he's homeless, but he lives in a rather nice terrace house not far from the town centre. He doesn't do anyone any harm despite being totally barmy. In fact, he often picks up litter, and he once floored a young guy who'd stolen a tourist's camera. He sat on him for about 20 minutes until the police arrived. Imagine the smell of cheese? The thief must have felt like a cream cracker. You made the mistake of sitting on his spot on the lawn. People weren't laughing at you in a bad way. They could just see what was about to happen and knew you had no idea."

"I'm not sure that makes us feel any better," replied Lily. "That was so embarrassing."

"And he really did stink!" added Oliver. "Does he not have a shower in his house? Come on, Lily, let's wander home now. I think I've had enough of Bridgeward for one day."

"Thank you for telling us about that odd man," Lily said to the stranger.

"No problem! Which way are you heading home? I'm on my way home too. I live up the hill near Bridgeward Estate."

"Oh, that's close to where we're staying," Lily replied.

"Great! I'll show you the quickest way home. My name is Colin. What are your names?"

"I'm Lily, and this is Oliver. We live in London, but we're here on holiday."

Oliver smiled awkwardly when his name was mentioned. He did not know what to say because he hadn't had much practice making friends with strangers. In London, Oliver had had the same friends since he started school.

"So, where are you both staying?" asked Colin.

"We're just visiting our Auntie," replied Lily. "She's renovating an old house she's recently bought. It's beside the estate."

"Not the Old Rectory?" said Colin. "That building is awesome! And right by my house. I live in one of the old workers' cottages opposite. The Old Rectory has been unoccupied for as long as I can remember. I used to explore the gardens. I'd love to have a look inside!"

"It's not that great," mumbled Oliver. "It's not got a TV, there's no internet, and the showers are cold."

"That's a bit naff," Colin replied. "Have you had a look around Bridgeward Estate yet? Nobody cares if you wander around the grounds since the Lord was kicked out. It's great fun, although very dangerous in places. Some of my best friends got lost in a cave a few weeks ago. Did you hear about it? A rescue team is still looking for them."

Colin tried not to show that he was worried about his friends, but Lily could tell he was. "That's so sad!" she exclaimed. "Our Auntie told us about it last night. I'm sure the rescue team will find them eventually. She said one of the teachers used to be in the SAS, and he'll look after them all."

Colin laughed. "Unfortunately, Mr Montero is a complete idiot. He was never in the SAS, not unless SAS stands for 'Stupid Arrogant Simpletons' or maybe 'Sham Army Storytellers'. I imagine he's about as much use in a cave as a solar panel. Anyway, what were you both doing in town today? Did you go into the cathedral to see the Spell Book, or the Great Map, or the clock?"

Oliver's eyes lit up. "Have you seen the big window? It's brilliant! There's a Giant smashing a load of knights with a huge club and another dude on a horse killing a green Troll."

"It's cool, isn't it?" replied Colin, who was pleased Oliver was joining in. "If you liked that, you must see the Great Map – it's nuts! It's supposed to be a map of the world with lots of little pictures of interesting landmarks and creatures, but it was made around 1400, so long before Europeans had explored the whole world. Back then, Europeans thought monstrous people lived in the far corners of the Earth. There are pictures of frog people, people with their faces in their chests, Giants, Trolls, Goblins, one-legged people and even people with heads like dogs."

"That sounds right up Oliver's street," replied Lily. "After the window, we went to see the Spell Book. It was quite interesting, I suppose."

"What page was it open on?" asked Colin. "Every month or so, the page is changed."

"There was an apple tree, a man with no head and three brightly coloured dragonflies," replied Oliver.

Colin stopped walking and looked surprised. "Did the headless figure have a bow and arrow? And maybe a satchel?"

"Yes," replied Lily. "Have you seen that page too?"

"That's odd. No, I've never seen that page, but it sounds like the Story of the Headless Archer. The story must be much older than I thought if it's in the Spell Book."

"A ghost story about an archer with no head?" replied Lily,

giggling. "That's ridiculous. How does he know where to shoot his arrow?"

"Well, it is the Spell Book," said Oliver. He waved an imaginary wand. "Iggedy, wiggedy, woggedy, zipples, give me the power to see through my nipples!"

The three friends laughed.

"All right, the story isn't perfect, but it's really famous. The story is set on the grounds of Bridgeward Estate behind your Auntie's house. Look over there; that pub is even called *The Headless Archer*." Colin pointed at a traditional pub with white walls and a wonky slate roof on the other side of the road. Cyclists and dog walkers were sitting outside enjoying cold drinks and packets of crisps.

"How about we show you the Spell Book tomorrow?" suggested Oliver.

"We can see the Great Map too," Lily added.

"That sounds great!" Colin replied. "Now, let me tell you the Story of the Headless Archer."

Colin told the Story of the Headless Archer as they walked home, and he finished just as they arrived back at the Old Rectory. "Interestingly, the Story of the Headless Archer started after the English Reformation when some people knocked the heads off the statues on Bridgeward—"

"MISTLETOE!" shouted Oliver as he staggered forward. "Where did you come from?"

Mistletoe had jumped out of a bush and almost tripped Oliver over. He gave a dismissive bark before running down the path to the Old Rectory.

"That's our Auntie's dog," explained Lily. "He's weird. Come and have a look around the house. I'm sure Auntie Dot won't mind. You could probably stay for dinner. No doubt there'll be enough food to feed that Giant in the cathedral window."

Colin followed the twins into the Old Rectory, where delicious aromas drifted along the hallway. The three friends followed their noses into the kitchen.

"Oh, hello, darlings!" blurted Auntie Dot with her mouth full. "I wasn't expecting you back so soon!"

Auntie Dot was sitting at the dining table, looking very

flustered. Her hands were behind her back, and there was something red on her chin and cheeks. She swallowed what was in her mouth in one big gulp.

"This is Colin," said Lily. "He lives nearby. We got chatting in town, and he told us all about the missing school group. Could he join us for dinner?"

"Yes, yes! Of course!" said Auntie Dot, noticing the food around her mouth. She removed one of her arms from behind her back to wipe her lips. As she did so, there was a loud *splat* followed by barking. Auntie Dot had accidentally leant back on the freshly baked and half-eaten doughnut she was hiding. The jam filling had squirted halfway across the kitchen, landing on Mistletoe's face.

"Goodness, how did that get there?" Auntie Dot exclaimed. "I must have dropped it! Silly me!"

"Brilliant!" exclaimed Oliver. "I love doughnuts! Wait... I thought you only drank smoothies? The doughnuts aren't made from cottage cheese and cauliflowers, are they?" Oliver was looking worried.

"Don't be silly, Oliver," Lily said. "They're for us. Auntie Dot just accidentally sat on one."

Lily knew this was not true, but it was clear Auntie Dot was embarrassed about being caught scoffing a doughnut. Lily could not understand why; it was just a doughnut, and they looked amazing.

"Colin, which house do you live in?" asked Auntie Dot, wiping doughnut jam from Mistletoe's face with a tea towel. It was the jam Mistletoe's tongue could not quite reach. "And will your parents mind you eating here tonight? Would you like to tell them?"

"I'll send them a message, but they won't mind," replied Colin. "They're both working on big projects, and they'll probably be happy they don't have to cook anything. We live in the end terrace house over the road. They're the old workers' cottages for Bridgeward Estate."

"Jolly good fun! Well, do tell your parents to pop by for a cup of tea whenever they fancy!"

Colin knew his parents never had time to drink a cup of tea

with their neighbours, but he nodded politely.

The three friends finished their delicious dinner and ate jam doughnuts for dessert. They then agreed to meet tomorrow morning to visit the cathedral. Colin went home, and Auntie Dot decided a brisk evening walk was in order. Mistletoe stayed at home with the twins. He still looked upset at being splattered with doughnut jam.

CHAPTER SIX

The Voice in the Chamber

Lily and Oliver sat down in the living room on an uncomfortable sofa that had long lost all plumpness and shape. The sofa's springs creaked as the twins tried to find a comfortable sitting position. Opposite them, a fireplace dominated the room. Hundreds of years of use had stained the hearth black with soot. The ceiling was also discoloured, particularly above the fireplace, and the old floral wallpaper was damaged and peeling. The floor was covered in a thread-bare patterned carpet, and the only other piece of furniture was a faded green armchair on which Mistletoe was curled up. It was beginning to get dark outside.

"Do you have to do that now?" exclaimed Oliver. Lily had hooked a foot up to her mouth and was chewing her toenails. "I'm sure Auntie Dot has some nail clippers. Do you even wash your feet before doing it?"

"Be quiet!" mumbled Lily with a big toe between her teeth. "I'll just be quick."

"I imagine they taste like really old brie," began Oliver, "the sort that is so ripe it saunters across the dining table, introduces itself, and then smears itself on your cracker. Have you not had enough of cheesy pongs after the weirdo outside the cathedral? Even Mistletoe looks put off, and he enjoys sniffing other dogs' bottoms!"

Lily glared at her brother but could not reply because her mouth was full of toe.

"Mistletoe, is this yours?" said Oliver, who had spotted an old tennis ball on the floor. "Do you like playing fetch?"

Mistletoe turned around in the armchair, so his back was facing Oliver. Oliver took this as a 'no' and started throwing the ball into the empty fireplace. It bounced off the floor, onto the wall and back to where he sat.

Thud-thud, thud-thud, thud-thud.

"Mistletoe is such an odd dog," said Lily as she changed feet. "He must be the most miserable dog I've ever met."

Thud-thud, thud-thud, thud-thud.

"That is until something mad happens, then he cheers right up. He seems to revel in chaos."

Thud-thud, thud-thud, thud-thud.

"I've never seen a dog so happy as when Auntie Dot was handing out slices of cheesecake to the Queen's Horse Guard."

Thud-thud, thud-thud, thud-thud.

"I also swear he was laughing at us when we were cycling on that tandem."

Thud-thud, thud-thud, thud-DONK!

Oliver paused with the ball in his hand. "Did you hear that?" he exclaimed.

"Did I hear what?"

Oliver resumed bouncing the ball.

Thud-DONK! Thud-DONK! Thud-DONK!

"That's odd," said Oliver. "There's a hollow sound coming from the fireplace."

Oliver stood up, walked over to the fireplace and knelt among the cobwebs. There appeared to be a small carving in the stone, but it was difficult to make out because of all the soot. Oliver adjusted his position to let more light reach the carving. It was a figure with no head, a bow in its hands and a satchel around its waist. Oliver ran his fingers lightly over the figure. To his surprise, the block of stone moved backwards with a grinding noise. "Lily!" he shouted. "You need to check this out! There's a secret passage!"

Lily jumped to her feet and joined Oliver in the fireplace. They peered into the small opening that had been revealed in the side of the hearth. Cold and stale air drifted out of the passage. Mistletoe leapt from his chair, sniffed the passage, and ran purposefully out of the room.

"Such a strange dog!" exclaimed Lily.

"This is amazing!" said Oliver. "A secret passage! Well... erm... ladies first, I suppose."

"Since when did you become such a gentleman?" replied Lily. "It does look cool, but maybe we should wait for Auntie Dot to get back from her walk?"

As Lily and Oliver were building up the courage to explore the passage, Mistletoe darted back into the room with two torches in his mouth. He dropped them at the feet of the twins, barked and then shot into the passage.

"Mistletoe, you silly dog!" exclaimed Lily. "Come on, Oliver. We've got to get Mistletoe."

Lily crawled quickly into the passage. Oliver followed, delighted that not only were they exploring the passage, but he did not have to go first. The twins had to crawl on their hands and knees to fit through the hole. It was full of cobwebs and rodent droppings. After about a metre, the passage led into a higher and narrower space. Lily could hear Mistletoe barking beneath her as she examined her surroundings by torchlight.

"You can stand up in this bit," Lily called back, "there are stairs going down beneath the house. I'm going to find Mistletoe."

Oliver entered the second space where he could just make out the warped timbers of the Old Rectory. The stairs had somehow been squeezed within the thick walls of the building. Oliver descended the stairs carefully and emerged into a large chamber.

"Well, here is the silly, little dog!" spluttered Lily, wiping cobwebs and dust from her mouth with the back of her hand.

"This must be a secret cellar or something," said Oliver, shining his torch around. "Now we have Mistletoe, maybe we should... erm... head back upstairs and wait for Auntie Dot to get back?"

"Let's have a quick look around first. We're covered in dirt and cobwebs, so we may as well. I don't fancy staying down here for too long though – it's a bit creepy."

The twins hesitantly moved further into the chamber, exploring with their torches. Long timbers spanned the ceiling, and the floor consisted of uneven stone slabs. The walls were made of old bricks, the air was lifeless and a thick layer of dust covered everything. No natural light found its way into the chamber. A rusty bed with moth-eaten sheets stood in one corner. At the foot of this bed was a set of shelves with comics and football sticker albums from around forty years ago. There were also model football players, colourful monster figurines and a jar of marbles. On the floor nearby, there was a sleeping bag and a skateboard. Lily gently pushed the skateboard with her foot. The dust fell off to reveal colourful patterns. It was clear a child of a similar age to the twins had turned this space into a den thirty or forty years before. Since then, these bright and vibrant belongings had been smothered and suffocated by the dust and darkness.

Lily directed her torch at the far end of the chamber, where there stood a chunky table made from dark wood. In this grey, miserable and dirty space, five marbles stood like beacons, gently glowing on the tabletop.

"Oliver, look over here," whispered Lily as she moved closer to the table.

Oliver turned to see Lily's torch lighting up the row of five marbles.

"They look like they're moving inside," Lily continued, "and they keep changing colour."

"They're also the only things down here that aren't covered in dust," added Oliver.

The marbles were the size of small apples, and each one gently glowed. Beautiful swathes of every colour moved gracefully inside them. Lily picked one up and watched as a peacock blue cloud drifted across the marble, like the smoke from a candle. The blue faded and was replaced by a vibrant daffodil yellow. This yellow transformed into a rich violet that swirled like a galaxy. Then there was a silent explosion, like a firework, of mint green. The green faded behind streaks of marmalade orange. Oliver was now beside Lily, and the twins stared deep into the marble, completely entranced.

BANG!

A loud noise startled the twins. Dust fell from the floorboards above, and Mistletoe began to bark. Lily and Oliver felt a sudden urge to flee the chamber, but not before they grabbed the marbles. Lily then turned quickly and accidentally knocked something off the table. She looked down and saw a sculpture of the Headless Archer lying on the floor. Oliver turned sharply too and knocked over a quill of arrows leaning against the table. As he caught his balance, Oliver then tripped on a canvas satchel lying on the floor. There was something heavy inside it.

Suddenly a muffled voice barked, "GET OUT! GET OUT OF HERE!"

The voice was coming from within the chamber. Shivers ran up the spines of the two twins. They shot towards the narrow staircase, leaving dust clouds rising behind them. Mistletoe bolted up the steps first, with Lily and Oliver close behind. The twins had a horrible sensation that something was close behind them. They dived into the passage behind the fireplace and scuttled through as fast as possible. The rough stone and loose grit ripped into their knees. The twins emerged breathless in the hearth. They quickly pulled the stone back into place and fell to the floor, gasping. Blood was seeping from their knees, and they were filthy.

"Oh dear! Did I surprise you?" exclaimed Auntie Dot, who walked into the living room moments later. "This looks like jolly good fun! Have you been on an adventure? Good for you! That's what I like to see."

"Auntie Dot!" blurted Oliver. "We've found a passage!"

"There's a hidden chamber under the house!" Lily added.

"And there's something down there!" Oliver continued.

"Jolly good fun! That's the spirit. You two seem to be getting the hang of this. To be young again!"

"No, Auntie Dot, we're serious," Lily asserted. "We've just been down there. I'm sure I heard a loud voice. Something is living under the house!"

Auntie Dot thought she was being invited to play an imaginary game. She hunched her shoulders and walked around with a dumb look on her face. "Was it an ogre? Nobody wants an ogre under the floorboards. Quick, let's hide!" Auntie Dot stumbled and fell as she hurried behind the sofa. There was a loud thump followed by a stifled groan. "It's okay... I'm okay... just not as young as I used to be."

"I don't think you're taking this very seriously! Look, we found these down there!" Oliver reached out a hand to show Auntie Dot some of the marbles.

"They're nice ones," said Auntie Dot as she pulled herself up from behind the sofa. "Your father and I used to play marbles. They were very popular back in our childhood." Auntie Dot paused. A childlike grin appeared on her face, and her eyes twinkled. "Or are they dragons' eggs?"

"Mistletoe was down there with us!" exclaimed Lily, gesturing towards Mistletoe, but Mistletoe was calmly lying on his chair, looking like nothing had happened. "Stupid dog! Well, if you're not going to believe me, I'm going to bed!"

Lily and Oliver left the living room and stomped upstairs. Behind them, Auntie Dot spoke from the doorway, "You can continue playing if you like. I'll leave you to it... sorry... I was just trying to join in..."

The twins had cold showers and went to bed, leaving a pile of filthy clothes on the bedroom floor. There was a gentle knock at the door.

"Darlings," began Auntie Dot gently, "I've brought you some hot chocolate. If you pass me your dirty clothes, I'll get them washed for you."

Oliver got out of bed and went to the door with the dirty clothes. "Thank you, Auntie Dot. Sorry for getting them so dirty."

"That's okay. I'm glad you were having an adventure. You've made a friend today and been exploring. That's jolly good. You don't need to tell me what you've been up to. I trust you to do the right thing, and if you make a mistake, well, that shows you're normal. A mistake is only bad if you don't learn from it. Good night."

Lily and Oliver wished Auntie Dot goodnight, and after she had left, talk turned to the marbles.

"They're so odd," said Lily. "I've seen marbles before, but these have no imperfections, and they seem alive. The moving colours inside them are amazing. I'm sure they became cold when we heard that voice."

"I think you're right," replied Oliver, examining the marbles. "I felt coldness too. We need to find out more about them, but I'm not sure I want to go back down into that chamber if there's something down there."

"But it didn't look like anyone had been down there for decades," Lily replied. "There was no sign of the dust being disturbed. As for that voice, if I didn't know you'd heard it too, I'd think it was in my head. Where could it have come from?"

"It sounded strangely familiar. If something is down there, shouldn't we call the Police? Especially as we're so close to where the school group went missing."

"The chamber had stone walls," Lily replied. "If we call the Police and tell them we're hearing voices, they'll think we're mad. We shouldn't do anything that will worry mum."

"We definitely need to take another look. We should speak to Colin tomorrow to see what he thinks. He seems to know a lot about Bridgeward and the estate."

The twins sat for a long time examining the marbles, chatting and drinking their hot chocolates. It was now completely dark outside. The lights in the neighbouring houses were off, and most people were asleep. The marbles glowed gently in the darkness, ethereal and in continual flux. Cool air drifted through an open window. Lily and Oliver were finding it difficult to get to sleep. Eventually, their conversations became shorter, their eyelids grew heavy, and they began to drop off to sleep with the marbles beside them in their beds.

The marbles became cold.

"GO AWAY! WHOEVER YOU ARE! GET OUT OF HERE!"

The twins awoke with a start.

"THESE ARE MY WOODS! GET OUT OF HERE!"

Lily and Oliver rushed to the window and looked out. It was the same gruff voice they had heard in the chamber, but this time it was coming from the woods of Bridgeward Estate.

"STAY AWAY. I WARN YOU!"

The twins peered out into the darkness but could see nothing. The voice stopped.

"I was struggling to get to sleep as it was," Lily whispered. "This isn't going to help."

"Isn't that the woods where the school group went missing?" Oliver asked.

Lily nodded. "Those are the woods of the Headless Archer."

CHAPTER SEVEN

Croissants

The sound of people chatting downstairs woke Lily and Oliver. "What's going on?" moaned Lily from beneath her duvet.

Oliver rolled over in his bed. "I don't know, but I barely slept," he said groggily. "I dreamt we were being chased through the cathedral by the Headless Archer. We were saved by a giant Boom-Box Bert, who tore the roof off the cathedral and scooped us up in his big hands. He boogied down the high street with us in his pocket."

"I don't want to imagine being in his pockets," said Lily, still hiding under her sheets. "I dreamt that a Troll dragged us into the woods and imprisoned us in a cave with the school group. Auntie Dot came to our rescue with a gun that fired doughnut jam."

The morning sun shone through the thin curtains onto the marbles on the bedside tables. The marbles cast the sunlight onto the bedroom floor, much like the stained glass window in the cathedral, but with motion and more intensity.

The twins got out of bed when they felt hunger pangs in their stomachs. They descended the stairs to find a gathering of people and dogs in the living room. Mistletoe was unimpressed with the company and had escaped to the kitchen.

"Good morning, darlings!" said Auntie Dot from the bottom of the stairs. "I forgot to mention yesterday; it's my turn to host the Canine Poetry Breakfast Club this morning. We meet every two weeks. You're more than welcome to join us. Trevor is about to begin his recital."

The members of the Canine Poetry Breakfast Club were an odd-looking bunch. There was a tall man with hunched shoulders and long grey hair. Beside him sat an Irish wolfhound. There was a lady with long, curly hair that reached down to her waist. She wore flared trousers and stood by the fireplace with a chocolate-brown spaniel. Also by the fireplace was an older man with tidy white hair, a well maintained white beard and a crisp white shirt. His dog was a Siberian husky. In fact, all of the Canine Poetry Breakfast Club members looked just like their dogs, except Auntie Dot and Mistletoe.

"Thank you, Auntie Dot," said Lily, "I think we'll probably just have some breakfast. We said we'd walk into town with Colin today."

"It's jolly good to hear you're meeting your new friend again," said Auntie Dot. "I've baked some croissants, but please don't eat them all. They're on the kitchen table. You might get a few visitors popping in from the poetry club. Enjoy!"

Lily and Oliver headed into the kitchen and sat down. There was an enormous pile of croissants at the centre of the table. The buttery smell was delicious. Surrounding the croissants was a selection of homemade jams with curious names like 'Scrumper's Crab Apple Jelly' and 'Forager's Hedgerow Jam'. The twins started eating. In the background, the poetry club members babbled, and their dogs occasionally barked.

A short and squat old lady appeared at the kitchen door leaning on a walking stick. She was wearing a flowery skirt, a blouse and a cardigan. Her grey hair was permed, and she wore horn-rimmed glasses with a cord around the back of her neck to stop them from falling off. Most old ladies have an air of kindness and charity about them, but this lady was the opposite; she seemed crafty and mean-spirited. She peered into the kitchen with a screwed-up expression on her face. There was a faint high-pitched sound coming from her malfunctioning hearing aid. Beside her stood her canine double; a tiny but very fat Chihuahua with pointy ears and bulging eyes. The old lady hobbled towards the kitchen table with her dog beside her.

"Don't mind me!" the old lady shouted over the sound of her

buzzing hearing aid. It was clear what she meant was 'get out of my way'. The old lady began shovelling croissants onto her plate, and her Chihuahua started barking. "I'm not forgetting you, Digbert! Marmalade for Digbert! Pass me the marmalade!"

"Sorry, are you talking to me?" responded Lily politely.

"What? Speak up, you silly little girl! Don't mumble!"

Lily spoke louder, "I said sorry. Are you talking to me?"

"Don't shout, you little moron! I don't see anyone else around here with the marmalade next to them."

Lily was taken aback, but she passed the old lady the marmalade. Oliver stifled his laughter.

"Knife!" yelled the old lady.

Lily and Oliver looked at each other.

"KNIFE!" the old lady repeated, staring at Oliver. Oliver handed her the knife, and the lady proceeded to smear a ridiculous amount of marmalade on croissant after croissant after croissant. Each time she finished applying the marmalade, she swept the croissant onto the floor for her fat Chihuahua to gobble up. When the Chihuahua finally looked like it had finished, the old lady ate a few croissants herself before stuffing a load more down her blouse, presumably for later.

"Do you brats read poetry?" the old lady said, brushing crumbs off her cardigan. She peered over her horn-rimmed glasses at the twins.

"Ummm, not really," responded Lily.

"What did you say? Speak up, you dimwit!"

"Not really, I said!"

"Don't shout, you cretin! I can hear you! What about you?" The old lady glared at Oliver.

"I've never really read any either," Oliver replied.

"You're a mumbler too, are you? Are kids not taught to enunciate properly at schools nowadays? Speak up!"

"No! Not really!" Oliver shouted.

"It's rude to shout! I'm not deaf, you know! Well, you should read poetry. You might learn something. Right, I'm off to listen to Trevor. He's completely rubbish, but I enjoy watching him squirm with nerves."

The old lady chuckled nastily as she hobbled out of the

kitchen. Her Chihuahua followed close behind, struggling to walk with its stomach rammed full of croissants and marmalade.

When the lady had reached the door, Oliver leant over to Lily and whispered, "Actually, I do know a bit of poetry…"

"An old lady once stopped for a chat,
Her dog was incredibly fat,
She was so rude,
We had to conclude,
That she was a nasty, deaf old bat."

"I HEARD THAT! You pair of little—"

"Gertrude, my dear!" interrupted Auntie Dot. She had entered the kitchen, oblivious to what had happened. "There you are! Do come along now. Trevor is about to start his recital."

The old lady's demeanour changed immediately. The nasty witch turned into a kind grandma. "Oh, thank you, Dot, my love," she said. "Could you please lend me an arm? I'm struggling to walk nowadays. What a lovely niece and nephew you have. Oh, and those croissants are delightful. You're such a good baker."

"I'm so glad you've had a chance to speak to the twins," said Auntie Dot with a smile. She turned to Lily and Oliver, "This is lovely Gertrude. She's such a sweet and kind— goodness me! What's happened to all of the croissants? How many have you two eaten? Please leave some for everyone else."

Auntie Dot turned and walked back to the living room with Gertrude on her arm. Gertrude scowled over her shoulder at the twins.

"Lovely old lady?" said Lily once she had stopped laughing at Oliver's poem. "She was revolting! And her hearing wasn't that bad. She heard your whispered poem from the other side of the room!"

"There are certainly some odd characters in Bridgeward," replied Oliver. He looked at the time on his phone. "I think we need to leave soon. Colin is probably waiting for us. I can't wait to show him the marbles."

The twins finished their breakfast and got ready to leave.

They gestured to Auntie Dot, who was in the living room, to tell her they were heading out. She acknowledged them with a smile and a wave before returning her attention to Trevor, who was awkwardly reciting a poem he had written:

> *"Oh hedgehog, oh hedgehog, how hedgehoggy you are,*
> *I almost hit you in my car,*
> *You should look both ways before you cross,*
> *It would have been such a loss,*
> *Snuffle, snuffle, snuffle away,*
> *Have a lovely hedgehoggy day."*

The recital was followed by polite clapping and thoughtful expressions as the other Canine Poetry Breakfast Club members considered the more profound messages contained in the poem.

Colin was waiting for the twins at the Old Rectory gate. It was another warm day. The sun was burning through the morning clouds, and long aircraft vapour trails streaked across the sky.

"Colin, you'll never guess what we found yesterday evening," said Oliver.

"There's a hidden chamber under the living room floor," Lily added. "We found it down the back of the fireplace—"

"And there was a weird voice telling us to get out—"

"And these cool marbles—"

"And some old children's toys—"

"And also a sculpture of the Headless Archer—"

"Calm down you two. One at a time, please!" Colin laughed. He was slightly overwhelmed with information. "Shall we start walking into town? You can tell me what happened as we go."

The friends headed off, with Lily and Oliver describing the passage in the fireplace and the chamber in as much detail as they could remember.

"That's cool," said Colin when the twins finished. "I think you've found a Priest Hole. Do you know what a rectory is?"

Lily and Oliver shook their heads. They knew the house was called the Old Rectory, but they had no idea what it meant.

"So it's a rector's house, and a rector is like a vicar. The house would have been built for the man who looked after the

Bridgeward Estate church."

"Where do you learn all this stuff, Colin?" asked Lily.

"We inherited lots of old books when my grandad died. My parents wanted to throw them out, but I persuaded them to keep them. I love reading books. Anyway, have you heard about the Tudor monarchs? You know, Henry VIII and all his wives?"

"Oh yeah," said Oliver, "he chopped off their heads and stuff, didn't he?"

"That's the one. In a nutshell, Henry VIII decided England should split from the Catholic Church in Rome and create its own form of Christianity. The Kings and Queens who ruled after him persecuted Catholics, except for Queen Mary, who decided to be Catholic, but that's a different story. During the reign of Queen Elizabeth I, Catholics were sought out by Priest Hunters. Wealthy Catholic families created hiding places for Catholic priests in their houses. The priests hid in these hiding places when the Priest Hunters knocked on the door."

"That's so stupid," said Lily, "why weren't people allowed to do things differently?"

"Ha!" exclaimed Colin. "People have been telling each other how to live their lives for thousands of years. I think we'd all be better off if we spent more time questioning our own beliefs and less time trying to convince everyone we're right."

"That's quite deep for this time of day," responded Oliver. "So we've found a priest's hidey-hole, but I'm still confused about why a priest would have a statue of the Headless Archer."

"Well, interestingly," began Colin, "the Story of the Headless Archer started after the English Reformation when people knocked the heads—"

"OUCH!" interrupted Lily. "What was that? Something just hit me in the face!"

There was a croissant on the pavement. The three friends looked around and saw a mini driving down the road with an old lady's arm hanging out of the window, gesturing rudely. They could hear Gertrude cackling.

"That horrible old lady!" exclaimed Lily angrily, "She's so nasty!"

Oliver thought for a moment and then spoke...

"There once was a lady in a Mini,
Who threw a croissant at Lily,
On her face it did land—"

"NOT NOW, OLIVER! It's your silly poem that got us into this situation in the first place. She's such a revolting old hag."

Despite Lily's annoyance, the thought of Oliver's original poem brought a small smile to her crumb-covered face.

"So why did an old lady just throw a croissant out of a car window at you, Lily?" asked Colin, trying not to laugh. "That's not something that happens every day."

"Well, it's quite a long story," began Lily. She then described the twins' interaction with Gertrude at breakfast.

"We also discovered these marbles in the hidey-hole," added Oliver, who was keen to talk about the Priest Hole, despite finding it hilarious that Lily had just been hit in the face by a croissant thrown by a vengeful pensioner.

Oliver took a marble out of his rucksack and gave it to Colin. Colin was amazed by what he saw. The marble had a dull glow, and the moving patterns inside reminded Colin of images he had seen of distant galaxies. Colin watched as clouds of crimson faded into a spiral of flamingo pink. There were also streaks of ice blue that shot across a smoky drift of copper. In front of all this, there was an explosion of mustard yellow.

"This is amazing," muttered Colin. "There are no chips on it, and it feels perfectly round. It can't have been used to play marbles. I have no idea what it is."

"The marbles are cool," said Lily, "but the voice was terrifying. You know you told us the Story of the Headless Archer yesterday? Well, I'm not sure that it's just a story."

"Think about it," Oliver continued, "the school group went missing in the woods on Bridgeward Estate – woods said to be haunted by the Headless Archer. Last night, we heard a strange voice in these woods, and we discovered a hidden chamber with a statue of the Headless Archer."

"And we opened the passage to the Priest Hole by pressing on a carving of the Headless Archer," added Lily.

"What if that voice was the voice of the Headless Archer? Oliver asserted. "Maybe he has kidnapped your friends?"

"I'm not sure," replied Colin, taking a moment to think. "I love ghost stories, but I don't think they're true. Didn't you say that no dust had been disturbed?"

"But we're talking about a ghost, not a human," replied Oliver. "He also hasn't got a head. Dusting his bedroom probably isn't a priority."

"Oh dear," exclaimed Lily with her eyes wide open. "A ghost with no head, and we've just stolen his marbles."

"If the Headless Archer wanted the marbles back, he'd have taken them back," said Colin, "and if the voice you heard was his, he was close enough to do something. It's just a ghost story, and there will be a sensible explanation. Anyway, I'm certainly very keen to see the image in the Spell Book."

"And I'm keen to see if anything in the Spell Book helps us understand how the Priest Hole, the marbles and the Headless Archer are connected," added Lily.

"Me too," said Oliver as he took the marble from Colin and put it in his pocket.

CHAPTER EIGHT

Marbles and Riddles

The centre of Bridgeward was busy again with visiting tourists, teenagers on their school holidays and locals going about their everyday business. The three friends walked towards the cathedral along a tree-lined path that bisected the lawn. Boom-Box Bert was in his usual spot, shimmying in time with his music. When he spotted the twins, he pointed with outstretched arms, winked and then jumped 90 degrees to continue his shimmying in a different direction.

"My fault," said Oliver. "I shouldn't have made eye contact."

The three friends joined the queue to enter the cathedral beside a family with two young children. Oliver overheard the eldest child speak, "I hate it here! It rains too much, and the food is really boring. How can all these English people wear shorts? It's too cold, and they all have horribly pasty legs."

Oliver looked at his legs and felt slightly offended. He did not notice the marble in his pocket becoming cold.

"The pizzas here are dreadful," responded the child's father, "but they're still better than English food. Fish and chips? Sausage rolls? There's a reason why the seagulls pinch all of the chips; they taste like bird food."

Oliver quite liked the idea of a sausage roll for lunch. The marble was getting colder.

"I couldn't believe people were swimming in the sea yesterday," added the mother. "It must have been freezing!"

Oliver thought the weather had been beautiful since they

arrived in Bridgeward. The marble was now ice cold.

The younger child nudged the older child and spoke, "If you don't like pasty English legs, I wouldn't look at these three behind me." The two children sniggered.

"Excuse me!" blurted Oliver. "We can hear what you're saying, you know! The weather has been lovely, and sausage rolls are brilliant, particularly if you dip them in ketchup." Oliver then gestured towards his legs. "And my mum says I tan up quite nicely after a few weeks of sun!"

The family went quiet and looked very embarrassed.

"Since when did you speak Italian?" exclaimed Lily, looking shocked.

"I'm so sorry!" said the father in English. "We didn't realise you spoke Italian. We're having a lovely holiday in your beautiful country. We were just joking, so please don't take offence."

"What did you say to them?" Lily asked Oliver with a nudge.

"He was right to speak to us," said the mother. "We were being very rude. I have to commend you on your Italian. Where did you learn to speak so fluently?"

"Erm, I… erm, I taught myself?" replied Oliver, completely baffled by what was going on.

"Well, you speak beautifully," continued the mother. "With a Tuscan accent too – we are from Tuscany. We are truly very sorry, and we won't bother you anymore."

With that, the Italian family sheepishly turned and entered the cathedral.

"What just happened?" Oliver asked Lily.

"You tell me! You're the one who just spoke fluent Italian to some tourists!"

"But I can't speak Italian."

"Well, you just did," said Colin, "and very well apparently because those Italians were impressed."

Without Oliver noticing, the marble in his pocket returned to room temperature.

The friends entered the cathedral and walked silently towards the wooden staircase that spiralled up into the library. Lily walked with her arms crossed. She was upset because she thought Oliver had been learning Italian without telling anyone, and she had always wanted to speak a foreign language. Meanwhile, Oliver was trying to understand what had just happened. As far as he was aware, he had just spoken English to some tourists who were also speaking English. Colin was in the unfortunate position of being with one person who was peeved and sulking and another who was consumed by his thoughts.

"I'd love to own a library like this," said Colin, trying to break the awkward silence when the friends reached the library. "Look at all these leather-bound books. I bet they all have that old book smell too; I like to think it's the smell of wisdom. I'd love to read some of them, although they're probably all written in Latin."

"I'm sure Oliver could help you with those," snapped Lily. Her arms were on her hips as she glared at Oliver. "He's probably been casually teaching himself Latin in the evenings."

"I can't speak Latin or Italian!" Oliver snapped back. "I spoke English to that family, and they spoke English back. I'm very confused by everything."

"Have you had a bang to the head recently?" asked Colin, trying to mediate. "I've read about people getting knocked out and then waking up able to speak a different language."

"No," replied Lily, still glaring at her brother, "he's not had a hard whack on the head… yet."

"Okay, let's go and check out the Spell Book," said Colin quickly.

Lily, Oliver and Colin walked across to the cabinet that displayed the Spell Book. The same man as yesterday was standing beside the cabinet talking to visitors.

"Fancy translating this one for us, Oliver?" whispered Lily. "Have you been practising your unknown languages recently too?"

"Shut up!" replied Oliver rather loudly.

The old man stopped speaking and glared over his glasses at Oliver.

"My apologies, Sir," said Colin. "He wasn't talking to you. He was talking to me. I was chatting, but he wanted to listen to what you're saying."

"Ah, hello, Colin," replied the man smiling. "It's nice to see you. Not a problem, but please do behave."

"Yes, Sir," replied Colin with a smile. He then whispered to the twins, "He's my old history teacher. He's retired now."

Colin squeezed into a small space among the tourists surrounding the Spell Book. He immediately spotted the picture of the Headless Archer beside an apple tree. The beautifully drawn figure stood with his legs astride, looking away from the viewer. He wore light brown trousers and shin-high black boots, but his torso was bare. The Archer's broad shoulders and powerful arms were contorting with the effort of drawing back the string of his longbow. An arrow was nocked and ready to fire. The archer's forearms were protected with laced leather guards, and a quiver and a satchel hung from his hips.

As Colin pondered the image, Lily joined him beside the display cabinet and spoke quietly, "That picture of the Headless Archer is so similar to the statue in the Priest Hole and the carving in the fireplace. The figure is in the same pose."

"It also matches the description of the Headless Archer in the story," replied Colin. "He even has the satchel in which he keeps his head, and those are the dragonflies from the story; electric blue, neon yellow and bright red."

Lily had a sudden realisation, and her eyes widened. "There was a satchel by the table in the Priest Hole! And a bow! And one of those things that hold the arrows!"

"Are you sure?" questioned Colin. "Did you look in the satchel?"

Lily gulped. "No. You don't think it contains his head do you?" Lily then remembered that Oliver had tripped over the satchel as he turned to flee the Priest Hole. She made a frightening connection, "The voice! It came from the Headless Archer's head! Oliver! Oliver!"

But Oliver did not respond. He was staring at the Spell Book with his eyes and mouth wide open. While Lily and Colin had been discussing the image of the Headless Archer, the marble in Oliver's pocket had become freezing cold, and unlike during the incident with the Italian family, this time, Oliver noticed. Oliver had watched as the mysterious letters and symbols in the Spell Book had gently drifted and flowed on the old, discoloured pages as if they were drops of ink in water. The images of the Headless

Archer, the apple tree and the dragonflies remained the same, but the shifting, ethereal patterns around them began to form words Oliver could read.

Lily nudged Oliver hard with her elbow. With his attention abruptly broken, he turned to her and whispered, "You're not going to believe what is happening. Come with me."

Oliver led the others to a quiet corner of the library, where he reached into his rucksack. "Right, do you want to learn to speak Italian? Or maybe Latin? Or maybe a mysterious language from hundreds of years ago? Put a marble in your pocket, and let's go back to the Spell Book."

Lily and Colin were confused, but they took a marble from Oliver and followed him back to the cabinet. They could feel the marbles getting colder in their pockets as they got closer. They squeezed in between the tourists, and as they looked at the Spell Book, the mysterious writing slowly began to move as it had for Oliver moments earlier.

"This is amazing!" whispered Lily. "How is this happening?"

"The words are being translated into English!" said Colin, giddy with excitement. "I think we've just cracked the undeciphered language! This is sooo cool. Just a moment more, and I think we'll be able to read the writing."

"It's the marbles," explained Oliver, "they grow cold in your pocket when something strange is about to happen. They made me speak Italian earlier, and now they are translating the Spell Book. They were also cold when we heard that voice yesterday."

The three friends watched as the characters completed their transformation into English. Together, Lily, Oliver and Colin read from the Spell Book of the Woodland Folk:

Follow the archer
Rome's last stand
The end of the world
Lelandis found
Beneath God's altar
The worship of the Headless

Follow the archer

A dragonfly creek
The end of the world
Lelandis found
Where apples fall
The Headless play their games

"They look like riddles," exclaimed Oliver.

"They certainly don't make much sense," added Lily, "but we now know for sure that the Spell Book, the Priest Hole, the marbles and the Headless Archer are connected. We just need to work out how and why!"

"This is really strange and very confusing," muttered Colin, deep in thought. "I'm starting to wonder if you are both right about the voice. We need to look in that satchel to see if it contains the head of the Headless Archer."

"I don't think I can do that," said Lily, turning slightly pale. Oliver pulled a face that suggested he was not keen either.

"My friends went missing two weeks ago," Colin continued, "and I've not slept properly since. What we've discovered must be connected to their disappearance. I was so close to falling into that hole, but my friend, Sam, saved me. This is my opportunity to do something that could find them. A stupid head in a bag isn't going to stop me. Anyway, what's it going to do?"

"I wouldn't be so complacent," said Oliver. "The head could nibble your toes, or maybe sneeze at you, or possibly burp angrily."

Colin and Oliver laughed.

"Thank goodness you're so untidy, Oliver," said Lily, exploring the inside of Oliver's bag. She pulled out a piece of crumpled paper and a pen. "Colin, would you mind turning around for me, please?"

Colin turned around, and Lily placed the paper between his shoulder blades. She then wrote down the riddles from the Spell Book.

The three friends descended the stairs from the library and left the cathedral, desperate to explore the Priest Hole. The walk back to the Old Rectory passed very quickly, with the friends talking excitedly about everything they had discovered. They arrived home late in the afternoon. As they walked up the pathway to the front door, they could smell delicious aromas drifting out of the open kitchen windows. Auntie Dot was cooking lasagne with fresh garlic bread. It was a meal that would have undoubtedly pleased the Italian family.

"Good afternoon, dears!" Auntie Dot sang as they entered the kitchen. "Have you had a good day? What have you been up to?"

"We visited the cathedral again, Auntie Dot," replied Lily. "There are so many fun things to do in Bridgeward. We're having a great time."

"What jolly good fun!" exclaimed Auntie Dot, both delighted and surprised. "It's nice to see you again, Colin. Will you be joining us for tea?"

Colin was almost drooling at the sight and smell of the delicious food. "I've never had fresh lasagne before. We always have microwaved ones. I'd love to stay, please."

"There's more than enough to go around! It'll be about 10 minutes, so you can pop home to tell your parents if you like."

"They're both in town today for important meetings," Colin replied. "They won't be home until very late."

"Not a problem," replied Auntie Dot. "I can give you some to take home for them if you like."

"Auntie Dot," began Lily, "would you tell us more about your house? We've loved exploring it and would like to know more about its history."

Auntie Dot was delighted by Lily's question. "Well, I don't know too much, really," she began. "I bought the house off Bridgeward Estate. Last year, Lord Bridgeward was investigated for financial irregularities. The Police found all sorts of odd things, and they still haven't worked everything out. Regardless, the Lord was kicked out, and the administrators began selling parts of the estate to repay debts." Auntie Dot sensed that Lily, Oliver and Colin were not interested in *financial irregularities*, so she changed tack. "This house hasn't been occupied for decades, apparently. A few locals have told me it's been empty since before the Lord's son went missing."

"What happened to the Lord's son?" asked Lily.

"He disappeared around forty years ago. Around the same time, a young girl from the town also disappeared. There was a massive Police hunt, but nothing was found. Apparently, it broke the Lord's heart, and he has never been the same since. The boy was his only child."

The three friends gave each other knowing looks. They had all connected the missing boy and the belongings in the Priest Hole.

Auntie Dot served up dinner, and the three friends chatted casually as they ate the delicious meal. The food suppressed their desire to explore the Priest Hole like a magic spell. When the friends finished their last spoonfuls of rhubarb crumble and custard, the spell lifted, and the urge to explore returned.

"I'm popping into town this evening," announced Auntie Dot. "The local amateur dramatics group is performing. Hopefully it's better than Peter Pan last Christmas. Trevor badly hurt his hip flying across the stage on a wire. I don't think he was the right choice for Peter Pan, although I must say, Gertrude was surprisingly good as Captain Hook."

Lily gave Oliver a wry look. She could imagine Trevor spinning around uncontrollably on a wire with Gertrude firing croissants at him from a pirate's cannon.

After dinner, the three friends helped Auntie Dot tidy the kitchen. Auntie Dot then went to her room to smarten up. The three friends waited. The moment Auntie Dot left the house, they planned to head straight down into the Priest Hole.

Outside, a halo of dark orange radiated from the setting sun. It pierced the soft clouds and blended into the darkening blue sky. Opposite the sun and beneath a full moon, dark clouds drifted menacingly towards Bridgeward. A storm was coming.

CHAPTER NINE

The Lost School Group

"Is everyone okay?" shouted Miss Wilson. She grimaced in the dark as she stood up. "Speak to me! Is everyone okay?"

Miss Wilson had landed heavily on a pile of soil at the bottom of the cavern. She felt winded and shaken, but her immediate concern was the welfare of the four students: Mia, Jay, Sam and Joe. Dragonflies darted around above her head, providing colourful and erratic light. The hole beneath the apple tree had disappeared completely, and water could be heard flowing nearby.

"Miss... Miss Wilson? Is t-that you?"

"Joe! Yes, it is me. Are you okay? Where are you? I'm here with you now. Let's just stay calm. The emergency services have been called, and I'm sure they'll be looking for us soon."

"The H-Headless Archer!" Joe shouted. "What if t-the Headless Archer is d-down here?"

"Don't be silly, Joe," replied Miss Wilson, scrambling across the dirt towards Joe's voice. "That's just a silly story."

"B-but what about all the d-dragonflies?"

"I don't think this is a time to be admiring the insect life."

"And the c-carving on the apple t-tree?"

"Just calm down please, Joe. I'm more concerned about everyone's safety right now."

"We're okay, Miss!" Mia called. Mia, Jay and Sam had landed on the side of the large pile of earth, and they had skidded down towards an underground stream.

"The dragonflies are part of the story, Miss," Sam pointed out. His colourful football shirt was now covered in soil.

"That's quite enough," replied Miss Wilson. She stood up with the torch that had been thrown into the cave for Joe. "It was silly, childish behaviour that got us into this situation in the first place."

"And Mr Montero's clumsiness," Jay added.

"Yes… well… quite," replied Miss Wilson as she shined the torch around the cave, looking for Mr Montero. She quickly spotted him lying completely motionless and face-down in the soil. "Oh, goodness me. Fred! Fred! Are you okay?" Miss Wilson scrambled down the bank of earth towards Mr Montero. "Can you hear me? Are you able to move? Can you talk?"

Mr Montero slowly lifted himself. There was a gash on his forehead, and blood was running down the side of his dirty face. The blood mingled with the muck and dripped onto the soil beside the stream. "Who are you, and where am I?" he replied. "The old lady's underwear… it's not mine… I promise."

"Old lady's what?" replied Miss Wilson. "You're talking nonsense. I think you're concussed, so please don't move. Help is on its way. You need to be checked out by someone medical."

Meanwhile, Mia, Jay and Sam had scrambled across to comfort Joe. The four students were less concerned by Mr Montero's head injury and more excited at discovering his name was Fred.

"Mr Montero once told us his first name was Flex," said Sam.

"What an odd first name," replied Mia. "Who names their child Flex?"

"I think Fred is a lovely name," Jay added. "Why would you pretend your name is Flex?"

"He probably thought it was cool," replied Sam. "I wonder if Montero is his real surname."

"What about the dragonflies?" interrupted Joe, bending his glasses back into shape. "They led me through the woods to the apple tree, and the apple tree had a carving of the Headless Archer on the trunk. This hole appeared when I touched it!"

"Really?" exclaimed Sam. "Surely the Headless Archer is just a made-up story?"

"I haven't heard the story for a long time," replied Jay, "but it can't be true. How does someone continue to live once their head has been chopped off? It's ridiculous."

"Well, if we do find him down here," replied Mia, clenching her fists, "there's six of us and one of him."

Mr Montero climbed to his feet, despite Miss Wilson's assertions that he should stay still until medical help arrived. When he noticed Miss Wilson, he quickly brushed the soil off his front, smiled awkwardly and held his hand out to greet her. "Hello. It's lovely to meet you. I'm Flex Montero, and your name is?"

"You are definitely concussed," replied Miss Wilson. "I'm Penny. You've had an unpleasant accident and hurt your head. You do know who I am, but you've temporarily lost your memory."

Mr Montero became aware he was in a cave lit by dragonflies. He also noticed the four students. "Ah, you have children," he exclaimed with disappointment in his voice. "Probably married too. Trust my luck."

The students began to giggle, and Miss Wilson raised an eyebrow.

"Right, it's all very odd hanging around in a cave," continued Mr Montero. "Let's get out of here and find a nice café to have some food. I'm starving."

"I don't think that's very sensible," replied Miss Wilson. "We should stay put. Emergency services have been called, and they'll be looking for us within an hour. We'll make it harder for them if we move."

Unfortunately for Miss Wilson, but not unsurprisingly, Mr Montero was not listening. He was striding along the side of the rolling stream towards a passage formed over millions of years by the flowing water. The dragonflies flew slightly ahead of him as if they were encouraging him in that direction.

"Come back, Fred!" Miss Wilson called. "This isn't a good idea. You've taken a hard bang to the head, and your brain isn't working at full capacity."

"No change there then," muttered Sam to the other students.

"Look, lady," replied Mr Montero as he stepped into the

stream and ducked to enter the passage. "You and your children managed to get in here easily enough, so let's just follow the river back out again. Even the dragonflies know I'm right. Look at them."

Miss Wilson took a deep breath. She was now in a difficult position. With every step Mr Montero took, the dragonflies flew further away, leaving Miss Wilson and the students with nothing but the feeble light of one torch. She was also very concerned for Mr Montero because he had no idea what he was doing. Miss Wilson reasoned that he would slowly recover from his concussion, and if she were with him, she could lead him back to where they fell into the cave. With a sigh, Miss Wilson beckoned for the students to join her, and they followed Mr Montero.

The passage they followed was like a blood vessel in the body of a stone Giant. It was roughly cylindrical, and the surface was smooth and undulating. In places, the meandering passage was tight, and the school group had to crouch down. In other places, it opened up. At times, the school group were knee-deep in water. At other times, they could walk beside the steadily flowing stream. The dragonflies led the way through the passage, closely followed by a determined Mr Montero. Miss Wilson stayed close to the students and constantly reassured, encouraged, and directed them.

Moving along the passage gave the students a distraction from their scary predicament. There was no more talk of the Headless Archer, and unspoken solidarity developed between the four students. Sam and Mia were naturally very adventurous, and once the shock of falling into the cave had subsided, the two of them began to revel in the adventure. They felt it would be a brilliant story to tell their friends when they found their way out, which was bound to be soon.

In contrast, Joe and Jay were keen to get out of the caves as soon as possible. Jay was very cautious, and the current predicament was far too dangerous for her liking. She knew there was a risk they would get lost, or the water levels would rise, or someone would trip and seriously injure themselves. Nonetheless, she had come to terms with her situation and was determined to play her part to make sure everyone found their way out of the cave safely.

Joe walked through the caves without saying a word. He had had enough excitement for one evening and just wanted to go home. He quietly observed everything he passed, and his mind kept returning to the story of the Headless Archer. The story still made him uneasy, but the presence of the others, particularly Miss Wilson, lessened his anxiety. Miss Wilson kept by his side and gave him the only torch.

After a while, the narrow passage opened out into a large cavern. The dragonflies shot into this much larger space and began darting around unrestrained. Their colourful light revealed a craggy ceiling above an undulating floor strewn with large boulders. Stones, rounded by the relentless flow of water, were amassed along the stream's route. The water burbled through the cavern, and there was a faint sound of buzzing in the distance.

The school group no longer needed to walk along the stream's path. Their wet feet squelched as they stepped out of the water and began walking past the large boulders. With the torch in his hands, Joe was the only person who noticed that the boulders were covered in simple and beautiful images painted in shades of ochre, red and grey. There were images of horses and deer in full flight pursued by men with spears. Joe also spotted horned cattle, pigs and other animals. One of the boulders was covered entirely in handprints.

The sound of buzzing grew as the group moved through the cavern, and the images on the boulders became stranger. There was one image of a group of men with bows and arrows chasing a Giant brandishing a club. Another boulder had pictures of people jumping around like kangaroos. Joe also spotted an image of oversized rabbits with spears hunting panicked humans. Then Joe's eyes were drawn to a very large boulder on the other side of the stream. A blue dragonfly zipped past the boulder, and its neon glow revealed a large image of the Headless Archer.

"Miss!" Joe cried, with his voice echoing through the cave, "The Headless Archer! Look!"

"Now, Joe," Miss Wilson began, "this experience must be very frightening for you, and you are doing so well, but these stories of the Headless Archer are not helping anyone."

"But look," Joe asserted, pointing the torch at the large boulder.

"Oh, that's definitely him," exclaimed Sam. "Look, there's his satchel where he keeps his head."

"He keeps his head in a satchel?" Jay replied. "Really? How silly."

"Yeah, it's in the story," replied Sam, "and he's supposed to haunt the woods of Bridgeward Estate. Did you notice the headless sculptures at the back of the manor when we were orienteering?"

"I never heard that bit of the story," replied Mia, sounding slightly frightened. "Do you mean the woods where we were camping?"

"Oh, please!" said Miss Wilson. "It's just a story!"

"She's right," agreed Mr Montero. "The Story of the Headless Archer started after the English Reformation when people knocked the heads off the statues on Bridgeward Estate because they disliked idols." Mr Montero finished his sentence and looked confused. He had no idea what he had just said.

"It's good to hear you were listening to the Head Instructor," replied Miss Wilson with a glare.

"It isn't the only image down here," continued Joe, shining the torch's light on the boulders nearest to the school group. "All of these boulders are covered with images of people, monsters and animals."

"Probably just local yobs with spray cans," said Mr Montero. "Compulsory military service is what they need. Anyway, it's a good sign; we must be close to the exit. The buzzing is getting louder too. It must be an electrical substation or something like that. No need to thank me! Not all heroes wear capes." Mr Montero turned and winked at Miss Wilson.

Miss Wilson contained her growing annoyance at Mr Montero's behaviour. His latest comment was particularly irksome because it was his fault they were all down in the cave. Miss Wilson's temper was building up inside her like the fizz in a shaken cola bottle.

At the same time, Joe was getting frustrated that the teachers were not taking the story of the Headless Archer seriously. He turned to the other students and whispered, "They're not listening to me, but we need to be careful. The dragonflies, the woods, the images of the Headless Archer – they all fit in with the story. What if the Headless Archer is down here? What if the dragonflies are leading us towards him as they led me to the hole?"

"I'm with you, Joe," replied Sam. "I think we need to be careful."

"Yeah, we need to stick together," added Mia, punching one hand into the other. "Remember, there are six of us and one of him. We could take him down. Let's keep alert."

Jay rolled her eyes. "Let's just stick together," she said.

The school group continued their journey through the cavern. The four students walked together, with Joe quietly pointing out the images with his torchlight, so Miss Wilson did not notice. Almost every boulder now had a picture of the Headless Archer. Mr Montero strode on ahead, whistling to himself. The buzzing was getting louder, and there was a glow of light on the cavern walls in the distance.

A short time later, the school group turned a sharp corner and discovered what was making the buzzing noise and producing the glow. A stone obelisk stood at the centre of a large pool of water, and above it, the air was thick with dragonflies. These dragonflies glowed in every imaginable colour. Joe even thought he caught a glimpse of a colour he had never seen before. This colour was vibrant like the orange of a tiger's stripe but mellow like the blue of a calm sea. The buzzing was incredible, the glow was intense, and the display was mesmerising. The students looked around anxiously for signs of the Headless Archer.

Mr Montero waded into the water towards the obelisk. As he got closer, he spotted a carving of a headless figure carrying a bow and arrow. The figure was lit by the kaleidoscopic light. Mr Montero reached out and touched the carving. Suddenly, the dragonflies disappeared, and the buzzing sound was replaced by crashing water. The students began to panic in the darkness. It sounded as if water was about to flood the cavern. Then, from the darkness, Mr Montero called out, "Aha! An exit!"

Relief overcame the students. They would soon be back home sipping hot chocolate and telling everyone about their exciting adventure. They noticed that moonlight was pouring into the cavern through a narrow passageway. Miss Wilson and Mr Montero were standing on the edge of a precipice behind a huge waterfall. The students ran to join them. Water was streaming down from somewhere high above and crashing into the water far below. The smell of fresh evening air reached their noses, and the night sky could be seen on either side of the falling water. The stars were incredibly bright, and a jagged, rocky pathway led down the side of the cliff beside the waterfall.

"There's no need to thank me," said Mr Montero to Miss Wilson with a smug look on his face. "I'm just happy to have saved a damsel in distress. I hope you've learnt that it's probably best not to explore caves with your children at night."

Miss Wilson turned and stared at Mr Montero. Her jaw was clenched hard, and her temper was rising inside her. The cola bottle was being shaken again.

"You know, you're not usually my type, and you do have four children, but how do you fancy going out for a drink sometime?"

Miss Wilson continued to stare. She was now clenching her fists as well as her jaw. The cola bottle was being shaken very hard.

"I know what you're thinking; why would a guy as handsome as me want to take you out on a date? Well—"

"You're a flunking TWERP!" Miss Wilson shouted. The bottle of cola had burst. "Firstly, these are NOT my children! They are students, and we are their teachers. One of them fell into a hole. The other three were pulled down into the hole by you – you great, big, clumsy idiot! You also somehow managed to bundle me into the hole when I had the situation under complete control. Well done, you absolute clonking prat!"

Miss Wilson was now prodding Mr Montero's chest with her index finger. She was frothing with anger.

"I have been diligently following you through this cave system because you're clearly concussed. It's a pity the blow to your head didn't knock some sense into you! So no, I will not be saying thank you, and I wouldn't join you for a drink even if you were the last person on Earth!'"

Mr Montero looked shocked, but Miss Wilson was not finished.

"Now, while I'm on a roll, I'm not going to continue feeding your insecurities by calling you by this stupid new name of yours. You're not *Flex Montero*. You're *Fred Broccoli*. You were never in the SAS, and you never had a trial for Manchester United. You definitely didn't knock out a heavyweight boxer, and the England Rugby team have never heard of you. Do me a favour, and stop being a total flunking BERK!!!'"

There was complete silence when Miss Wilson finished. She turned to find that the students were frozen with their mouths open and their faces pale. The cave passage also seemed to have disappeared.

"How odd," Miss Wilson exclaimed. Her voice had become calm again. "Oh, come along now, you lot. I didn't swear. Now let's get moving. We'll be home soon."

The students remained silent, and Miss Wilson noticed their focus was on something behind her. She turned and quickly realised it was not her rant that had shocked the children. Against the background of the full moon and the starlit sky, high on the rock beside the waterfall, there stood the silhouette of a figure with broad shoulders, large arms and no head. His open shirt fluttered gently in the wind. There was a canvas satchel over his shoulder, and he had a quiver of arrows around his waist. He stood with his longbow drawn and the arrow pointing straight at the school group.

CHAPTER TEN

Lelandis

"I'm off now, darlings," announced Auntie Dot. "Mistletoe has been fed. He often goes out for a little walk in the evening, but he always returns. I'll be back quite late, so don't stay up for me. Help yourselves to the fresh lemonade in the fridge, and have fun!"

Lily, Oliver and Colin acknowledged Auntie Dot with smiles and nods. Auntie Dot then stepped outside and saw the black clouds in the distance. Bridgeward was strangely silent and still. No birds were tweeting, and there were no vehicles on the roads. The town seemed to be waiting for the storm.

"I thought Auntie Dot would never leave," exclaimed Lily.

"I've been thinking," Oliver began. "I'm not going into the hidey-hole like this if the Headless Archer has anything to do with the missing school group. I'm taking something to defend myself."

"This is Auntie Dot's house, Oliver," responded Lily. "It's not somewhere in one of your computer games. What are you hoping to find? An assault rifle? A sawn-off shotgun?"

"Of course not," Oliver said. "Although I'm impressed with your gun knowledge. I'm going to have a quick search around the house to see what I can find. I'll only be two minutes."

Lily shook her head as Oliver left the room. She then turned to Colin. "Do you think we'll find the Headless Archer in the Priest Hole?"

"I'm not sure," replied Colin, scratching his head. "If you had asked me that question two days ago, I would have thought you were mad, but we've seen some pretty weird things today."

"Both riddles say *follow the archer*," said Lily. "I wonder what this could mean. I don't fancy following the Headless Archer if we find out he exists."

"Even if his head is in the satchel," said Colin, "where would we find the rest of him? We'd need to find the body if we wanted to follow him. Oh, listen to me – this is so ridiculous!"

"Perhaps we need to follow the voice—"

"I'm ready!" interrupted Oliver. He burst into the living room and sent the door swinging into the wall with a loud crash that echoed through the house. He was wearing a pink bicycle helmet and brandishing a cricket bat with its handle grip falling off. "It's amazing what you can find when you have a good root around. I've got some things for you too."

Oliver went back into the hall and returned with two torches, a yellow hard hat and another bicycle helmet. He was also carrying a mop and a wooden play sword. He threw them all on the sofa and then placed his hands proudly on his hips. Colin invited Lily to choose first.

"If I have to take something, I think I'll take the sword," said Lily, clearly unimpressed. "Although I don't think it will do much good. The last sword used against the Headless Archer chopped off his head, and that doesn't seem to have stopped him."

Colin then put on the hard hat and swished the mop around like a sword. Lily rolled her eyes. There was a distant crack of thunder, and the living room lights buzzed and flickered. The three friends slowly approached the fireplace with feelings of trepidation and excitement. They crouched down with their torches directed at the carving of the Headless Archer. Then suddenly, the marbles become cold in their pockets.

"GET OUT OF MY WOODS!"

It was the mysterious voice coming from outside.

"I'VE TOLD YOU! THESE ARE MY WOODS! GET OUT!"

Lily, Oliver and Colin ran to the window. They could see nothing.

"YOU ARE NOT WELCOME HERE!"

The Priest Hole could wait. The three friends knew they needed to follow the voice. They grabbed their torches and ran out of the Old Rectory. Colin led the trio through a small gap in a hedge and onto Bridgeward Estate.

"GO AWAY! GET OUT!"

Rain began to fall, and the thunder was getting closer. The wind whistled through the trees. Acorns and leaves from the oak trees began to fall to the ground.

"THESE ARE MY WOODS!"

Still, the trio ran side-by-side towards the voice, becoming breathless as they ran through the clearing where the school camp took place.

"WHAT ARE YOU? GO AWAY!"

The rain was now falling heavily. The last light of the setting sun was slowly disappearing, and the rain clouds blocked out the moon's light. The trio continued through the undergrowth beneath the canopy of the trees. An old wall appeared in front of them.

Oliver felt something brush the back of his legs. He turned quickly. There was movement in the undergrowth, but nobody was there. "There's something near us!" he shouted. "Something invisible!"

Lily and Colin span around in panic. They could barely see through the falling rain. The grass was moving, but there was no sign of anyone. Then Lily exclaimed with surprise, "Mistletoe? Is that you?"

"Of course it's floomin' me. Who else would it be? Floomin' humans. What are you lot doing here? I thought you hated rain."

Mistletoe emerged from the long grass with his brown, white and caramel fur dripping wet.

"Since when have you been able to talk?" asked Oliver as he wiped the rain from his eyes.

"Been able to talk? What's the lanky one gibbering on about? Floomin' humans."

"This makes so much sense!" exclaimed Lily. Her hair was drenched, and water dripped down her face. "We've been hearing Mistletoe's voice! He was in the Priest Hole when we found the marbles! He was telling us to get out!"

"Floomin' humans! What are they talking about? This time it's the one who bites her toenails. Disgusting human." Mistletoe started barking into the woods again, "GET OUT OF HERE!"

"Excuse me!" said Lily. "I don't think you should be criticising my habits. I saw you sniffing another dog's bum yesterday when all those dogs were in the house."

Mistletoe stopped barking and turned to face Lily. "How do you know what I just said?"

"We can hear what you are saying," explained Oliver. "You keep calling us *floomin' humans*."

"What? I don't floomin' believe you! If you can understand me, repeat this saying my mother taught me: *you can lead a horse to water, but you can't make it wear socks*."

Lily, Oliver and Colin repeated the peculiar phrase together.

Mistletoe shook his head. "Well, these are floomin' strange times. Chatting with humans, talking green foxes in the woods, people going missing, hidden rooms in the house…"

"So these marbles translate things!" said Colin, who had been thinking. "They helped Oliver understand the Italian family, they helped the Italian family understand Oliver, then they translated the Spell Book for us, and now we find out they've been translating Mistletoe's barks."

"Hold on a moment, Colin," said Lily, turning to speak to Mistletoe. "What did you say about green foxes? We thought you were barking at deer."

"Not a floomin' deer! There's a talking green fox in the orchard. I've never seen anything like it. I saw her snooping around the garden a few nights ago. She must have fallen in a paint pot while rummaging through someone's bins. Foxes are horrible creatures; floomin' garbage-raiders! They have an enchanting smell that will befuddle your mind." Mistletoe shook his head and muttered to himself, "You're talking to humans, Mistletoe. Are you going mad?"

Meanwhile, Oliver had been looking into the woods. He brought his hands to his mouth and shouted, "GREEN FOX! We want to speak to you!"

Lily, Oliver and Colin were now soaked from head to toe, and the last light of day had almost disappeared. The faint silhouette of a fox's head could be seen in the twilight through the falling rain. It was peering out from behind a distant oak tree. Oliver beckoned for the fox to come closer.

"I don't think you should be doing this," Mistletoe whispered, "As you humans say: *don't shove a rocking horse in the moat.*"

"Erm… do you mean *don't stare a gift horse in the mouth?*" replied Colin.

"I mean exactly what I said," replied Mistletoe haughtily. "Why would anyone stare into a horse's mouth?"

"Why would anyone want to shove a rocking horse in a moat?" responded Oliver.

A fox tentatively emerged from behind the oak tree and walked slowly through the long grass towards the three friends and Mistletoe. When the fox saw that the humans were not threatening and Mistletoe did not bark, she ran towards them, hopping gracefully and silently through the undergrowth.

"It's wonderful to meet you, humans," the fox said with a bow of the head. "My name is Lime Fox, and I'm delighted to make your acquaintance."

The name certainly suited the fox; she looked like a fox in every way, except she was lime green instead of rusty red.

"A formal greeting from a funny coloured woodland animal," Oliver said. "I wasn't expecting this today. Just when we thought we were working out the puzzle, we discover that we've been hearing Mistletoe's voice, and there's a talking green fox in the woods. I'm more confused than ever."

"It's wonderful to meet you, Lime Fox," said Colin with an air of grandeur. "Can you assure us that you are a good fox? Or are you up to no good as Mistletoe suggests?"

"Oh no, human, I am indeed a good fox. I found my way to this land about a week ago by accident. I simply wish to find my way home. If you could help me, I would be most grateful. My friends will never believe what I tell them if I ever get home. Humans! Real humans! And such kind and generous ones at that."

"Let's get back to the Old Rectory before it gets completely dark," said Lily. "Will you come with us, Lime Fox? We'd love to know more about you. We will try out best to get you home, and

I'm sure you can help with something that has been bothering us."

Lime Fox, Mistletoe, Lily, Oliver and Colin made their way back through the woods to the Old Rectory in the pouring rain. Mistletoe kept his distance from Lime Fox but watched her closely. It was completely dark by the time they arrived home. The wind was howling, and lightning occasionally lit up the sky. Mistletoe and Lime Fox shook out their wet coats at the door, and Lily ran upstairs and found three towels. Before long, Lily, Oliver and Colin were sitting wrapped in towels in the living room. Mistletoe was sitting curled up on his favourite seat, and Lime Fox was lapping water from a bowl she had been given. The electricity had cut out, so the three friends lit beeswax candles that Auntie Dot kept for such occasions. The candles cast irregular, flickering shadows in the dark.

"So, Lime Fox," said Lily, "I don't know where to start. I suppose it would be nice to know where you are from. Foxes are usually red and don't tend to make conversation."

Lime Fox lifted her head from the water bowl and spoke, "Yes, I tried to speak to a few of your red foxes, but they were all Dumb-Tongues. Your dog friend is the only talking animal I could find, and I tried to reassure him that I am just a lost animal from Lelandis."

Lily, Oliver and Colin sat forward quickly when they heard 'Lelandis'. They remembered this strange name from the riddles in the Spell Book.

"Did you say *Lelandis*?" asked Colin.

"Yes, Lelandis, it's the only land I have ever known. A few weeks ago, I was hunting in the woods around the waterfall. I spotted brightly coloured dragonflies on the river. The dragonflies led me along the riverbank to a steep path up a cliff. The path climbed up to a ridge cut into the rock behind the waterfall. With the water crashing down beside me, the dragonflies drew me towards a strange carving on the wall; it was of a human. I reached out and touched it. Suddenly the sound of crashing water disappeared, and I found myself in a cave lit only by dragonflies. They led me deeper into the cave and along a passage. Eventually, I reached a stone obelisk beside a pile of soil. On the obelisk, there was another carving of a human. I pressed the carving, and an opening appeared beneath an apple tree. I emerged to find it was nighttime. I thought I was still in Lelandis. The sky looked the same, but the stars weren't as bright. As my eyes adjusted, I realised the trees and plants were slightly different, and the animals were not quite the same. Certainly, none of them spoke. Except for the dog you call Mistletoe."

Lily, Oliver and Colin listened intently to Lime Fox. They were fascinated by everything she said.

"What Lime Fox described matches one of the riddles from the Spell Book," said Colin.

Lily shrugged off her towel and found the scrap of paper in her pocket. She read the second riddle aloud: *"Follow the archer. A dragonfly creek. The end of the world. Lelandis found. Where apples fall. The Headless play their games."*

"It does!" replied Oliver. "The *dragonfly creek* must be the river beneath the waterfall in Lelandis."

"And *where apples fall* is the orchard on Bridgeward Estate!" added Lily. The friends were becoming excited.

"*Lelandis found* is very easy to understand," said Oliver. "But what about *the end of the world?* Do you think Lelandis is a completely different world?"

"It sounds that way," replied Colin. "So the riddle is describing a passage from Earth to Lelandis."

Lily turned to Lime Fox, "Have you heard of the Headless Archer? And do you know anything about a group of humans lost in Lelandis?"

"I'm afraid not," Lime Fox replied. "Before today, I had never seen a human, although there was an odd smell in the passage between the waterfall and the apple tree. It was an animal smell that was unfamiliar to me." Lime Fox paused and sniffed the air. "It was similar to how you smell."

"We need to find that passage in the orchard," exclaimed Lily. "It must be where the school group went, but before that, we need to explore the Priest Hole again. We need to find out more about the Headless Archer. At least we now know it wasn't his voice we were hearing."

"Just a moment," replied Oliver. "Can you read the other riddle, Lily? I wonder whether it describes another passage."

Lily recited the first riddle: *"Follow the archer. Rome's last stand. The end of the world. Lelandis found. Beneath God's altar. The worship of the Headless."*

"The key part of the riddle is *beneath God's altar*," said Oliver. "If we think the second riddle describes a passage to Lelandis under the apple tree, then this riddle must describe a passage to Lelandis under an altar."

"If the chamber is a Priest Hole, maybe the table is an altar?" suggested Lily. "And if the table is an altar, there could be a passage beneath it."

"It would fit in with the bit that says *Rome's last stand*," said Colin. "Priest holes were made for Catholic priests, and the heart of the Catholic Church is the Vatican in Rome."

Lily stood up and walked purposefully towards the fireplace. "There's only one way to find out," she exclaimed boldly.

"Wait," called Oliver. "You're forgetting your helmet and weapon."

Oliver handed Lily the bike helmet and the wooden sword. At the same time, Colin was putting on his yellow hard hat. Oliver then started swinging his cricket bat around like a cricketer warming up.

"Well, I feel like some protection is better than none," conceded Lily as she put on the helmet and grabbed the wooden sword, "and I don't think I will ever look as ridiculous as you two."

The three friends approached the fireplace with Mistletoe and Lime Fox close behind. Lily crouched down with her torch in her mouth to find the carving of the Headless Archer. She pressed the carving lightly, and the limestone block moved backwards. As she bent down to crawl through the hole, Mistletoe darted past her into the passage. Lily followed, Oliver and Colin were next, and Lime Fox was last.

CHAPTER ELEVEN

Beneath God's Altar

Lily could hear the rain hammering against the walls of the Old Rectory as she descended the narrow staircase to join Mistletoe in the Priest Hole. The others were close behind. The twins' footprints from the night before, along with Mistletoe's paw marks, could be seen in the dust on the stone floor. The statue of the Headless Archer lay where it had fallen. A quiver, a longbow and a satchel lay beside the table.

The friends focused their torches on the satchel, worried it contained the Headless Archer's head. They would not be able to think about anything else until they looked inside. The friends edged closer with makeshift weapons at the ready. The complete darkness beyond the beams of their torchlight did not help their unease.

"What is it you fear, humans?" said Lime Fox softly. The darkness did not bother Lime Fox, nor did it concern Mistletoe, who was still watching Lime Fox suspiciously from a distance.

"It's the bag," whispered Oliver without taking his eyes away from the satchel. "We think it might contain a human head."

"Would you like me to take a look?" Lime Fox said casually.

The three friends looked at each other, and the tension in their bodies seemed to disappear instantly.

"Oh, if you wouldn't mind," said Lily.

Lime Fox skipped over to the satchel and used the corner of her mouth to loosen the cord that tied it shut. Lime Fox then squeezed her head inside.

"Well, humans, there is no head," said Lime Fox, emerging with what looked like an item of clothing in her mouth.

"Are you sure?" asked Colin.

Lime Fox nodded.

"In that case, let's have a look!" Colin strode forward, picked up the satchel and shone his torch inside. "Lime Fox is right; there's no head. Well, that's a relief, but it doesn't bring us any closer to understanding what the Headless Archer has to do with all of this." Colin then reached into the bag and pulled out a packet of crisps, a tube of sweets and a water bottle.

"Hardly the most frightening things in the world!" exclaimed Lily.

"I wonder if the Lord's son used this bag," said Oliver.

"There's one more thing," said Colin, "and it's a bit more interesting."

Colin pulled an object out of the satchel and showed it to Lily and Oliver. It consisted of two short and broad barrels, like a pair of binoculars. Unlike binoculars, these barrels were attached to a light fabric cap, clearly designed to be worn on the head. A solid ridge ran from the barrels over the crown to the back of the neck. It was made from a brown, leathery material and was like something you might see displayed in a museum, yet it had sharply defined edges that made it look futuristic. It was like nothing the three friends had ever seen before.

"Who fancies trying it on then?" asked Colin.

Oliver was quick to volunteer. He handed his torch to Lily, took the item in both hands and placed it on his head. Oliver felt the cap shrink to fit his head perfectly. The two barrels also felt incredibly comfortable against his eyes. In fact, it felt as if the object had become part of his head. At the same time, Lily and Colin gasped. They had watched the cap disappear, and disconcertingly, Oliver's eyes had merged into one large eye above the ridge of his nose.

"Are you okay, Oliver?" Lily exclaimed. "You're looking a bit different right now, and I'm not sure it suits you too well."

"What do you mean?" replied Oliver with his big eye blinking. "These binocular things are amazing! I can see everything in the Priest Hole. It's like someone has just switched on a light, and if I want to focus on something, they just zoom in. It's incredible!"

"Try taking them off again," suggested Colin. "It would be nice to know if you go back to normal."

Oliver took the object off his head, and both eyes reappeared. "Why are you looking at me like that?" he asked.

Lily thought that a demonstration was better than an explanation. She took the object and placed it on her head.

"Oh, that's weird," exclaimed Oliver as Lily's eyes merged into one. "Possibly an improvement though."

"These are fantastic!" said Lily. "My vision is amazing, like some sort of superhero!"

"A superhero?" said Colin laughing. "What would your name be? Lighthouse Lady?"

Oliver laughed. "You're right, Colin. She does look like a lighthouse. It's a pity she's not wearing her red and white hooped shirt."

Lily took the object off and handed it to Colin, who inspected it closely with his torch. "There's something written on the inside," he said. "It's similar to the writing in the Spell Book, and the marble must be translating it because it's starting to move. It says... *Woden's Eye.*"

"Cool name," exclaimed Oliver. "Now try it on, Colin. It's amazing."

Colin took off his glasses and tucked them into his pocket. He placed Woden's Eye over his head, and just as with Lily and Oliver, the object disappeared as Colin's eyes merged. Colin was amazed by the change in his vision. He scanned the Priest Hole and could see everything perfectly, including the item Lime Fox had pulled from the satchel moments earlier. "Lily," he said, "there's something Lime Fox found in the bag by your foot. It looks like an item of clothing. We need to see if it does amazing things too."

Lily picked up the item from the floor. It was shaped like an open waistcoat with two large holes for arms. Unlike a waistcoat, there was not much fabric to cover the wearer's chest, and the back was shaped like an inverted teardrop. The item was golden, like a wheat field, and was incredibly light. Lily swung it around as if it were a coat and put her arms in the holes. The back floated in the air like a feather. Slowly and gently, it fell to Lily's back. As it did so, the item disappeared like Woden's Eye, and feathered wings sprang from Lily's back. They were the same gold as the fabric, and Lily had complete control over them. She stretched the wings out to their full width and shook them like a swan beside a lake.

"I so wish it wasn't raining right now!" Lily said with a beaming smile. "I knew how to fly the moment I put these wings on."

"We're never going to get those off her," said Oliver to Colin. "You know London is really boring compared to Bridgeward. We've been here three days, and we've found magic marbles, a talking beagle, a polite green fox and these cool things. What's more, I get the feeling we're about to find another world. London is rubbish."

With all the excitement of finding Woden's Eye and the wings, combined with the relief of knowing the Headless Archer did not haunt the Priest Hole, the three friends momentarily forgot they were trying to solve the riddles of the Spell Book. Fortunately, Mistletoe and Lime Fox had been sniffing around.

"Humans," Lime Fox began, "were you planning to look under the table? I cannot see anything interesting here or smell anything strange, but then I don't really know what I'm looking for."

"Not much floomin' use are you, Fox?" said Mistletoe with a sneer. "Look what I've found. There's another carving of the Headless Archer in the stone behind the floomin' table. It's the same as the one in the fireplace. Come and take a look."

Lily, Oliver and Colin joined Mistletoe behind the table. They crouched down and directed their torches at the wall. It was undoubtedly the Headless Archer.

"I know!" exclaimed Colin, "the riddles are telling us to follow the *carvings* of the Headless Archer, like a trail!"

As Colin spoke, the marbles became cold in everyone's pockets, and the friends knew what to do.

"Are you ready?" said Lily.

Oliver and Colin nodded.

"Well, here goes then!"

Lily pressed the carving, but nothing happened. The three friends looked at each other confused. Colin placed a hand on the carving and pushed hard. Again, nothing happened. Oliver drew closer to the carving, traced it with his index finger and then pushed as hard as possible. Still, nothing happened.

"Okay, I didn't expect this," said Colin.

"If there's a second passage down here," said Lily, "why doesn't anything happen when we press the carving?"

"*Beneath God's altar*," recited Oliver thoughtfully. He turned to look at the table in the hope of finding inspiration. He found much more. The table was indeed an altar, and beneath it was a stone staircase that spiralled down into darkness. In contrast to the uneven, dust-covered floor of the Priest Hole, this staircase was clean and perfectly formed. Every line was straight, every angle was precise, and every surface was flawless. It looked like it had been fashioned out of one colossal stone monolith. Like Woden's Eye and the wings, it appeared both ancient and futuristic. Oliver nudged Lily and Colin, who were still examining the carving. He pointed to the staircase. Beneath God's altar, at the edge of their world, the three friends had found a passage to Lelandis.

CHAPTER TWELVE

Into the Darkness

"I guess it's time to find your friends, Colin," said Oliver, whose nervousness was just perceptible in his voice.

"And hopefully take Lime Fox home," added Lily.

"Kind humans! Have you found another passage?" exclaimed Lime Fox, skipping to where the three friends were crouched behind the altar. "I don't understand. Where is it?"

"She's not the only one who's confused," barked Mistletoe, sniffing for clues under the altar. "Where's this floomin' passage?"

To the surprise of Lily, Oliver and Colin, Mistletoe stood floating above the staircase.

"I'm sensing more marble magic," said Lily. She walked over to the altar, crouched down and stepped into the spiral staircase.

"Where's your floomin' foot gone?" exclaimed Mistletoe.

Oliver and Colin now understood what Lily had realised moments before; the passage to Lelandis was visible only to marble holders. Colin turned to Mistletoe and Lime Fox, "If you want to come with us, you'll need a marble each."

Oliver found the last two marbles in his backpack, and he placed them on the floor in front of Lime Fox and Mistletoe. The marbles glowed gently in the darkness. Lime Fox and Mistletoe gave the marbles a sniff and tentatively touched them with their paws. The marbles were cold, like walking on snowy ground, and the passage appeared.

"Well, I floomin' never!" exclaimed Mistletoe. "*Blow me up,* as you humans say!"

"*Blow me down*," corrected Colin. "I don't think you want to be blown up."

"I suppose we need to find you both a way of carrying the marbles," said Lily, shining her torch around the Priest-Hole, looking for inspiration.

"Good idea," said Oliver. "Some little bags would do the trick."

"Or perhaps those little jackets you see dogs wearing in the winter," suggested Colin.

"I was thinking of something they could hang around their necks," said Lily.

Without the friends noticing, Mistletoe picked up a marble in his mouth, flicked his head back, and swallowed the marble whole. It was not the easiest thing to ingest, and for a moment, Mistletoe looked quite ridiculous with his eyes bulging, his brow raised and his neck muscles tensed with the effort of forcing it down.

"You don't need to worry about me!" announced Mistletoe proudly as he felt the marble plop into his stomach.

"Why's that?" responded Lily, still scanning the Priest Hole.

"I've found somewhere safe for it."

"Oh, brilliant!" said Colin. "Do you have pockets in your fur or something?"

"Don't be ridiculous. I've swallowed it. As you humans say, *one in the ear is as good as two in the washing basket.*"

Lily, Oliver and Colin stopped what they were doing and looked at Mistletoe in disbelief.

"Firstly," said Lily, "that phrase is total nonsense. Secondly, what happens now if we need that marble back?"

Mistletoe thought for a moment and then spoke, "Well... I... I didn't really think that far ahead."

"For the record," added Oliver, "I'm not going to be the one searching for that marble in a few days."

"What a disgusting thought," muttered Lily.

"At least that's Mistletoe sorted," said Colin, "even if it isn't quite what we had in mind. I'm sure we can find an item of clothing somewhere that will fit Lime Fox, and we could then tuck the marble in somewhere secure."

"Sorry, humans," began Lime Fox, "did you say *clothing*?"

"Yes, that's probably the best way, isn't it?" answered Lily.

"You are very kind and generous humans, and I'm so thankful for your help, but I am NOT wearing clothes." Lime Fox's gentle voice became surprisingly forceful.

"Why's that?" asked Lily, taken aback by Lime Fox's tone.

"Well, it's rather peculiar. Animals don't wear clothes. If my friends in Lelandis found out I'd been wearing clothes, I'd never live it down. Besides, they must be so uncomfortable."

"I hate to agree with the fox," said Mistletoe, "but clothes are floomin' strange. What's even weirder is you humans seem obsessed with putting clothes on animals in your books and television programs. Have you ever seen a real rabbit bouncing around in a denim shirt? Or a floomin' toad in a waistcoat? Don't get me started on cats in wellies. You humans can be very odd. I don't know what you're all hiding. Auntie Dot exercises most mornings in the nude, and she looks perfectly norm—"

"Okay! Let's move on!" interrupted Oliver.

"...she starts with a few stretches."

"That's enough!"

"...followed by some squats."

"Enough!"

"...and she finishes with 50 star jumps."

Oliver glared at Mistletoe. "Are you finished yet?"

Colin returned the conversation to the marbles. "So what do you suggest, Lime Fox?"

Lime Fox peered into the distance as she thought. She then looked down at the marble. "Well, I have eaten worse."

"You can say that again," muttered Mistletoe under his breath.

Lime Fox picked up the marble in her mouth, tossed her head back, and swallowed the marble whole. She did this with slightly more decorum than Mistletoe, but the marble still did not look like the easiest thing to ingest.

After finally resolving the marble problem, the five companions readied themselves to descend the mysterious spiral staircase. Woden's Eye was put in Oliver's backpack, helmets were put on, and makeshift weapons were picked up. They then began their descent.

The staircase was steep, and the steps were very narrow. The companions descended carefully, keeping to the outside of the spiral. Even Mistletoe and Lime Fox found it tricky. As they corkscrewed further into the Earth, steps kept appearing out of the darkness. Oliver led the way, hoping that the end of the staircase would appear imminently. Down and down they went until finally, a simple archway appeared.

The archway was made from the same stone as the spiral staircase. Like the staircase, it was perfectly formed with faultlessly straight edges and flat surfaces. Oliver shone his torch through the archway and cautiously led the others forward. The light from Oliver's torch got lost in what appeared to be a vast cavern. The air was moist and cold. It was so dark that not even Mistletoe and Lime Fox could see beyond the feeble torchlight. Mistletoe sniffed the air keenly in the darkness, and Lime Fox's ears were pricked up, listening for the slightest sound. The companions stood by the archway, unsure how to proceed and nervous about what lay ahead.

"Our torches aren't going to be much good down here," whispered Oliver as he peered into the blackness.

"One of us needs to wear Woden's Eye," suggested Colin.

Lily had thought the same thing a moment earlier, and she was very keen to get her hands on Woden's Eye first. She jostled past Colin and reached into Oliver's bag. "I think as I ended up with the stupidest weapon, I should be the one with the super sight."

Lily put on Woden's Eye. Immediately, she could see everything in magnificent detail. They had stepped from the symmetry and precision of the staircase into an enormous cavern where glistening stalagmites and stalactites grew haphazardly from the floor and ceiling, and water dripped into irregular pools of water. A path made from the same stone as the staircase weaved through the enchanting landscape

"What can you see, Lily?" asked Colin, who was feeling very uneasy in the darkness. He desperately wished he was the one wearing Woden's Eye.

"We're in a big cavern, and there's a path," replied Lily, unaware of the nervousness in Colin's voice. "You're going to have to follow me closely. The path is winding, but it's just like a pavement, so you shouldn't trip on anything. You may as well turn your torches off too. The batteries will just run out, and they're not much use down here."

"That's easy for you to say," replied Oliver. "You're not going to be walking in complete darkness. How come you get Woden's Eye and the wings?"

"Stop moaning!" snapped Lily. "You'll get your chance."

"I think... we should hold hands," suggested Colin. "You know... like school children walking to the library."

Colin grabbed Lily and Oliver's hands before they could agree or disagree. Initially, the touch of Colin's hands felt uncomfortable, but the twins soon relaxed when they accepted it was a sensible idea.

"Is there any sign of the Headless Archer or the school group down here?" Oliver asked with a faint trembling in his voice.

"I don't think you should be worried about the Headless Archer," said Lime Fox. "I can't see much, but my hearing is sharp, and all I can hear is dripping water."

"I can't smell anything odd," added Mistletoe. "I'll keep sniffing. Just keep that fox away from me. She won't cast her floomin' spell on this dog."

The companions began their trek through the subterranean landscape. Lily led the way, with Colin next and Oliver third in the line. Lime Fox walked by their side. Mistletoe's sense of smell was so good he could walk a few paces behind.

Woden's Eye made Lily's journey through the cavern easy, but it was very different for Oliver and Colin. Their journey was uncomfortable and unnerving. Every step they took was a step further into the darkness, and their safety was utterly in the hands of Lily. Without their sight, they became more aware of water dripping into pools and gentle drafts of cold air on their skin. Colin found the journey particularly difficult. He tripped over Lily's heels more than once, and the twins noticed his hands were sweaty and trembling. But Colin continued, trying hard not to show his new friends he was scared.

The path took the companions up a long, weaving slope to a broad ridge. When they reached the top, Lily stopped to enjoy the view, and she explained that they were about to descend.

"Is it… is it much further?" asked Colin.

"I can't see a way out yet," replied Lily, "but the path is clear. I'm sure we just need to follow it. The view is amazing."

"Why don't you let someone else wear Woden's Eye now?" suggested Oliver.

"Well, I suppose so," replied Lily with a huff. She took off Woden's Eye and passed it to Oliver, who put it on without delay.

"This is brilliant," Oliver announced. "This is so much better than walking in the dark. I can't believe we've been walking through this landscape all this time."

Colin let out an involuntary yelp of despair.

"Can I make a suggestion, humans?" interrupted Lime Fox. "Perhaps you need to be a little bit more aware of how each other are feeling."

"What do you mean?" said Oliver.

"I think it might be wise to let Colin wear Woden's Eye."

Oliver was taken aback. "But I've not had a go either."

"Use your floomin' brains," interrupted Mistletoe. "There is a strong smell of fear, and it's not coming from you."

"Walking through this darkness is not pleasant for any of us," Lime Fox continued, "but Colin is clearly finding it harder than you and your sister."

"Fine!" exclaimed Oliver. He turned to Colin, who was tremoring in the darkness, and pushed Woden's Eye into his stomach. "You're leading the way then, Colin."

Colin felt relieved but also embarrassed because his new friends now knew he was battling his fears. He had hoped one of the twins would notice and quietly offer him Woden's Eye. Colin put on Woden's Eye and immediately felt more comfortable. He held his mop upside down like a walking stick and began to lead the others down the ridge. Lily, who was now second in line, was surprised at how unpleasant it felt to be led through the darkness. Oliver stayed at the back, sulking.

Colin attempted to make conversation, "How come you can

talk, Mistletoe? Do other dogs on Earth talk?"

"Apart from my mum, I've never met an intelligent dog on Earth," answered Mistletoe. "Of course, they floomin' speak, just not in sentences. They repeatedly shout the same floomin' words like *food* or *walkies*. My mother taught me. She also taught me how to understand what humans say. I don't know why I can talk and other dogs can't – maybe it's a lost dog skill. As you humans say: *don't count your biscuits in the snow.*"

"Do you mean: *don't count your chickens until they hatch?*" replied Colin.

"I mean exactly what I said," replied Mistletoe defiantly. "Biscuits and snow."

"Your ability to talk does explain a lot about your behaviour," said Lily, "particularly incidents like the one in London."

Mistletoe began to laugh hysterically. "I'll never forget that! Floomin' brilliant! I'll let you in on a secret; Auntie Dot didn't buy me my favourite dog food at the supermarket, so I kept changing the page in the map as she was driving home. It worked out so much better than I could have planned. I tell you what, the Queen's corgis were odd. You'd think they'd be posh and well-spoken, but I've never heard so much doggy swearing in all my floomin' life!"

The companions continued through the landscape of lifeless pools, glistening stalagmites and dripping stalactites. In the distance, Colin spotted that the path was leading to another archway in the cave's rock walls. The archway looked the same as the one they emerged from after descending the spiral staircase from the Priest Hole.

"It looks like we might soon be out of this cave," explained Colin to his companions.

"There is the faintest smell of something peculiar drifting through this cave," warned Mistletoe. "At first, I thought it was a human smell, but it's slightly different. I can't floomin' work it out."

"Maybe the Headless Archer," Oliver whispered.

"Or perhaps the missing school group?" suggested Lily.

"I can't see anyone," said Colin, "but we need to keep on our guard."

"YOU need to keep on YOUR guard," said Lily sharply. "We can't see anything."

"I'm sure we'll be out of here soon, humans," said Lime Fox calmly. "Let's work together."

Colin led the companions more slowly than before. When he reached the archway, Colin peered through and discovered a passage in the rock with a tight bend a short distance along.

"I think it's best if you stay here," Colin said, letting go of Lily's hand. "There's a passage ahead, and I'm going to check it out. I'll come back when I know it's safe."

"Hold on!" exclaimed Lily. "I don't want to be left alone in complete darkness!"

But Colin was not listening. He was slowly walking through the passage with his mop held out in front of him.

"Colin!" shouted Oliver, "where have you gone?"

Oliver and Lily reached out, hoping to find their companion.

"We're here with you," reassured Lime Fox. "Stay calm."

Colin reached the corner in the passage. He leant against the rock and took a deep breath to compose himself. Holding the mop out in front of him, he swiftly rounded the corner. The passage ended a short way ahead, and beyond it, there was light. Colin turned around and shouted back down the passage, "Everything is okay! It looks like we're out of the darkness!"

At that moment, Colin's marble became colder than it had ever been before. He turned around and discovered a figure at the end of the passage.

CHAPTER THIRTEEN

The Bridge over the Infinite Void

The twins had also felt their marbles become ice cold, and they began to panic. Oliver raised his bat above his shoulders and was twitching, ready to swing. Lily held her wooden sword out in front of her. The blade quivered as Lily's arms trembled. Mistletoe barked.

"HALT!" bellowed a gruff voice from the end of the passage. "Who wishes to pass?"

"It's... it's... the Headless Archer!" exclaimed Lily, stuttering with fear. "Colin! Where are you?"

"What's going on? Colin!" Oliver shouted into the darkness.

"Stay calm!" Colin called back. "It's not the Headless Archer!" Colin turned to the figure standing at the end of the passage, "Who a-are you?"

"I am Marius, Centurion of Rome and guardian of this passage at the command of the Spirit of the Cave." Marius lowered his large, rectangular shield and beckoned with his short sword. "Come forward if you wish to pass."

"How d-do we know we c-can trust you?" responded Colin.

"If you have a marble, I have no quarrel with you. If you don't have a marble, you must turn around, or we will kill you."

The threat was declared in a chillingly casual way. Nine more imposing figures emerged and stood in a tight unit behind Marius.

"We each have marbles!" shouted Colin quickly.

"Then come," replied Marius. "The gods have sent you here for a reason."

At that moment, Colin remembered that his companions were alone in the dark cave. He ran back down the passage, turned the tight corner and saw Lily and Oliver back-to-back, braced nervously with their weapons at the ready.

"It's okay, everyone! It's okay!" Colin called.

"Colin!" Lily shouted. "Where have you been? You just left us!"

"Nice move, Colin," said Oliver angrily. "Just fly off without us, why don't you?"

"I'm sorry," responded Colin, "but everything is okay. I just wanted to make sure the passage was safe. Look, there's light at the end of the passage. There's a load of Roman Legionaries too. I have no idea what they're doing there, but they're happy for us to pass. I'll lead you there."

"Anything to get out of this horrible darkness," replied Oliver.

"And don't you dare run off again," said Lily, still angry.

Colin led the others through the passage. Marius was still standing in the same spot with the nine Legionaries shoulder-to-shoulder behind him. The Legionaries had red, rectangular shields on their left arms, javelins in their right hands, and short swords hanging from their waists. They wore leather sandals, silver helmets and red tunics. Their torsos and shoulders were protected with silver armour. All of them had limbs that were lean, strong and covered in battle scars. As a Centurion, Marius also wore a red cape, and there was a plume of feathers on his helmet.

Marius and the Legionaries watched as a boy with one eye, a yellow hard hat and a mop emerged from the darkness. Behind him, there was another boy with a bike helmet and a cricket bat. Next, there came a girl with a toy sword, another bike helmet and golden wings. Finally, there came a green fox and a beagle. They were all blinking as their eyes adjusted to the light.

"Finally!" exclaimed Mistletoe, "some floomin' light—"

"And a talking dog," interrupted Marius. "The gods have sent an odd-looking band of heroes into the Underworld."

"You know what they say, Marius," said one of the Legionaries, "the gods work in mysterious ways."

"Please show your marbles," commanded Marius.

Lily, Oliver and Colin removed their marbles from their pockets and showed them to Marius.

"The dog and the green fox swallowed their marbles," Lily explained nervously. "It was the only way they could carry them."

"I'm sorry," Lime Fox added, "but it was the most sensible thing to do."

"So the green fox talks too," said Marius. "You've got a dog and a fox that speak perfect Latin. They must be carrying marbles somewhere."

Marius made a gesture encouraging the companions to come forward. The Legionaries stepped aside to reveal the space beyond the passage.

The companions stood on a wide ledge on the brink of a void. There was a rock face that stretched into infinity above and below them. The stone path bridged the void to another ledge protruding from another infinite cliff face. In this void, bright colours of every shade ebbed, flowed, streaked and exploded. It was the same stunning display as could be seen in the centre of the marbles, except this time, it was everywhere and in every shade of every colour.

Colin's eyes were drawn to a globular turquoise fog that drifted upwards like it was in a lava lamp. The fog dispersed in a cinnamon brown sprinkle. Oliver watched a blast of creamy white followed by apple green and thistle blue sparkles. At the same time, Lily watched as a seaweed green swirled into a mix of mango and mahogany. Then the companions spotted colours they had never seen before, mingling and merging with the colours they knew. One such colour bobbed across the void like a helium balloon. It was deep, like blood red, but it had the bitter sharpness of lime. Then a colour spiralled past that was soothing like lavender, with subtle variations in tone like fallen autumn leaves, but it was darker than the darkest shadow.

"Welcome to the Bridge over the Infinite Void," explained Marius. "You are currently on Earth. On the other side of the bridge lies Lelandis. You are free to cross the bridge".

The companions moved closer to the bridge and peered down into the Infinite Void. An unpleasant churning sensation in their stomachs made them step back quickly.

"I feel so embarrassed," whispered Lily. "Look at us with our stupid weapons and armour. We must look like a bunch of idiots to them, and yet we're hoping to save the school group from a distant world by defeating the Headless Archer."

"I didn't see you coming up with any good ideas in Auntie Dot's house," responded Oliver with his arms crossed. "I was just trying to protect us."

"Protect us?" replied Lily. "With a toy sword and a mop? The only half-decent weapon is in your hands."

"Well, why don't you go to find your own weapon then?" Oliver responded. "Or were you planning to fight the Headless Archer bare-knuckle?"

"No," Lily responded with her hands on her hips, "I think I'll use the mop to clean his kitchen floor!"

"You'll be lucky if Colin gives it to you," responded Oliver sharply, "he's been hogging Woden's Eye."

"Do you want it now?" replied Colin. "I led you for ages, and I checked out the passage on my own to keep you lot safe, and this is the thanks I get!"

"You're right, Colin," Lily began in a sarcastic tone, "thank you oh so much for leaving us in the complete darkness with no idea what was—"

"SILENCE!"

The trio stopped immediately and looked back at Marius, who had bellowed the command. He did not look impressed, and nor did the other Legionaries.

"Do you know what lies beyond that bridge?" continued Marius. "You are about to enter a completely new world where there are great dangers. You are not the first to cross the bridge. Many have come before you, and many have not returned. If you cannot walk through an empty cave without bickering and fighting, you will not survive a day in Lelandis."

Lily, Oliver and Colin stood like children being told off in a headmaster's office.

"What is your mission?" Marius asked.

"We… we are looking for a Headless Archer," replied Oliver, who realised how stupid these words sounded the moment they left his lips.

"And we're hoping to find a group of students… and their teachers, who… who we think are lost in Lelandis," added Lily.

"So, what is your plan?" asked Marius.

"Well… we don't really have one," answered Colin. "We were just… well… we were just having a little adventure following clues."

"Marius," Lime Fox began, "I have witnessed these humans showing kindness and courage so far on their journey. They are young, and this adventure is presenting challenges they have never encountered before."

"If you want to succeed in your mission, you will need more than just courage," replied Marius. "To begin with, you need to work together. You also need to be more focused and better prepared. You've already found two artefacts of the gods; Woden's Eye and the Wings of Icarus. You also have intelligent animals with you, so make use of them. You do not need those peculiar weapons. Avoid combat because you are not fighters."

The three friends were not offended. They knew they were not fighters. This became obvious the moment they saw the Legionaries. The friends now began to doubt themselves. Their journey up to this point had been kindled by curiosity and a sense of adventure, but now they were on the brink of entering a dangerous and unknown world far from the security of Auntie Dot's house. All three friends considered turning back, yet they felt a sense of responsibility. Two teachers and four students were lost in another world, and the companions were close to discovering where they were.

As the friends realised the gravity of their situation, the Legionaries began sitting down in alcoves that had been roughly hewn out of the cliff face on either side of the passage. All colour disappeared from their clothing, armour and complexion. They became cold and motionless, like statues carved from the same rock as the cliff face. The Legionaries were returning to their eternal sleep, awaiting the next travellers.

"Marius was right," said Colin as he put his hard hat and mop on the floor. "We are clueless. I shouldn't have left you all alone in the darkness."

"I have to admit I'm starting to feel out of my depth," said Lily. "What happens if we get lost in Lelandis? What we're doing is very dangerous. You were right to find some weapons, Oliver. It was a sensible thing to do. I just don't think they're going to help us anymore." Lily took off the Wings of Icarus and placed her helmet and wooden sword on the floor.

"You were really struggling in the dark, weren't you, Colin?" said Oliver. "We should have noticed. I think both of us were being a bit selfish." Oliver threw his cricket bat on the floor. The crash echoed between the cliff faces.

"Well, do we go home, or do we continue?" Lily asked after a moment of silence.

"You continue."

The companions turned around to see a figure bathed in kaleidoscopic light approaching them. It was one of the Legionaries. His cheeks were hollow, his limbs were lean and his eyes were piercing blue. He must have been in his early twenties, but he carried himself like an older man. He peered at the friends from beneath his helmet and spoke, "I am Titus. Come with me. I have something to show you."

Titus led the friends towards the Infinite Void. He placed his shield on the ground, removed his helmet and stood with his toes only millimetres from the cliff edge. Titus patiently watched the magnificent colours changing in front of him. Then he drew his short sword and reached into the Void. Titus collected an ethereal blue syrup on the end of his blade with a slow stirring movement. He brought the sword to his upturned helmet and let the weightless substance drip in. Titus turned to the three friends who were standing back from the edge. "You spoke with Marius about courage. This is reckless courage. Take it and breathe it in."

Titus beckoned for the friends to come closer. Oliver and Colin hesitated, but Lily stepped forward. Titus reached out with his helmet and gestured for her to breathe in the substance. Lily took the helmet and scooped up some of the sky-blue essence in her hands. It was weightless, but Lily could control it. She lifted her hands to her face and breathed in. Immediately her body was flooded with a feeling of invincibility. She stood taller and puffed out her chest. Lily thought about the lost school group; she could find and rescue them easily. Once she had done that, Lily knew the school group would adore her for being so brilliant. The Legionaries no longer intimidated her either. She felt she could defeat all of them in a fight if she wanted to. Lily walked forward confidently and stood next to Titus. He took hold of the shirt between her shoulder blades without her noticing.

"Be careful, Lily," shouted Oliver. "Step back from the edge!"

"Don't be silly, Oliver," Lily replied. "You're such a sissy. I'm not going to fall over the edge. I've got very good balance."

"I'm sure you have," said Colin nervously, "but you are being a bit silly!"

"You're a right pair of softies!" replied Lily. She then stood on one leg and smiled back at Oliver and Colin.

The two boys gasped, and their stomachs turned unpleasantly as Lily wobbled on the edge of the Infinite Void. Titus braced himself with her shirt in his hand. Then the reckless courage began to fade. Lily peered down into the void and panicked. She lost balance, and her body lurched forward. Lily screamed as she felt herself falling forwards. Then, with a firm tug, Titus pulled her back to safety. She ran back to Oliver and hugged him.

"What were you doing?" said Oliver. "You almost killed yourself!"

"It was reckless courage that almost killed her," replied Titus.

"You've got an interesting teaching method," said Colin in a surprisingly assertive tone.

"Courage will make you stand up for what is right, and it will help you overcome challenges, but it isn't always a good thing. It takes courage to steal and cheat." As he spoke, Titus reached his sword into the swirling colours again, and this time he collected some pine-green light on his blade. He let it drip into his helmet. "Who would like to know what it feels like to be a coward? This is cowardice, and it is less likely to kill you and more likely to kill other people."

Colin stepped forward. He was disappointed with himself for

being so scared in the dark cave. He had never considered himself very brave, but was he a coward? Titus handed him the pine-green essence.

"Be careful, Colin," warned Lily. "We'll watch out for you."

Colin tentatively breathed in the weightless substance. To his surprise, he immediately felt quite warm and smug. It was a rather pleasant feeling, like when you get out of trouble at school by blaming someone else for something you have done. These feelings quickly passed and were replaced by feelings of guilt, regret and embarrassment. These were not fleeting feelings, like when you accidentally trip and fall in front of your friends. These were deeper feelings that arise from a deliberate and avoidable act of self-preservation, an action that causes other people great difficulty, harm, or even death. Colin sat down and hugged his legs. He just wanted to curl up in a ball and disappear. As quickly as these feelings came, they disappeared, and Colin felt normal again. He realised that Lily had placed a comforting hand on his shoulder.

"Are you okay, Colin?" said Oliver.

"Yes," replied Colin. "As a matter of fact, I feel much better than before. It wasn't nice for a moment, but I feel good now."

"What did it feel like?" asked Oliver.

Colin explained what cowardice felt like, but he did not tell the others why he felt good. Colin now knew he had not been a coward in the dark cave. His feelings in the cave had been very different. He had been fearful of the dark and of letting his friends down, but he had battled these fears. He had not been a coward.

"That sounds very different to my reckless courage," said Lily when Colin had finished. "I just felt invincible, like I could do anything. I was blind to risk, and I was being selfish too. Everything was about me."

Titus now offered the three friends a sapphire light. "Try this," he said. "I've collected courage and mixed it with virtue, and I've added some self-respect and self-control."

The three friends took the sapphire light and breathed it deep into their lungs. They were not overwhelmed with a wonderful feeling. There was no shallow and self-indulgent desire to be admired, and there was no urge for self-preservation at all costs. Instead, there was a steadfast devotion to treating people with respect and a willingness to stand up to bigotry and cruelty. The three friends felt deep contentment.

Titus spoke again as the feeling faded, "There are infinite shades of every colour in the Void, even colours you have never seen before. There are infinite ways in which they can mingle and merge. The thoughts and feelings that govern your actions are very complicated. Embrace complexity and shun glibness. You will need courage to succeed in your mission in Lelandis, but try to understand what courage is. Courage is not running headlong into a futile battle. Only fools fight battles they cannot win. If you cannot win a battle, turn the battle into one you can win. When you are confident a battle can be won, win it. If your judgement is poor and you make mistakes, accept responsibility and learn from them. Endeavour not to make the same mistake again. Remember; embrace complexity and shun glibness. It is time for me to leave my post. My guardianship has ended, and the Spirit of the Cave will let me go. You are not well prepared for what you will find in Lelandis, but I sense your mission is righteous. May I join you?"

CHAPTER FOURTEEN

The Sanctuary of Games

Lily, Oliver and Colin accepted Titus' company without hesitation. When they looked into his bright blue eyes, they saw beyond his tough exterior and sensed his true character. This was a man who was dependable, smart and honest. The friends did not know what they would find in Lelandis, but they knew they would be better off with Titus by their side.

Crossing the bridge to Lelandis was scarier than being led through the dark cave. It was nothing more than a continuation of the path the companions had followed since the spiral staircase. The difference now was it spanned the Infinite Void, and there was no barrier to stop the companions from falling into the colourful abyss. Titus led the way, seemingly unaware of the drop. Lime Fox and Mistletoe were also untroubled and occasionally peered over the edge. In contrast, the three friends walked across as if they were on a tight rope, fearful they might lose their balance at any moment.

On the other side of the bridge, there was another ledge with another passage through an archway in the rock. There were more alcoves on either side of the archway with statues of resting Roman Legionaries. One figure was sat forward with his elbows on his knees and his chin resting on his hands. Another was slouched in the corner of his alcove with his arms crossed and his head back. The three friends paused, unsure whether they were allowed to continue.

"You are free to pass," instructed Titus. "These Legionaries guard those coming from Lelandis. It has been a long time since I have seen their faces, and I have some very good friends among them."

"Why do you guard this bridge?" asked Colin as they entered the passage.

"Why do *they* guard this bridge," Titus corrected. "I have served my time. The Spirit of the Cave does not stop us from leaving. Our story is long and deserves to be told around a campfire under a starlit sky. I will say this; our boat was blown off course, and we found ourselves lost on an unknown island somewhere north of Gaul. We wandered for weeks, surviving on what we could hunt and fish. We were harassed by barbarians and were at the mercy of terrible weather. We kept together, but we began to give up hope of ever returning to our homes. We were then invited into a cave by the Spirit, who offered us eternity guarding the Bridge. We thought this was the will of the gods, and so we agreed. The Spirit of the Cave told us we were free to leave whenever we wished. I am not the first to leave."

The companions entered the passage as Titus spoke. They could just discern another spiral staircase in the distance. It was identical to the spiral staircase in the Priest Hole, and the three friends knew it led to Lelandis. It was agreed that Oliver would wear Woden's Eye, and Lily and Colin would use their torches.

"Would you be happy to follow Oliver up the stairs?" Lily asked Titus. "If we encounter anything hostile, we'll need you. You can borrow one of our torches."

"The threat is ahead of us and not behind," replied Titus, "so what you suggest is sensible. Where are the torches you speak of? And have you something to light them?"

"We've got something you won't have seen before," said Colin as he switched on a torch.

Titus took the torch and inspected it closely with a look of wonder on his face. "What is this? Have you captured a thunderbolt of Zeus? A magnificent artefact, as wonderful as Woden's Eye and the Wings of Icarus."

Lily turned to Mistletoe and Lime Fox, "Do you want to follow Titus? Your hearing and sense of smell have been very useful so far. Perhaps you could let Oliver know if there is anything ahead."

"An excellent idea," said Lime Fox, excited at being so close to Lelandis. "I will do as you wish."

"I'm happier at the floomin' back, thank you very much," said Mistletoe.

The companions began their ascent of the spiral staircase. Within a few minutes, Lily, Oliver and Colin could feel their legs burning and their hearts pumping. In contrast, Titus did not even break a sweat despite carrying his shield, weapons and full armour. The armour rhythmically clanked as they went around and around, ever upwards. Eventually, Mistletoe smelt the faintest trace of fresh air drifting down the staircase. Oliver slowed his pace and climbed more cautiously than before. Everyone else followed him in complete silence. Soon, all of the companions could smell the fresh air. It felt invigorating after being underground for so long. After a few more steps, Oliver emerged from the staircase into a small, warm chamber made of large stone blocks. Titus was close behind and alert to any threats. The chamber was different from the staircase and the underground path; it was less precise and not made from marble-like stone. There was an opening, and bright moonlight poured in. The rest of the group quickly joined Oliver and Titus.

"We have reached Lelandis," exclaimed Lime Fox quietly. "I can smell it in the air!"

"There must be other humans around," whispered Oliver, who stood at the chamber entrance. "There are fires everywhere and very old looking buildings."

"It feels like we're in an ancient city," agreed Lily as she joined Oliver at the entrance.

"The buildings look medieval," muttered Colin, "like the buildings in the centre of old English towns. They've all got wonky walls and thatched rooves. There aren't any cars either or street lights. It's like we've gone back in time."

"I have no idea how this all fits in with the Headless Archer and the missing school group," whispered Oliver.

"There's only one way to find out more," said Titus. "We're going to need to explore. Fortunately, it is nighttime."

The thought of exploring this unknown place made the three

friends apprehensive, but still, they were drawn forward by the excitement of the adventure, the prospect of discovery and the responsibility they felt to look for the lost school group.

"Let me take a look first," announced Lime Fox excitedly, "I am the lightest on my paws, and I shouldn't draw any attention."

"I'll come with you," added Mistletoe quickly, not wanting to let Lime Fox out of his sight. They scampered from the chamber and were soon lost to view.

"Lime Fox is fearless, isn't she?" said Lily. "I don't know why Mistletoe is so suspicious of her."

"She is a bright green talking fox," said Oliver, "but then again, Mistletoe is a grumpy beagle who keeps coming out with stupid phrases. He can't be too judgemental."

"It seems odd that Lime Fox could get to Earth without a marble," said Colin. "If the passage beneath the apple tree is guarded like the passage of the Romans, she wouldn't have been let through."

"The passage entrance must also appear without marbles," added Lily. "It's all very confusing!"

Colin turned and spoke to Titus, "What do you know about the passages? Did the Spirit in the Cave tell you anything about why they exist?"

"My memories of guarding the Bridge over the Infinite Void are fading fast," Titus replied. "I clearly remember seeking shelter in the cave with the other Legionaries. I also remember joining you, but the period between is very cloudy. I recall the Spirit of the Cave, but I cannot remember what it said. I recall travellers between the worlds, but I cannot remember who they were, what they looked like or what their purpose was."

Lime Fox and Mistletoe returned as Titus finished. "Come with me," Lime Fox whispered. "You'll want to see what is above you!"

"But be careful," added Mistletoe. "There are definitely people around. We haven't seen any yet, but I can smell them, and they smell floomin' weird."

The companions followed Lime Fox and Mistletoe out of the chamber. They emerged onto a stone porch, about the size of a basketball court, which surrounded the chamber. The chamber entrance disappeared behind them. Fire pits crackled and burnt around the perimeter of the porch, and steps led down to a cobbled road with patches of grass sprouting from the gaps between the stones. It was warm, like it had been in Bridgeward, except there was no storm. Bright stars and a full moon shone in the sky. Lime Fox led the companions down the steps and across the road to a narrow gap between two buildings. The companions crouched in a shadow beneath a small tree. Vines clambered up the uneven and cracked walls of the buildings on either side of them.

The companions looked back and were amazed to discover that the chamber was actually in the plinth of an enormous statue of the Headless Archer. The Archer stood with his legs astride, a satchel over his shoulder and a longbow pointing into the distance. There were flowers, wreaths and burning candles surrounding it. The statue was beautifully crafted, remarkably life-like and the height of a cathedral. The surrounding buildings may have reminded Colin of medieval England, but this statue looked like it belonged in Ancient Rome, Athens or Constantinople.

"This is not all, humans," whispered Lime Fox. "Come with me."

The companions were viewing the statue from behind. Lime Fox led the group from building to building, crossing cobbled roads quickly to avoid getting spotted. As they moved, the front of the statue was slowly revealed.

Up until this point, Lily, Oliver and Colin had not seen the front of the Headless Archer. The picture in the Spell Book showed his back, the stone carvings were just an outline, and the statue in the Priest Hole had fallen on the ground face first. The Story of the Headless Archer had consumed their imaginations. Throughout their adventure, the companions had tried to reconcile this story with what they had discovered. How could someone without a head shoot an arrow? It was ridiculous. The companions now realised the Story of the Headless Archer was just fiction, but it had developed out of something very real: the Headless Archer did not have a head because his face was in his chest.

The Archer's shoulders were far broader than those of a human, giving ample room on his chest for a large face. There was a patch of shaggy hair above the Archer's shoulders where a human's neck would be. The position of the face meant the Archer's ears were near his armpits, and his chest and sternum were below his face and close to his belly button. The Archer's arms were large and muscular, but his legs were short and stumpy.

The companions were processing this revelation when they heard noises nearby. They stepped back into the shadows between the two buildings. Two headless figures were staggering towards the statue with their arms over each other's shoulders like they were drunk. The figures were about the same height as an adult human and wore small, brown boots and baggy, striped trousers. Like the statue, they were bare from the waist upwards. They had broad shoulders, large arms, short legs and, most striking of all, faces on their chests.

"Hey! Watch this!" slurred one of the headless men as he staggered up the steps to the front of the statue. He picked up some of the flowers, which had been placed as offerings, and put them on the shaggy hair above his face. "I'm Apollon, God of Archers, and I'm going to sprain your wrist the day before the Games, so you can't compete because I'm a big, smelly GIT!"

The other headless man found this very funny. "Apollon the God of Big, Smelly Gits!" he shouted as he too placed some flowers on his shoulders.

"Sssshhhhh!" exclaimed the first headless man with a finger over his mouth. "We're near Agon Agathon's residence. Don't nake a moise!"

The other headless man started laughing again. "You said *nake a moise!*"

"No, I didn't. I said *nake a moise.*"

"You said it again!"

"Said what?"

"*Nake a moise!*"

"Make a noise? Alright then!" The headless man then let out an enormous burp that made the ground rumble and the statue shake. "Was that noud elough?"

The other headless man fell to the floor and started rolling around laughing. "No, it wasn't!" he replied when he had recovered enough to speak. "You burp like a softy. This is how a real *Blemmy* burps… BELLLCCCCCCHHHHHHHH!"

This burp made the first burp seem like the burp of an amateur. Dust fell from the building around the companions, and birds flew up into the night sky, squawking.

In front of the statue, there stood several large buildings that reminded Lily, Oliver, and Colin of the cathedral in Bridgeward. The grandest was surrounded by a veranda with an angled roof held up by columns. Two lines of marching figures emerged from this building. They carried bows over their shoulders, quivers around their waists, and flaming torches in their hands. Between these two rows, there strode an older headless man. He wore a gold chain around his waist, bronze cuffs around his wrists, and purple and white striped trousers. His nose was squashed and disfigured as if it had been broken many times. It was Agon Agathon, and he looked fearsome.

"Drunkards!" Agon Agathon boomed. "In the Sanctuary of Games! Desecrating the Statue of Apollon! You should be ashamed of yourselves."

The two drunks were no longer laughing; they were quivering with fear.

"For thousands of years, this sanctuary has been the meeting place of *Blemmies*," continued Agon Agathon, "and for thousands of years, alcohol has been banned. We are gathered here for the Great Games; strength, athleticism and skill, not drunken idiocy!"

Agon Agathon gestured to the guards who stood beside him. They approached the drunken pair and grabbed them roughly by the hair above their faces.

"It looks like we have two more competitors for tomorrow's Death Match – the highlight of the Games! Count yourself lucky we no longer practice sacrifices to the gods. If I had my way, you'd be sacrificed to Apollon this very night. At least in the Death Match, you have a slim chance of survival, although I think I will be watching you die beneath the setting sun."

The two individuals were dragged away down the narrow, winding streets of the Sanctuary of Games. Their cries of despair slowly faded into the silence of the night. Agon Agathon returned to his residence, and all was quiet again around the Statue of Apollon. The companions stood aghast in the shadows.

CHAPTER FIFTEEN

Blemmies

"This adventure keeps getting weirder and weirder," Oliver uttered.

"So the Headless Archer is... er... a *Blemmy* god?" Lily questioned.

"I suppose so," whispered Colin. "The Story of the Headless Archer must be based on their god Apollon. People and these Blemmies must have been using the passage from Earth to Lelandis for thousands of years. This is amazing!"

"Titus," Lily began, "have you seen Blemmies passing through the passage?"

"My memories have completely disappeared," Titus replied. "I remember the passage, and I know I guarded it, but I cannot remember the travellers. It must be the will of the Spirit of the Cave that I do not carry my memories with me. What I do know is that when I was a child in Rome, merchants told stories of creatures like these Blemmies. They were thought to live far beyond the Empire, in the farthest corners of the Earth."

"Yes!" exclaimed Colin. "Now I think about it, these creatures are on the Great Map in the cathedral too. I also wonder if the headless statues at Bridgeward Manor are Blemmies rather than statues with their heads knocked off."

"Didn't we also see these Blemmies in the cathedral window, Lily?" asked Oliver. "They were alongside the strange frog people, the Trolls and the goblins."

"I think we did," said Lily, "but what about those poor

Blemmies? Agon Agathon seems terrible!"

"I'm not sure what's worse," said Oliver, "the ghost of a man who carries his head in a bag or that horrible Blemmy."

"If Blemmies think a Death Match is the highlight of their Games," said Colin, "I doubt Agon Agathon is the only Blemmy we need to worry about. At least we now know the Headless Archer doesn't exist. Instead, we're facing a city full of blood-thirsty creatures with faces in their chests."

"I don't think this is a city," said Titus. "It feels like we are in the centre of a religious sanctuary to the Blemmy gods. Somewhere similar to the sanctuaries of the Greeks, places like Olympia and Delphi. Blemmies will come here to honour the gods and seek glory through sport."

"One thing's for sure," said Colin, "the riddles of the Spell Book make complete sense now. They were definitely instructions on how to get to Lelandis."

Oliver found the riddles in his bag and recited the first one: "*Follow the archer. Rome's last stand. The end of the world. Lelandis found. Beneath God's altar. The worship of the Headless.*"

"So we were right about the other riddle," said Lily, "it must describe the passage in the orchard that Lime Fox found. Can you read it, please, Oliver?"

"*Follow the archer. A dragonfly creek. The end of the world. Lelandis found. Where apples fall. The Headless play their games.*"

"The last line," began Colin, "*the Headless play their games*. It refers to the sanctuary. The lost school group must be somewhere near here."

Oliver turned to Lime Fox, "Do you know anything about this Sanctuary of Games? Have you ever been here before?"

Lime Fox hesitated before speaking, "No, I'm sorry, but I haven't."

"Have you ever seen these Blemmies in the woods near the waterfall?" asked Lily.

Lime Fox shook her head and looked away as she spoke, "No, I haven't. I'm sorry I can't be more helpful."

"Are you sure you're telling the floomin' truth?" challenged Mistletoe.

"Don't be nasty, Mistletoe!" Lily exclaimed. "So the second

riddle doesn't add up completely, but we're definitely on the right track."

"There's still a lot to understand," said Titus. "I expect things will become clearer in time. We need to look around. Things are in our favour; it is very late, and I imagine most Blemmies will be indoors. The sanctuary also looks like a labyrinth which is perfect for us if we want to keep hidden. The moon will provide us with enough light, so we shouldn't need your thunderbolts of Zeus."

"They're just torches, Titus," explained Oliver. "They're not a big deal."

"Remember, this is reconnaissance only," continued Titus. "We are not in a position to fight. We stick together and retreat to the statue if we are spotted. My shield will only be a burden. I need to take it back to the chamber, but the chamber is now closed to me because I have no marble."

"I'll take it," offered Oliver. "I have Woden's Eye and a marble."

Titus handed the shield to Oliver, with Colin looking on enviously. Oliver threw it over his shoulder and darted through the shadows to the rear of the statue. The chamber entrance appeared, and Oliver placed the shield inside before returning to the others.

"I think it's time for someone else to use Woden's Eye," said Oliver. He took the artefact off his head and offered it to his friends. Colin gestured that it was Lily's turn, and she put it on.

"Are we ready?" asked Titus.

The companions nodded.

"Then follow me."

Titus led the others through the winding streets of the Sanctuary of Games. He flitted between the shadows, light-footed and alert, with his short sword in front of him and his armour clanking lightly as he moved. Titus did not know where to go, so he relied on his instincts. Once beyond the grand buildings in front of the Statue of Apollon, the companions found themselves creeping past small, rustic buildings with exposed timbers, irregular walls and low thatched rooves. As the companions moved, they occasionally heard talking, snoring and other noises coming from open windows. In the distance, orange light could be seen rising into the night sky above the buildings. They moved towards this light, and the sounds of voices and activity grew louder.

The companions peered around a building and discovered they were next to a wide river. There were docks on one section where boats were moored and wooden cranes towered over run-down warehouses. Hundreds of fire pits lighted the whole scene. The warehouses were surrounded by fishing nets, baskets and coils of heavy rope. A small number of Blemmies were guiding a long, wide and open barge into port. The barge was full of Blemmies sitting and lying in every available space. There were two rows of six individuals standing on either side of the barge. These Blemmies held long oars in their hands and rowed in time with a drum being struck at the rear of the boat. When the barge reached the dock, everyone disembarked and entered the sanctuary. The companions looked upriver and could see the silhouettes of more barges drifting towards the docks.

On another stretch of water, a swimming pool was set into the riverbank. It was about five times the size of the swimming pools on Earth. A grandstand ran the entire length of the pool, and it was lit by yet more fire pits. With Woden's Eye, Lily could see that the pool was fed by the river. The water had a greenish tinge, and beneath the surface, fish swam through plants that gently swayed in the aquatic habitat. Waterlilies grew along the sides of the pool, and Lily even spotted a frog jumping into the water after being disturbed by Blemmies swimming back and forth at great speed. They created bow waves that intersected each other before crashing against the sides.

"Look at those Blemmies training," observed Lily, "I've never seen a human swim as fast as them."

"Their arms are so powerful," added Colin.

"Do Blemmies not sleep?" Oliver asked. "It seems odd training so late."

"We shouldn't hang around for long," said Titus. "Let's move parallel to the river and see where it leads. I can see more firelight in the distance."

The companions moved on, still keeping to the shadows created by the narrow streets. The top of a colossal building began to emerge above the thatched rooves. They headed towards it and realised it was a stadium consisting of four rings of arches. Above these rings, wooden scaffolding created even more seating for spectators. The companions stopped and knelt beside a low wall that was cracking due to the roots of a nearby tree. From here, they could see the stadium was surrounded by large grass fields bordered by lines of trees.

Stocky, hairy Blemmies were grappling and wrestling in one of these fields. Perspiration covered their bodies, and steam was evaporating from their backs. As the companions watched, a red-haired wrestler manoeuvred himself behind his opponent. He placed his enormous arms around his opponent's torso, arched his back and threw him over his shoulders. The Blemmy flipped in the air and landed heavily on the turf about five metres away. An older Blemmy, with a squinty eye and a limp, was observing the bout. He looked furious.

"You useless chump!" the old Blemmy shouted. "The first rule of wrestling: never get turned! Once you've been turned, you're finished! You better not do that tomorrow in any of your matches. It's bad enough in training."

The companions turned their attention to another field where archers were practising. They all looked the same as the Statue of Apollon, with quivers and satchels around their waists. They were firing longbows at circular targets that must have been a distance of two football pitches away. The arrows flew at such speed that they barely rose above the height of the targets in flight. The Blemmies reached into their satchels between firing, and their hands came out covered in chalk to improve their grip.

"They're amazing wrestlers and archers, but I think I've spotted their weakness," said Colin, pointing at a group of Blemmies running around the perimeter of the fields between rows of trees. "I think I could run faster than them, and I always come last in the school cross-country."

The jogging Blemmies were huffing and puffing despite running not much faster than Lily, Oliver and Colin could walk. These were the lightest built of all the Blemmies the companions had seen, but were still very top-heavy. Unlike the archers and wrestlers, these runners wore shorts that revealed how little their legs were.

Titus was keen to keep moving, so the companions skirted around the sides of the training fields, along an avenue of trees and towards the stadium. The colossal structure loomed over them as they got closer. The open space surrounding the stadium, where spectators would gather before taking their seats, was dotted with statues. Some of these statues were carved expertly, and others were not. Some looked very old and were covered in lichen, but many looked freshly chiselled. Each sculpture had an inscription, and the companions could not help but read them.

"*In honour of Boofus Booma*," Lily read from the plinth of a statue of an archer. "*He was robbed of his victory. May the umpires forever find slugs in their porridge.*"

"What a strange thing to write on a statue," said Colin.

"Listen to this one," said Oliver, standing by a statue of a Blemmy with a gormless grin. "*Lest we forget the Magnificent Diblon Dago. He voluntarily fought in three Death Matches and won them all. He lost the fourth. We told him to stay at home, but he wouldn't listen.*"

"Here's another," said Lily, "*In memory of Ploggon Plodga. He won the wrestling with two broken arms, a broken leg and most of his teeth falling out.*"

"Do you think he ever wondered if it was worth it?" added Oliver as he looked at this ridiculously disfigured Blemmy, leaning heavily on his only good limb.

"*Honouring brave Flumbum Bumflum and Gorga Grothpot,*" read Lily. "*They died at the same time in each other's submission holds. It looked rather painful.*" This statue depicted the two wrestlers entangled in their final moments. The two Blemmies had their eyes screwed up and their mouths wide open as if they were releasing great screams of pain.

"Look at this one," said Oliver. "He's got a weird physique – if they weren't weird enough already." Oliver was pointing to a statue of a very tall Blemmy with a torso like a surfboard. His incredibly long arms dangled by his sides, and he had hands like shovels. Oddly, he had tiny legs and long feet like a clown. The inscription read '*Big Barry: the greatest swimmer ever to grace the sanctuary.*'

"Humans, do you think we have seen enough?" Lime Fox asked politely. "I don't think we should hang around here for much longer in case we get spotted."

"Lime Fox is right," said Titus, much to the disappointment of Lily, Oliver and Colin, who were having great fun. "We need to return to the Statue of Apollon to form a plan."

The companions moved on through the statues, around the stadium and into another district of small, rustic buildings. Occasionally they spotted a Blemmy walking through the streets, but it was easy to stay hidden. The enormous Statue of Apollon soon appeared above the buildings, and Titus led them towards it. When they got closer to the statue, they realised they were next to Agon Agathon's grand residence.

"I feel we need to find out more about Agon Agathon," suggested Lime Fox quite abruptly. "He seems important, and I wonder if he knows anything about the missing school group. After all, the passage behind the waterfall is only a short distance upriver from here."

"Are you sure we should do that?" replied Colin. "It seems very dangerous."

"I don't fancy finding myself in the Death Match," added Oliver.

"Only because you know I'd win," responded Lily with a nudge.

"Follow me," continued Lime Fox. "I think I can see a way onto the veranda's roof, and from there, we should be able to look in through the windows."

Lime Fox darted off towards the rear of the building before anyone could offer an opinion. This was the first time any of the companions had taken the lead from Titus, and Titus saw that the others were looking at him for guidance. "It's worth a try," he said. "The fox could be right, but we must remain vigilant."

Lime Fox was soon on the tiled roof of the veranda that surrounded Agon Agathon's residence. When the others reached the building, they spotted a series of rectangular stone blocks that looked like headstones in a graveyard but only much bigger. They were inscribed with the names of victorious Blemmies from past Games and were positioned between the columns that held up the veranda roof. It was easy to use these stones to climb up. Lily and Oliver clambered up first, followed by Mistletoe. Colin was up next with help from Titus, who subsequently pulled himself up with ease.

Once on the roof, the companions realised how exposed they were, particularly with a full moon above them. They crept carefully along the narrow, sloping rooftop in the small shadow provided by the main building. Lime Fox guided them towards a window with a carved stone lattice. The companions looked down through the gaps in the intricate lattice over a large room with sumptuous purple seats, gilded tables, bronze fire pits and an elaborately detailed floor made from different coloured marble slabs. Agon Agathon sat speaking to a female Blemmy. She had a puffy face and a resting expression of pompous repulsion. She had bright red hair that curled down her back and stripy trousers covering her little legs. A fabric band covered her waist and chest, and gaudy jewellery adorned her fingers, wrists and ears.

"Agon Agathon," began the female Blemmy with a voice affected by the slimy spittle that collected in the corners of her mouth, "there is much excitement in the sanctuary about this year's Death Match! Word has spread to the neighbouring cities, and Blemmies are desperately trying to get here for tomorrow evening. The stadium will soon be sold out."

"Good, Doria!" said Agon Agathon, rubbing his hands together. "I must admit, I am very excited too. The prison guards have reported that training is going well. We have quite a selection this year."

"It's been a long time since we've had a Giant and Trolls in the same match!" said Doria. She grinned, and her crooked yellow teeth were revealed.

"Yes! And it is finally time to kill the King of Monopods. I've held him hostage for three years now. The doddery old fool doesn't stand a chance. The Dwarves will be fun too; persistent little things. They always work well together."

"Now I have a few pieces of important news," said Doria, as if this was the purpose of her visit. "There has been talk among the merchants in the ports of a king gaining power across the

Endless Sea. We all know what these merchants are like – they get drunk and share silly stories of nonsense lands – but there is something about these stories; they are being discussed everywhere."

"Thank you for letting me know, Doria," replied Agon Agathon. "Probably just nonsense, as you say."

"On another matter, more Trolls have been discovered making homes under bridges in the north. The nobles of the frontier are concerned the Trolls might be looking to invade again."

"It's been a few years since we've had problems with the Trolls," replied Agon Agathon, "I'll speak to the nobles. Most of them are here for the Games."

"Finally, I'd like you to consider selling the young humans to me now." Doria sat forward in her chair and began rubbing her knees. "Just name your price. I know you were planning to auction them, but I am willing to pay you handsomely right now. That way, you don't have to stress about the whole auction palaver. I've always wanted to have human slaves."

Lily, Oliver and Colin felt their hearts skip a beat.

"I admire your boldness Doria, but I have made it known to all the nobles at the Games that there will be an auction."

"I can also arrange for your athletes to win the wrestling tomorrow, and the archery finals! Come now, Agon Agathon! What is your price?" Doria looked agitated and desperate. Spittle flew from her mouth as she spoke. She looked like a spoilt child being denied chocolate for the first time in her life.

"No, Doria," Agon Agathon replied sternly. "They will be sold after the Death Match. I want them to know that the adult humans have died in the stadium. It's has been centuries since we had humans competing. The female is raising a few eyebrows; she keeps knocking out her trainers. The male is rather a disappointment, but we'll have him ready. It's amazing what happens to the combatants when the Death Match starts and they realise only the winner will survive."

Lily, Oliver and Colin looked at each other in shock.

"So the school group is here!" whispered Colin.

"And we've got less than 24 hours to save them," added Lily.

"Lime Fox, you were right," whispered Oliver. "The passage behind the waterfall must be very close to the sanctuary."

Lily had a sudden realisation. "Lime Fox, you said you had never been to the sanctuary before. How did you know the passage behind the waterfall was just upriver from here?"

There was no response.

"Lime Fox, are you there?"

Still, there was no response.

"Where's Lime Fox?" Lily whispered.

The full moon was directly above the buildings of the sanctuary, and a small cloud had drifted across its face. The grey-blue moonlight created an eerie landscape of silhouetted buildings, dark shadows and softly illuminated rooftops. There was complete silence as the companions looked around for Lime Fox. Mistletoe broke the silence with a hushed growl, "The treacherous floomin' mongrel! I knew we couldn't trust her!"

Through the lattice, the companions watched aghast as Lime Fox approached Agon Agathon and sat beside him on his purple seat. Agon Agathon stroked her green fur gently, and she edged closer and whispered in his ear. He turned sharply and glared straight at the window with a ferocious look on his face. For a fleeting moment, the companions met his terrible gaze.

"It's time to flee," said Titus. "To the passage, and fast!"

CHAPTER SIXTEEN

The Wings of Icarus

There was not enough time to process the betrayal of Lime Fox; the companions needed to move quickly to the statue to escape capture. Titus slid quickly down the tiles and off the roof. He turned as he did so and caught the edge of the roof with his hands. He then released his grip and fell silently to the floor.

"Don't expect me to do that," whispered Colin as he scrambled to the edge of the roof with the twins.

"Throw the dog!" commanded Titus, standing with his arms outstretched.

"Throw the floomin' dog?" replied Mistletoe. "I have a name you know, and nobody is throwing me." Mistletoe then launched himself off the roof into Titus' arms. His large ears flopped around as he flew through the air.

"Now, follow my instructions," said Titus. "Slide off the roof backwards and grip hard onto the edge. When you drop, I'll catch you."

The friends felt uneasy but did not have time to hesitate. Lily took a deep breath and slid off. Titus caught her over his shoulder and lowered her to the ground. Oliver was emboldened by his sister's success and launched himself off. This left Colin, who was feeling very nervous.

"It's not as hard as it looks, Colin," whispered Lily.

"I'm not built for jumping off buildings," Colin replied with his voice shaking, "I can barely run."

"It's like when we were in the cave," called Oliver. "You need to trust us."

The twins were itching to run to the statue, but they knew Colin needed their help. Colin crept on his hands and knees to the edge of the roof. He peered down at the others, gulped and then gripped hard with his hands. At that moment, noises could be heard coming from the building. Without further hesitation, Colin spun around and slipped off the roof with a yelp. Titus caught him and lowered him to the floor. Colin was relieved when he realised he had not landed like a sack of potatoes.

Titus bounded off with Lily and Oliver close behind. Colin puffed along at the back, moving as fast as possible, with Mistletoe providing unwelcome encouragement, "Pump those floomin' arms! Lift your knees! Breathe!"

"Breathe? That's a good one... I hadn't thought of that," replied Colin between breaths. "Have you ever... met Mr Montero? I think... you'd get on... well together."

The companions soon found themselves in the shadow of a tree opposite the Statue of Apollon. They looked back and saw Lime Fox standing between the fire pits in front of Agon Agathon's residence. The shadows of marching Blemmies were cast on the wall behind her. These Blemmies would soon emerge from the building. There was no time to waste. The companions sprinted across the cobbled road on Titus' command and disappeared into the chamber beneath the statue.

"Treacherous, green mongrel," Mistletoe muttered under his breath.

"Why is Titus not joining us?" exclaimed Oliver.

"Titus!" Lily called. "Get into the chamber. They won't be able to see us in here!"

Titus did not respond.

"Titus!" shouted Oliver. His voice echoed around the chamber.

"He hasn't got a marble," Colin realised. "He can't get in."

"We can't let the Blemmies capture him!" exclaimed Lily. Thinking quickly, she reached inside Oliver's bag and removed the Wings of Icarus. She swung the fabric over her shoulders, and the wings emerged. "We know the school group are somewhere in the sanctuary," Lily continued, "but we need to know exactly where to form a rescue plan. I've got the Wings of Icarus and Woden's Eye. I'm going to fly high above the sanctuary and scope it out. The Blemmies won't see me in the darkness. I'm also going to give my marble to Titus. You work something out with him, and keep alert for me returning."

Lily darted out of the chamber, taking Titus by surprise. She gave him her marble and then took off into the sky with a few graceful beats of her wings. Within a few seconds, she was gently gliding on air currents high above the sanctuary. The stress of the escape to the chamber was quickly replaced with the most tranquil feeling Lily had ever experienced.

The stars above Lelandis looked like they had multiplied tenfold. Those that had been visible from the ground now sparkled twice as bright. The fainter stars came together in a band of gentle light that arched across the night sky. The moon was full, and Lily could see its cratered surface in remarkable detail. Lily had never taken much notice of the night sky on Earth, but everything felt familiar.

The Sanctuary of Games was spread out below Lily. To her surprise, there was no activity around the Statue of Apollon. Lily expected to see Blemmies rushing to the statue under orders to search for her and her companions, but all she saw was Agon Agathon standing on the steps of his residence, scowling. Lime Fox was by his side.

Lily wondered what Lime Fox had been doing. Had Lime Fox deliberately led her and her friends to Agon Agathon, so he could capture them and sell them as slaves? Or had Lime Fox been on a mission to discover where the school group had come from? Either way, Lime Fox had misled Lily and her friends terribly. It was clear Lime Fox's loyalties lay with Agon Agathon. He now knew about two passages to Earth and was in possession of a marble. What did Agon Agathon have planned?

Lily turned her attention to the rest of the sanctuary. She could see more barges filled with Blemmies arriving at the docks. The swimming pool was still bustling, and so were the training fields beside the stadium. The stadium was enormous even from this height. The arena was large and circular, with a surface of thick grass dotted with patches of small, red flowers. It was surrounded by a high wall that had a large entrance with a portcullis. Lily could see hundreds of rows of stone seating surrounding the arena and additional wooden seating at the very top of the stadium. A long, wide and straight plaza ran from the stadium to the docks, bisecting the training fields.

The streets between the stadium and the Statue of Apollon were just as maze-like from above as they were on the ground. Lily could see other large statues of Blemmy gods in different districts of the sanctuary. They were all surrounded by flowers and candles. Lily could also now see that the sanctuary was nestled in a large forest. The forest spread into rolling hills in one direction and a patchwork of different coloured agricultural fields in the other. Lily could see the different crops swaying gently in the coastal breeze. In one field, on the far side of the river, there were tents of different shapes and sizes. Lily reasoned that this must be where Blemmy competitors were staying. Beyond the fields lay the river's estuary and a rugged coastline where waves crashed relentlessly against jagged rocks.

Lily glided over the stadium on a current of air. Not far from the stadium and beside the plaza, there was a large complex of walled enclosures and buildings that reminded Lily of a zoo. The largest of the enclosures had an odd-looking object in one corner. Lily flew lower and was disgusted when she realised it was a man curled up with his wrists and ankles in chains. Had she found Mr Montero? There was nothing else in the enclosure but a bowl. How could someone be so cruelly imprisoned? Lily felt sick. Lily then spotted a Blemmy walking along on the other side of the enclosure wall. He was whistling and fiddling with a large bunch of keys. Either this Blemmy was tiny, or the man was enormous. Lily looked again and discovered it was a Giant. He must have been five times the size of the Blemmy.

The Giant, apart from his size, looked just like a human. His hair was short and curly, and his face was beardless. He wore a beige tunic that reached his thighs and a rope around his waist that must have been the length of a skipping rope. He was sleeping barefoot, but there were two enormous brown boots the size of dining chairs beside him.

Lily was pleased that she was now looking in the right place despite her disgust at seeing the imprisoned Giant. She spotted two other very peculiar creatures in another enclosure. They were pacing monotonously in circles and were chained up like the Giant. These creatures walked on two legs and were smaller than the Giant but still much bigger than a Blemmy. They had large bellies, hunched shoulders and muscular arms. Their skin was a mossy green colour with patches of brown. Short horns emerged from their heads, and they had large ears. Their faces were dominated by broad noses and wide mouths with irregular teeth, some of which overlapped their lips. Lily had no doubt these were the Trolls spoken about by Agon Agathon.

Both enclosures had high walls upon which Blemmies with longbows kept guard. Between these two enclosures, there was a wide corridor with rusty metal cages. In one of these cages, Lily spotted the Dwarves. They were about two-thirds of the height of a human and had long, wiry hair and beards cascading down their fronts. Braces kept up their colourful but dirty trousers, and they also wore thick, button-up shirts and shin-high boots. A couple of the Dwarves were pacing around quietly while the others slept on the hard floor. Once again, Lily was shocked by the brutality of their imprisonment.

Lily noticed a lone figure asleep in the corner of another cage a short distance away. He looked like an elderly man with a patchy beard and grey hair on his head. Lily was surprised to discover that instead of two legs, this man had one large leg with a big symmetrical foot. The leg looked a bit like a kangaroo's. Lily quickly realised this was the King of the Monopods. He was dressed in rags and looked very frail. Lily could not believe he was expected to fight a Giant and two Trolls.

A Blemmy guard was now wandering along this corridor. A chunky hand emerged from one of the cages. It looked like someone was asking for food. The Blemmy guard stopped and removed a short cane from his belt. *WHACK!* He hit the hand sharply, and it retracted quickly between the bars.

Lily glided on the winds and drifted into a different position where she could see that the hand had come from one of the drunken Blemmies. They were slumped awkwardly against the metal bars of their cage. Traces of vomit could be seen on their legs, and their eyes were red and bloodshot. Everything about their demeanour told Lily they had given up hope. They looked like they had come to terms with their brutal fate: to be killed in front of baying crowds in tomorrow's Death Match. Lily felt despair too. If the missing school group were in this prison complex, their rescue would be almost impossible. To make things worse, Lily and her companions had less than 24 hours before the Death Match.

At that moment, Lily spotted what she had been seeking. In a cage at the far end of another corridor, there were two girls and two boys that looked the same age as her. Lily felt a surge of joy rush through her body. She had found Mia, Jay, Sam and Joe. The four students had messy hair, faces smudged with dirt and clothes that were filthy and torn. They were in a completely different world, far from the comfort and protection of their homes, imprisoned in a rusty cage and surrounded by barbarous Blemmies. It was a hopeless situation. Lily felt a strong urge to fly down and reassure them that help was coming, but then she remembered how reckless courage had made her behave next to the Bridge over the Infinite Void. She had the courage to fly down to the students, but the risk of being caught was too great. It would be foolish and irresponsible to attempt to communicate with the students at this moment.

Lily then witnessed something that created a surge of admiration that tingled up her spine and warmed her heart. It was like the feeling you get when a team-mate scores a goal or a friend comes from behind to win a running race. When the Blemmy guard walked past their cage, the students pretended to be asleep on the floor. The students became active again when the guard walked away. One began scratching marks on the bars of the cage, and the others gathered around a coat placed on the floor. The coat was removed, and there was a small hole beneath it. The students then formed a chain of workers. Two were digging, one was collecting the soil, and another was scattering it outside the cage. There was purpose and determination in their actions. They were sticking together, and unlike the drunken Blemmies, they had not capitulated. Lily felt inspired. If the students had not given up hope, she would not give up hope.

Lily remembered she needed to return to the Statue of Apollon quickly. Before doing this, she needed to know where the two teachers were. She scanned the prison complex one more time, and to her delight, she spotted two adult humans and knew immediately they were the teachers. They were both asleep on benches set back into the thick walls of an enclosure. Miss Wilson was lying on her back with her arms across her chest, perfectly still and sleeping soundly. She looked like a statue on a tomb of a medieval knight. Her hair was braided in two piggy tales, and her clothes had been deliberately torn at the shoulders and knees to make it easier to move. She had wrapped some of the cut-off fabric around her hands. Cuts and bruises could be seen on her exposed skin. In another corner, Mr Montero was twisting and writhing in a restless sleep. His clothes were dirty, torn and stained with blood.

CHAPTER SEVENTEEN

Strengths and Weaknesses

"I can't believe Lime Fox!" exclaimed Oliver. "The backstabber!"

"We should have listened to you, Mistletoe," added Colin.

"You know what they say," replied Mistletoe, *"the squeaky wheel gets the cheese."*

"Grease", responded Colin. "The squeaky wheel gets the *grease*, and even then, it's not a particularly good phrase in this situation. Anyway, we should have listened to you. We trusted Lime Fox, and now she knows two routes to Earth and has a marble. I wish I knew what Agon Agathon has planned."

"It's only one marble," said Titus. "We can easily take on a single Blemmy. I'm more concerned about the passage behind the waterfall. Any number of Blemmies could travel through if it isn't guarded. Regardless, our immediate concern is finding and rescuing the school group. We only have a day to achieve this."

"The odds feel stacked against us," muttered Colin with a shake of his head.

"When Lily returns," Titus continued, "I will immediately switch positions with her. It is then up to you to form a plan. I will ensure you are not immediately followed through the passage. Then I will make my way out of the sanctuary. You must return between noon and sunset tomorrow, when the sun is at half its height. I will be here to meet you."

"How can we possibly rescue the school group from a sanctuary filled with Blemmies?" questioned Oliver. "Especially when the teachers are the highlight of the Death Match, and the students will fetch such a high price as slaves?"

"We cannot take a confrontational approach," began Titus, "we will be quickly outnumbered and overpowered. Only I am a trained fighter, and the Blemmies in the sanctuary will be the strongest and fittest of their kind. Agon Agathon now knows about us, but he will not know our plans. We need to dictate where, when and how things unfold, and we must not fight battles we cannot win. Tell me, where do we have an advantage over the Blemmies? What are their weaknesses?"

"Well, they're not very good runners," joked Colin awkwardly.

"That's a good observation," Titus replied to Colin's surprise. "What else have you noticed?"

"That old Blemmy," began Oliver, "the one coaching the wrestlers, he said something about not being turned."

"That makes sense," replied Colin. "Their faces are in their chests, and they have no necks, so they must turn their entire body to see things beside them."

"Now you're beginning to think," said Titus.

"Aha!" exclaimed Oliver. "They must find it hard to twist and turn, yet their sanctuary is full of narrow, winding roads."

"Oh yes!" exclaimed Colin, "and they're really slow. We should be able to outrun them through the sanctuary. Escaping is now starting to sound a bit easier."

"All of the Blemmies will want to watch the Death Match tomorrow evening," explained Oliver. "That means they'll all be in the stadium, so the rest of the sanctuary will be almost empty."

"I think you're right," said Titus as he peered out of the chamber entrance. "Just before the Death Match is the moment to attempt the rescue. Don't forget Woden's Eye and the Wings of Icarus; these are powerful artefacts, and you must find a way to use them. As for the marbles, I feel that they do more than you currently know. Interestingly, Agon Agathon has not sent any Blemmies to watch this passage. Lime Fox knows it exists, and surely she would have told him. Ah! Your sister has returned so I must go. Good luck, and remember; meet me between noon and sunset, when the sun is at half its height." Titus then left the chamber, handed the marble to Lily and disappeared into the shadows.

"I've found them," announced Lily as she joined Oliver, Colin and Mistletoe in the chamber.

"That's brilliant!" exclaimed Oliver as he high-fived Lily.

"Well done, Lily!" said Colin smiling. "Where are they then? And what else did you find?"

"They're being kept in a prison," replied Lily in a less upbeat tone than Oliver and Colin. "The Blemmies are horrible brutes. I have no idea how we're going to rescue the school group. The prisoner walls are so high, and the enclosures are well guarded. The students are being kept in a cage, like animals."

"That's dreadful," replied Oliver. "Did they seem injured or unwell?"

"The students actually look like they're in good spirits," Lily began. "They are secretly tunnelling under their cage. Miss Wilson also seems to be full of fight, but Mr Montero did not look so good."

"Can I make a floomin' suggestion?" interrupted Mistletoe. "You need to form a plan, but humans don't think straight when they're tired and hungry. Let's get back to Earth. You can discuss what you've discovered as we walk through the passage. We've got a floomin' big day tomorrow, and we'll need full stomachs and a decent night's sleep."

Lily, Oliver and Colin agreed this was a good idea. They had been so engrossed in their adventure that they had not noticed how hungry and tired they were until Mistletoe had mentioned it.

The friends began their walk back to the Earth. Colin was growing in confidence and offered to lead the group down the spiral staircase wearing Woden's Eye. The companions soon reached the Bridge over the Infinite Void, where the Legionaries allowed them to pass. Colin then confronted his fears by letting Lily and Oliver lead through the dark cavern. They reached the other spiral staircase and ascended to the Priest Hole in the Old Rectory. As is often the case with journeys to new destinations, the return journey felt much quicker than the outward one.

All through the passage, the friends had discussed the Sanctuary of Games and the missing school group. Lily described everything she had seen on her flight. Oliver and Colin then detailed the weaknesses of the Blemmies and how they might be exploited. Rescuing the school group felt like an enormous challenge, but the friends sensed it might be possible with a well-formed plan.

"I'm really feeling tired now," muttered Oliver, who was the first to emerge into the Priest Hole. Lily yawned as she joined him.

"I'm starving as well," said Colin, "but I think there's one more thing we need to do. If Lime Fox or a Blemmy manage to follow us, we need to stop them getting into the Priest Hole."

"I agree," replied Lily with a yawn. "Titus was only going to watch the statue entrance for a short time."

The friends lifted the altar upside down and placed it over the hole.

"That'll stop Lime Fox, but I doubt it will stop a Blemmy," said Colin. "It will only take five minutes to pile other things on the altar. Best to be cautious."

The friends picked up the bed and placed it on the upturned altar. As they did so, clouds of disturbed dust went up their noses. The twins then approached the shelves on which the children's belongings were stored. The twins lifted the shelves and placed them on the upturned altar. The barrier was not perfect, but it would have to do.

Meanwhile, Colin had been otherwise engaged. He had spotted a pile of old books stored under the bed. He blew the dust from their covers and flicked through them.

"A bit of bedtime reading?" asked Lily. "Is it not late enough for you already?"

"Not quite," replied Colin. "I've been thinking about what Titus said about the marbles being more powerful than we currently understand."

"Yes, but Titus also thinks our torches are the thunderbolts of Zeus," replied Oliver. "Imagine what he'd think if he saw a mobile phone."

Colin laughed and then continued, "The Lord's son used this Priest Hole all that time ago, and other people must have used it before him. Surely these people learnt more about Lelandis and the marbles than us. We only discovered the marbles a few days ago. Think about the Spell Book too. We've only read two of its pages, and they described both passages to Lelandis. What else would we discover if we read the other pages?"

"Unfortunately, I don't think we're going to be able to look through the pages of the Spell Book any time soon," responded Lily.

"Exactly!" exclaimed Colin. "That's why I'm going to have a quick look around here. I'll also take these books with me and read through them in the morning."

Lily and Oliver turned to each other and shrugged. They then began shining their torches around the Priest Hole, searching for anything that might be useful.

Colin went to the shelves that the twins had moved onto the upturned altar. He flicked through the old comics and football sticker albums. The haircuts of the football players were amazing, but he found nothing useful. Colin then took a closer look at the small and brightly coloured figurines of monsters. They had all been knocked over when the twins had moved the shelves. Colin recognised Cerberus, the three-headed dog, Frankenstein's monster and an Egyptian mummy walking with outstretched arms. Then Colin spotted a figurine that was a little larger than the rest and not brightly coloured. On closer inspection, it was made from stone, like an old chess piece. It was a large monster with six burly arms that spread from its body like spokes from the hub of a wheel. The creature also had three heads but only two legs. Colin's instincts told him this figurine was worth looking at in more detail, so he put it in his pocket.

Lily was examining the jar of marbles. The marbles were a variety of colours, styles and sizes. Some were pearly white with strokes of bright colours, and others were transparent with spaghetti-like swirls of colour inside them. A few were full of tiny bubbles. Lily then spotted a bigger marble that was not inanimate like the others. She reached into the jar and grabbed it. "Aha," she exclaimed, "another magic marble. It was stored with these playing marbles."

"Sneaky," said Colin. "Perhaps a spare, just in case someone found the others."

"There's doesn't seem to be anything else useful, though,"

said Oliver, "unless either of you fancies going to a roller disco." Oliver held up a pair of retro blue roller skates with rainbow stripes down the sides.

"Perhaps we should give them to Boom-Box Bert?" joked Colin.

The friends left the Priest Hole and emerged in the living room fireplace. The thunder and lightning had stopped, but it was still raining outside. Water dripped from above a window into a puddle on the windowsill. The Old Rectory was completely quiet until a grandfather clock in the hallway chimed. It was 3am. The friends were now feeling very tired and hungry. They quietly walked through the house to the kitchen, where they each drank a glass of orange juice and ate some buttered bread with Auntie Dot's marmalade. Colin started flicking through the books he had found in the Priest Hole, but he was so tired his mind struggled to comprehend what he was reading. He gave up and decided to wait until the morning.

The door to the kitchen quietly opened halfway through their feast, and Auntie Dot appeared in a fluffy nightgown with matching slippers. "Jolly good idea," she whispered with a smile. "A midnight feast." She then glanced at the clock on the microwave, "Goodness me. It's 3 in the morning. Did I not cook enough lasagne last night? I'm terribly sorry. I'll make more next time. Oh, hello, Colin. You three haven't been up all this time, have you? You were very quiet when I got home. I didn't hear anything from your room."

"We were playing board games," Lily quickly replied. "You have a good collection."

"And we were reading stories," added Colin in an attempt to explain the pile of antique books on the dining table. Lily and Oliver both nodded overzealously.

"Erm, how was the play?" asked Oliver, changing the subject.

"Oh, yes, jolly good! It was the story of Robin Hood this year. Gertrude is a wonderful actress. She was very convincing as the Sheriff of Nottingham. Trevor wasn't bad as Maid Marion either. Although I think we could have done without seeing the Merry Men in green tights, none of them had particularly good legs."

"I really must be leaving now," said Colin between yawns.

"Thank you very much for inviting me over. Shall I meet you here tomorrow morning?"

"You can stay if you like," said Auntie Dot. "It is very late. Perhaps Lily and Oliver could top and toe, and you could sleep in the other bed."

"Really?" exclaimed Oliver. "I'm not going to sleep with Lily's cheesy feet in my face."

"And I am not lying in the same bed as you," Lily retorted. "It's bad enough being in the same bedroom."

"It's quite alright," said Colin laughing. "It's a very short walk, and I'll sleep better in my own bed. Thank you very much for the offer though."

"Jolly good," exclaimed Auntie Dot. "Well, I'll watch from the door to check you get home okay. Oh, and have any of you seen my mop? This house doesn't cope well with heavy rain, and I couldn't find it anywhere."

Chapter Eighteen

Geryon

When Lily and Oliver went to bed, they forgot to open a window and close the curtains. Their bedroom was filled with sunlight and uncomfortably warm when they awoke. The rain clouds had passed, and the sky was once again clear and blue. Oliver got out of bed and opened a window. Cool, fresh air drifted into the bedroom, along with the faint scent of rain drying on the roads and pavements. The twins could hear birds tweeting and cars on the streets of Bridgeward. Last night's adventure felt very distant in this more familiar environment. They were almost like a dream. The twins lazily tossed and turned. It crossed their minds they could probably go back to sleep for a little longer. It was the summer holiday, after all.

TING!

Something hit the window.

TING!

Oliver got out of bed and went to look outside. Colin was standing below with a handful of acorns.

"Oh, hello, Colin," called Oliver in between yawns. "What's the matter? Are you planning to serenade us from down there? Auntie Dot has this thing called a front door, and someone usually lets you in if you knock."

"Ssshh! I'm trying to avoid this odd girl from school," replied Colin. "For some reason, she's having a cup of tea in the garden with your Auntie and an old lady. The old lady must be her grandma or something."

"Oh no, it's 11:30am!" exclaimed Lily when she looked at her phone. She leapt out of bed and joined Oliver at the window. "I didn't realise it was this late. I've got loads of missed calls from Mum; we forgot to call her last night, and we've only got until sunset to try to save the school group. What were we thinking? We need to get moving!"

"11:30? Are you serious?" exclaimed Oliver. "I didn't realise it was so late. Wait there for us, Colin. We'll be with you as soon as possible."

The twins both felt disgusting. Neither of them had washed after last night's adventure, and they had fallen asleep in their dirty clothes. Lily's hair felt full of cobwebs, and Oliver's hands and face were filthy. They showered quickly and changed into clean clothes. Then they crept downstairs with a plan to have a quick breakfast before setting off to find Colin.

"Here are the sleeping beauties," announced Auntie Dot the moment Oliver's foot touched the bottom step of the staircase.

"How did she hear us?" Oliver asked Lily quietly.

"We're on the patio," Auntie Dot continued. "There's some brunch on the kitchen table. Help yourself and join us. There's a lovely young lady here who is dying to meet you."

"So much for our sneaky getaway," Lily muttered. "It's probably midday now, and we've got so much to do. We'll have to say hello very quickly and then leave immediately."

The twins went into the kitchen, where they found bread, crumpets and croissants alongside jars of jam, a bowl of fruit and a big tub of yoghurt. Oliver filled a plate with freshly baked croissants, and Lily buttered some crumpets. The twins poured some orange juice and walked quickly through to the patio. It was a wonderfully warm morning.

"Did you not fancy any more croissants?" Oliver said to Lily as they headed outside. "I thought they were your favourite?"

"I'm temporarily off them after having had one thrown in my face by that horrible—"

"Who's been throwing croissants at you, my dear?" interrupted Gertrude, sitting on the patio with a cup of tea on her lap. She looked like the sweetest Grandma you have ever seen. "Are you being bullied? Other children can be terrible."

Oliver suppressed his laughter, and Lily suppressed an urge to give Gertrude a piece of her mind.

"You've already met Gertrude," said Auntie Dot. "This is her granddaughter, Ingrid. She's inherited Gertrude's sweet nature for sure! She's been dying to meet you both."

Lily and Oliver smiled awkwardly at Ingrid. She was sitting in the same way as Gertrude: on the front of her seat with her back upright and a cup of tea on her lap. When Gertrude sipped from her cup, so did Ingrid. Between them sat Digbert, Gertrude's ugly and fat Chihuahua.

"Now, what were you saying about croissants hitting you in the face?" Gertrude asked with a voice full of concern.

"It's nothing to worry about," replied Lily. "Just some nasty, horrible, two-faced toad we encountered yesterday." Lily was staring hard at Gertrude, and Oliver almost choked on his croissant.

"How unpleasant," replied Gertrude sweetly. "You should be careful about making enemies so quickly in Bridgeward. It's a peculiar place." Ingrid nodded in agreement with her grandmother.

"So we must be heading off soon," said Oliver.

"Why's that?" Auntie Dot answered.

"Nothing really, just meeting someone," Oliver replied.

"Can I come?" Ingrid said in a squeaky voice.

"Well... I don't know..." babbled Oliver, who was taken off guard. "You see... that might be a bit tricky..."

"Don't be silly. Of course she can!" exclaimed Auntie Dot. "Are you meeting Colin again? You've already made one friend, and here's another for you! Isn't making friends jolly good fun?"

Oliver looked at Lily for help. She shrugged her shoulders, not knowing what to do.

"I think that's a wonderful idea, Dot," added Gertrude. "Ingrid is a lovely girl. She is very well-mannered and respectful, unlike many other children I encounter." Gertrude stared at the twins, and Ingrid smiled and clapped her hands together like a seal.

"So, that's that settled!" said Auntie Dot. "When are you meeting Colin?"

"Well…" responded Oliver, "we were hoping… we were planning… he was going to meet us—"

"I bet he's waiting at the gate again like yesterday, isn't he?" interrupted Auntie Dot, trying to be helpful. She walked to the patio's edge and leant around the house over a low bush. "Colin, are you there?"

There was a moment of silence, and then Colin popped his head up from behind the wall where he had been sitting on the pavement. "Oh, hello," he called back. "Are Lily and Oliver coming out?"

"Why is everyone in such a rush this morning?" Auntie Dot said cheerfully to herself. "Come on over for some food, Colin."

Colin reluctantly joined the brunch party on the patio. Like the twins, he was itching to find somewhere quiet to discuss the rather pressing issue of rescuing a school group from a mysterious world before the students were sold into slavery and the teachers made to fight to the death. He did not want to be sitting on a patio sipping tea with Gertrude and her slightly odd granddaughter.

"Hello, Colin," said Ingrid as Colin stepped over the low hedge onto the patio. "I'm coming with you today."

"Oh… great… hello, Ingrid," Colin said with forced politeness.

"And this is Gertrude," added Auntie Dot.

Colin waved awkwardly at Gertrude and then looked across at the twins. Their expressions made it clear they were desperate to get out of this situation, but they could not work out how to do so without being rude.

"Would you like a crumpet, Colin?" Auntie Dot asked with her usual jollity. Before Colin could answer, Auntie Dot had headed back into the house to get him a plate.

The moment Auntie Dot stepped into the house, Gertrude's demeanour switched from a sweet grandmother to an evil witch. She reached over to a plate, picked up two buttered crumpets and threw them at Lily and Oliver. Colin watched in shock. The crumpets hit the twins square in the face.

"You evil old hag!" replied Lily, spitting with anger. She picked up the crumpet from her lap, stood up and threw it straight back at Gertrude. It hit her on the nose and dislodged her horn-rimmed glasses.

"You little turd!" hissed Gertrude with pieces of buttery crumpet smudged all over her face. "So you've developed some courage, have you?" She turned to Oliver. "What about you? You're the clever little poet, aren't you?"

Oliver was still recovering from having had a crumpet thrown in his face when a croissant hit him on the ear. It had been thrown by Ingrid, who had watched her grandmother and concluded this must be the right thing to do in the circumstances.

"What is wrong with you two?" Oliver retorted. "Who throws crumpets and croissants at people?"

Oliver stood up, took aim and launched a croissant as hard as possible at Gertrude. Oliver's throw was much more powerful than Lily's, and it knocked Gertrude backwards off her chair into a small bush. He then launched a croissant at Ingrid. Ingrid deftly dodged the croissant, picked up another off her plate and threw it back at Oliver. Meanwhile, Gertrude had rolled over in the bush and picked herself up with remarkable athleticism. The nearest thing to her was a bowl of Greek yoghurt with a large serving spoon. She grabbed the spoon and flicked a big glob of yoghurt at Lily. It hit Lily in the face. Gertrude followed this up with a volley of yoghurt aimed at Oliver and Colin.

Colin had watched the food fight unravel with a look of complete bemusement on his face. This look of bemusement was soon covered with three large globs of Greek yoghurt that hit him in quick succession. Colin stepped backwards in the confusion and tripped over Digbert, the fat Chihuahua, who was having a great time eating all the pieces of crumpet and croissant that were scattered over the floor. Colin still had in his pocket the six-armed and three-headed monster he had discovered in the Priest Hole. The figurine fell out of his pocket and smashed on the patio floor as Colin fell backwards into a bed of lavender.

What followed put an immediate stop to the food fight. The smashed figurine vanished, and out of thin air appeared a real, three-headed Giant with six arms. The creature's heads were just below the Old Rectory's second-floor windows. It had brawny arms and blue skin, and it was wearing what looked like a kilt. The creature's three faces were very similar, like brothers' faces.

"I am Geryon, and I am at your service," announced the middle head.

"What is it you wish for me to do?" said another head.

"I am very good at smashing things up!" added the final head.

Lily, Oliver and Colin were surprised by the sudden appearance of this monstrous man, but they had become used to these unusual surprises since discovering the Priest Hole. Gertrude and Ingrid, meanwhile, were completely frozen in shock with their eyes and mouths wide open. Ingrid was midway through launching a croissant, and Gertrude still had the yoghurt serving spoon in her hand. The yoghurt slowly dripped off the spoon onto the head of Digbert, who was tucking into a particularly buttery piece of crumpet.

"Where did you come from?" asked Lily.

"I came from the Hide of Courage," replied Geryon's middle head.

"I'm right. That's exactly where I came from."

"Would you like me to smash something now?"

"What's all this floomin' noise?" interrupted Mistletoe, who had come running out of the building to see what was going on. He spotted Geryon and began running around his feet, barking. Geryon did not look very bothered.

"It's okay, Mistletoe," responded Colin from his position sitting in the lavender. "He says he's at our service."

"Well, if he's at our floomin' service, tell him to disappear immediately! Auntie Dot's about to come out with some more crumpets!"

Colin looked up at Geryon, "Erm... please will you disappear?"

"At your service."

"Whatever you say, I do."

"I can smash things later."

Geryon disappeared, and his figurine reappeared on the floor intact. A moment later, Auntie Dot stepped back onto the patio and discovered the twins covered in yoghurt, Colin sitting in the lavender surrounded by bees, and croissants and crumpets all over the floor. Gertrude and Ingrid were still frozen in shock. Mistletoe stood in the middle of the mess.

"By Jove! What happened here?" blurted Auntie Dot.

Lily, Oliver and Colin looked at each other, not knowing what to say. Then Oliver had an idea, "A deer! Mistletoe spotted a deer — a really big one — he went nuts."

"A deer in here? Oh dear, how queer!" exclaimed Auntie Dot. "Gertrude, is everything okay? Did the deer take you by surprise?"

Gertrude slowly began to move. It was like watching an ice statue thaw. She turned to Auntie Dot. "Yes... yes, my dear, I'm fine. It... it must have been a deer. Monsters don't just... appear out of nowhere, and dogs... don't talk do they? No... of course they don't. A deer... yes, of course it was. That makes sense... a deer. "

"What about you, Ingrid?" Auntie Dot asked. "Are you okay?"

Ingrid was also regaining her senses slowly. "I think... I'm fine. Was it... a deer Grandma?"

"It... it must have been Ingrid," Gertrude replied, "and... I don't think I will be eating any more Greek yoghurt for a while."

CHAPTER NINETEEN

The Hide of Courage

The unexpected appearance of Geryon at brunch immediately put a stop to Gertrude's unpleasantness and also meant Ingrid no longer fancied spending the day with Lily, Oliver and Colin. The three friends washed the food off their faces and briefly helped Auntie Dot tidy up the remains of the food fight. They then headed hastily onto Bridgeward Estate to find somewhere private to talk.

"Wow, that Gertrude is a fiery character," exclaimed Colin as the friends ducked through a gap in the bushes onto Bridgeward Estate. "I don't think I've ever seen a pensioner start a food fight before."

"I hate her," hissed Lily.

"You don't say?" responded Oliver. "You disguised it very well, particularly when you launched a crumpet in her face."

The three friends laughed.

"Her and Agon Agathon are two of the most revolting creatures I've ever met," continued Lily. "Although I do feel sorry for Ingrid. Imagine having a grandmother like that? I really wouldn't have minded her joining us on any other day, but we've got a lot on our plate."

The friends sat down under an oak tree surrounded by wild meadow flowers. Crickets were buzzing all around them.

"This morning, I quickly flicked through the books I found in the Priest Hole," said Colin. "They're very old books written in Latin. Luckily I had my marble to translate them. Someone in the past discovered Lelandis and tried their hardest to work out why it exists. A few of the books were written by people who travelled to Asia in the Middle Ages expecting to find weird, monstrous peoples. Guess what? They write about Blemmies, Giants and Monopods! There were also books from Ancient Greece and Viking sagas. I opened one book to a page marked with a piece of folded paper. The page was about Woden. He was an Anglo-Saxon god who only had one eye. 'Wednesday' is named after him."

"So we've been wearing a god's eye?" replied Lily. "That's a bit freaky. I hope Woden doesn't mind."

"I also looked up Icarus in my encyclopaedia," continued Colin, who was in his element. "He's from an Ancient Greek myth about a father and son who tried to escape prison by making themselves wings. The wings worked, but Icarus flew too close to the sun, and the glue in his wings melted. He fell to his death."

"Well, that's uplifting," said Oliver.

"It was until the glue melted," replied Lily.

"I've brought the books with me in case they become useful," said Colin, "but we don't have enough time to look through them in detail. However, this Geryon creature definitely needs more investigating. Shall we ask him some questions? He says he's at our service."

The twins were impressed with Colin's research and agreed that it was a good idea to talk to Geryon. Colin took the figurine out of his pocket and threw it hard against the ground.

"Ouch!"

"Oooph!"

"Corrr!"

Geryon had appeared beneath the oak tree, and because he was so tall, he bashed his three heads against the tree's branches. Acorns fell around the friends, and Geryon rubbed his three heads with his six hands.

"Geryon," said Colin, looking up, "would you like to sit with us and answer some of our questions?"

"As you please!"

"I am at your service."

"I will do as you ask. May I suggest smashing stuff?"

Geryon lowered himself from among the branches of the oak tree and sat down next to the friends. Mistletoe eyed him suspiciously.

"Where did you say you were from?" asked Lily.

"The Hide of Courage."

"I'm right about that."

"Yep, that's the place. Lots of things to smash there!"

"And where is the Hide of Courage?" asked Oliver.

"It leads to the amphitheatre of the Romans."

"That is where I demonstrate my skills to marble holders."

"If you show me where it is, I will show you my strength by smashing things." Geryon flexed his six large arms.

"I wonder if he means the old amphitheatre in Bridgeward?" said Colin, turning to the twins. "I've been there before, but I have no idea what the Hide of Courage is."

"Well, we've seen plenty of weird things in Bridgeward in the last few days," replied Lily. "I wouldn't be surprised if we discover something odd at the amphitheatre too."

Oliver turned to Geryon, who by now had stopped flexing his arms. "What is the Hide of Courage?" he asked.

"The Hide of Courage is a sanctum for marble holders," replied Geryon's middle head. "At the Hide, there is the Avenue of Legends."

"If marble holders need help, they will find it from the creatures who line the Avenue. I am one of those Legends."

"Damn right! I am a Legend!" finished Geryon, fist-pumping himself.

"This is just what we need!" exclaimed Oliver. "If we find the Hide of Courage, we can request help from the Legends, and they can come with us to Lelandis to help rescue the school group."

"There's one problem with this," replied Colin. "The amphitheatre is a long way away from here, and we don't even know if it's the right place. I doubt we can get there and back and still have enough time to get to Lelandis before the Death Match."

"When did Titus tell us to meet him?" asked Lily.

"Between noon and sunset," replied Oliver, "when the sun is at half its height. I guess Romans didn't have digital watches, did they?"

"So, noon is when the sun is highest in the sky," explained Colin. "Which is about now, so 1pm. Sunset is when the sun goes below the horizon, and that's around 9pm at this time of year."

"So we need to be in Lelandis by about 5pm," added Lily. "I think it took us about an hour to get through the tunnel, so we need to be in the passage by 4pm."

"Let's make that 3pm just to be sure," suggested Oliver.

"So that only gives us a couple of hours," responded Colin. "It's going to be hard to walk to the Roman Amphitheatre and back again in that time. I'm not sure this is a good idea."

"Why can't Auntie Dot just have a car like a normal person?" Oliver exclaimed.

"I never thought I'd say this," Lily began, "but Oliver, we could use the tandem, couldn't we?"

"I suppose we could. You've got a bike, haven't you, Colin?"

"My parents never taught me to ride a bike," Colin replied, feeling slightly embarrassed. "They were always too busy with work. So no, I don't have one."

"In that case, a tandem bike is a great way to learn," exclaimed Lily cheerfully. "I'm sure Auntie Dot will let us borrow her bike too. That way, we can take Mistletoe."

The friends agreed this was a good idea. Colin asked Geryon to disappear, and the friends headed back to the Old Rectory.

Gertrude and Ingrid had gone home to have a quiet afternoon, and Auntie Dot had cleared up the mess on the patio. She was now looking at two flattened patches of lavender, wondering how big the deer was.

"Auntie Dot," said Lily. "I was wondering if we could borrow your bike today."

"What a jolly good idea," replied Auntie Dot. "Are the three of you planning to go on a bike ride?"

"Yep," replied Lily. "Mistletoe also seems to enjoy our company, so we thought we'd take him with us if that's okay?"

"Absolutely! What a kind suggestion. I knew you'd like the

tandem. There's only one problem; I had a bad puncture last night cycling home from the play in that terrible storm. I've also got no spare inner tubes, so I'm afraid the bike is out of action for a while."

"Do you have any other bikes?" Oliver asked.

"No, I'm sorry, I don't," said Auntie Dot. "I used to have the bikes your dad and I played with as kids, but I got rid of them a while ago. I should have kept them."

Oliver turned to Lily and Colin, "You two get the tandem, and I'll be back in five minutes. Auntie Dot's comment about her childhood has given me an idea."

Oliver disappeared into the house while Lily and Colin went to find the tandem. Meanwhile, Auntie Dot made the three friends a late lunch to take with them.

Lily and Colin were standing by the gate when Oliver ran out of the house with his rucksack over his shoulder, cobwebs in his hair and a pair of retro roller skates in his hands. "I think we've already lost enough time this morning," he said. "These are about the right size for me. Let's get going."

"Since when have you been able to roller skate?" exclaimed Lily with a smile. "I think this is a bit much to ask of the marbles."

"If you take the front seat of the bike, Colin can sit on the back, and I'll hold on to the luggage rack with the roller skates on. You can pull me along, and I can help Colin keep his balance."

"Ha!" exclaimed Lily, "or help him lose it! Look at the size of my thighs. Am I supposed to pull both of you along?"

"Yep," replied Oliver, "and Mistletoe too. Here he comes now. I told him he could go in my backpack."

"I'll peddle too once I get the hang of balancing," replied Colin. His sense of urgency was masking his nervousness at learning to ride. "Come on, let's give it a go. We'll look pretty silly, but we haven't got time for anything else."

Lily and Colin mounted the tandem bike as Oliver grabbed the luggage rack over the back wheel and crouched down with his legs splayed. He quickly realised how difficult it was to balance on roller skates. Colin explained how to get to the

Roman amphitheatre, and with a big push from Lily, the friends began to move.

The bike was wobbly to begin with, and Lily had to shift her weight side-to-side to get the pedals moving. Her thighs quickly began to burn, but the friends were moving, and everyone was managing to stay in place. Colin was gripping his handlebars far harder than was necessary, but despite his nervousness, he was beginning to enjoy the sensation of riding. He had always wanted to ride a bike, but his parents had never taken the time to build his confidence. Colin now realised the faster they went, the easier it was to balance. The bike suddenly accelerated. Colin had started pedalling with full force, and Oliver almost flew off the back.

"This is great fun!" Colin shouted with a big smile on his face. "We'll be there in no time at this speed!"

"You need to pace yourself, Colin!" shouted Oliver. "You can't keep this pace up the whole way."

"Don't worry about me," Colin replied. "Just make sure you don't fall off. Next left, Lily!"

Lily was now barely pedalling, and they were flying along the road. Colin's pace did not wane despite him breathing so heavily it felt like there was an angry bull on the bike. Colin loved the sensation of the wind against his skin and the sound of the chain whizzing around. He felt like he had finally found a form of exercise he was good at. Lily and Oliver were a little sweaty when the friends reached the Roman amphitheatre, but Colin was drenched.

"So here we are," Colin announced, guzzling from a bottle of water that had been in Oliver's bag.

"Well, that was impressive, Colin," said Lily. "I think you need to get yourself a bike."

"And now what are we floomin' looking for?" asked Mistletoe. "I can't see anything but grass and mounds."

"This is it," explained Colin. "Those mounds are all that's left of the amphitheatre. They form a circle around where the arena would have been."

The friends wandered across the grass in the direction of the Roman amphitheatre. The remains of the building were in a clearing surrounded by woods. The grass was bisected with well-trodden paths that led around the amphitheatre and up onto the mounds where there was an information board. The sound of traffic could be heard on a stretch of motorway beyond the woods. Birds were busy flying between trees, an elderly man was walking his dog, and two young men drank from cans on a bench.

The friends had almost reached the amphitheatre when they felt their marbles growing cold. They looked at each other excitedly. They knew something was about to happen, and it had been worth their while cycling here. With every step they took towards the remains of the amphitheatre, the original Roman structure began to emerge as if it had been cloaked in a thick fog. It looked very similar to the stadium in the Sanctuary of Games, only much smaller. It consisted of two rings of stone arches, one on top of the other. Around the top of the amphitheatre, colourful flags on long wooden poles gently fluttered in the wind. The companions followed a tunnel lined with racks of weapons into the arena. There were spears, swords, pikes and maces. They were all different sizes, and every weapon was unique.

In the arena, there was a pile of enormous stone spheres, three round archery targets and a selection of large, hay-filled sacks hanging from wooden frames like boxing bags. There were also barriers like those at equestrian show jumping events. Another tunnel led out of the amphitheatre on the other side of the arena. The friends could just make out a long avenue lined with statues of mysterious creatures. They knew straight away this was the Avenue of Legends.

"Well, I think we've found what we were looking for!" said Lily as the friends walked through the tunnel and into the arena. "Good instincts Colin. You spotted the figurine of Geryon in the Priest Hole, and now you've found the Hide of Courage."

"This place is awesome!" Oliver said as he picked up a broad sword from the rack. He swung it around clumsily.

"Didn't Geryon want to show us some things in the arena?" asked Colin. "This must be what he meant. It looks like a weird gymnasium in here."

"Well, shall we take him up on the offer?" Oliver said

excitedly. "I'd like to see what he can do."

Colin took the figurine of Geryon out of his pocket and smashed it against the floor. Geryon materialised in front of the friends.

"Aha! You have brought me to the arena."

"Would you like to see my talents?"

"Just give me the command, and I'll start smashing stuff!"

"Yes, please," answered Colin. "You show us what you've got!"

The three heads of Geryon looked delighted. He rushed to the weapons racks and picked up three of the largest swords; each was bigger than a human. He also grabbed three large shields that were each the size of a rowing boat. Geryon then rushed at the hay-filled bags and started slashing and stabbing. Lily, Oliver and Colin were taken back by the frenzied display. It did not take Geryon long to rip the hay-filled bags to shreds. He then dropped his swords and shields and ran to the enormous stone spheres. One by one, with grunts that shook the whole amphitheatre, Geryon lifted the rocks above his head with his six brawny arms. He looked back at the friends, smiling through the exertion contorting his faces, and then slammed the stones against the arena floor, making huge craters.

"I am Geryon!"

"And I have the strength of a hundred men!"

"If you choose me to come with you, you will not be disappointed."

There was a moment of awkward silence.

"Erm... thank you, Geryon," replied Colin. "That was excellent. We are now going to discuss your... erm... application. Please return to your figurine."

Geryon immediately vanished, and the small figurine reappeared on the gravel floor of the arena.

"That was like a bizarre job interview, wasn't it?" said Lily. "Now, I know you boys probably love this – monsters with weapons and all that – but can I remind you why we are here? We need to make a plan to rescue the school group, and we only have a matter of hours before we need to get back to Lelandis."

"You're right, Lily," responded Oliver. "We do need to keep

focused, but this is just what we needed. Think about how much Geryon could help us in the sanctuary."

"I think we need to take a look down the Avenue of Legends," said Colin. "I have a feeling Geryon isn't the only creature we can ask for help."

CHAPTER TWENTY

The Avenue of Legends

The friends walked across the arena, stepping over the half-buried stone spheres Geryon had smashed against the ground and past the gently swinging remains of the hay bags Geryon had ripped to shreds. When they reached the middle of the arena, the friends began to appreciate how intimidating the amphitheatre was. The wall surrounding the arena was the height of a bus. Above this, there was tiered seating, and the friends could easily imagine the cacophony of shouting, chanting and groaning coming from a crowd of Romans watching gladiators fight to the death. This dreadful fate would befall Miss Wilson and Mr Montero if the friends were unsuccessful in their mission.

The friends exited the arena through the other tunnel. The Avenue of Legends stretched into the distance in front of them. The avenue was made of large stone slabs, and where the slabs met, wild grasses and flowers sprouted. There were statues of humans, animals and monsters on either side of the path. The statues stood on plinths that bore their names. On the edges of these plinths, there stood figurines of the statues, like the one of Geryon Colin had discovered in the Priest Hole.

"So I guess we choose who we want to help us," said Lily as she stood looking at a statue of a centaur. The centaur was standing on its hind legs, with its front legs in the air and an arm pointing a sword skyward. His torso was turned slightly, and his mouth was wide open as if he were shouting to other centaurs.

"But there are so many to choose from," replied Colin. "We

haven't got the time to go through all of them."

"As much as I'd love to watch these Legends all day," began Oliver, admiring the statue of a knight swinging a mace around his head, "I think we need to narrow things down by making a plan first."

Without the friends noticing, a creature had appeared behind them. Mistletoe sensed the creature's presence first and turned around. He then began barking loudly, just like when Geryon first appeared. The friends turned around to find themselves face to face with a huge brown bear.

"Do not be worried," said the bear in a gentle, feminine voice. "I am Arto, and welcome to the Avenue of Legends in the Hide of Courage. What is it you seek?"

Mistletoe stopped barking and returned to the three friends. *"Knock me down with a sausage!"* he exclaimed. "All this discovering enormous creatures isn't good for my floomin' nerves."

"Oh, hello," said Colin, with his heart rate slowly settling. "We've come looking for help to rescue our friends."

"You have come to the right place," said Arto in a voice that seemed too gentle to come from such a fierce and powerful creature. "There are one hundred Legends along this Avenue, each with their individual strengths. They are brave and loyal to their marble holders, but only if their marble holders are deserving of their support."

"Do we just take their figurines?" asked Oliver.

"Yes," replied Arto. "When you have decided who will be of most assistance, you just need to take their figurine. Smash the figurine when you need the Legend's help, and they will appear."

"That sounds easy," Oliver replied. He then turned to the others. "Let's fill up my bag with figurines. We'll smash them all in the Sanctuary of Games, and the Legends will demolish the place. We're going to be invincible!"

"It's not that simple," replied Arto. "You are in the Hide of Courage. The gods created this Hide before time began to help marble holders, but you do not help people by encouraging laziness and cowardice. The Legends will fight with you, but not for you. If you do not show courage, then they will not show courage. Tell me about your mission, and I will tell you how many you may choose."

The friends told Arto about the Sanctuary of Games, the Death Match and the missing school group.

"Your mission is a righteous one," Arto said when the friends had finished. "You may take two figurines with you, and that includes the figurine of Geryon in your pocket if you want his assistance. Come with me now, and I'll lead you to the highest seats of the amphitheatre. The views from there should help you with your plan. I imagine the amphitheatre is similar to the stadium of the Blemmies you have described."

Arto led the friends around the back of the amphitheatre and up a stone staircase to the spectator seating. The elderly man, who was still walking his dog on the grass, was oblivious to what was going on only metres away. Arto explained to the friends that the Hide of Courage was like a bird hide; marble holders could enter and see out, but it was invisible to everyone else.

The friends could now see the arena from the viewpoint of a spectator. Oliver opened his rucksack and took out lunch. Finally, the companions began to make a plan.

"We agreed yesterday that the best time to rescue the school group would be just before the Death Match starts," said Colin. "This is when all the Blemmies will be concentrated in the stadium."

"And remember the winding streets of the sanctuary," added Oliver. "It shouldn't be hard to stay away from the Blemmies once we've escaped with the school group. We'll be much faster than them."

"But we don't know where to go once we've got the school group," said Lily. "We can't all go through the passage beneath the Statue of Apollon because it's only for marble holders."

"So we'll need to look for the waterfall passage," added Oliver. "Did you see where it was when you flew above the sanctuary, Lily?"

"No, but I wasn't looking for it. I could see where the river went though. Once we're out of the sanctuary, we're into fields and woodland, which will again suit us more than the Blemmies. The bad news is Agon Agathon knows about the waterfall passage."

"It will be interesting to know what Titus discovered last night around the sanctuary," said Colin. "I'm sure he'll have some suggestions when we tell him about our plan."

"So if we forget the escape for the moment," said Lily, "let's think about the hard bit; how will we get the teachers and students out of Blemmy hands?"

"If we try to rescue the teachers as they're being moved to the stadium," Oliver began, "we're going to have to defeat a large number of Blemmies who are guarding them and somehow unchain the teachers in the confusion. Or, we could wait until they are unchained in the stadium and rescue them just before the Death Match starts. The problem is we're going to be surrounded by hundreds of thousands of Blemmies, and the entrance to the stadium will be locked and guarded."

"Neither seems like an easy option," replied Lily with a sigh.

"But if we had Geryon with us, he would make short work of opening the portcullis to the arena," Colin pointed out. "He'd probably make short work of any Blemmies guarding the portcullis too. Put yourselves in the shoes of the Blemmy guards. Once they've got the combatants into the arena, they're going to think their work is done, and they're going to want to watch the Death Match."

"But we've then got to perform a magic trick to get the two teachers out of the arena," added Oliver, "with every Blemmy in the sanctuary watching them."

"What about the four students?" said Lily. "They've got an escape plan, I'm sure of it."

"I think we need to take advantage of the confusion caused by rescuing the teachers," suggested Oliver. "If the students already have an escape plan, we might just need to give them the signal to escape at the same time."

"We should definitely try to communicate with the students before the Death Match," suggested Colin. "We could let them know our plan and find out what their plan is. Could you fly down to the prison without being spotted, Lily?"

"Maybe," replied Lily, trying to remember what she saw last night, "but it will be twilight, remember? I'll be much easier to spot."

"This isn't easy, is it?" Colin exclaimed. "There are so many things to consider; so many unknowns."

"Maybe there's a ninja or something similar along the Avenue?" suggested Oliver. "We could use them to communicate with the school group."

"We could also tell the other combatants our plan," added Colin. "Surely they're going to be pretty open to the idea of an escape. Imagine if we had the Giant on our side."

"So we need a Legend to sneak into the prison and a Legend to break into the stadium," summarised Lily. "Geryon would love the job of breaking in. I'm not so sure about rescuing the other creatures though. We don't know why they're being made to fight in the Death Match. They could be murderers, pirates, or other nasty criminals. Maybe we should just let them loose to create some chaos?"

"But what if they're not murderers and pirates?" said Oliver. "Those Blemmies were put into the Death Match for getting drunk and having a competition to see who could burp loudest. What if they're all innocent? Miss Wilson and Mr Montero haven't done anything wrong, have they? They're in the Death Match because humans draw the crowds."

"Unfortunately, we're probably never going to know if the other combatants are good or bad," said Colin. "It's a bit of a dilemma. If we never discovered Lelandis, those creatures would have been made to fight to the death anyway, and nobody would have been sitting here considering saving them. People are treated cruelly everywhere, all the time. You can't stop every bit of cruelty, can you? You can't save every life that is in danger."

"What a horrible thing to consider," exclaimed Lily, "and if we try to save the other creatures and the school group, we might fail to save anyone. We might also get caught ourselves. This is horrible. Who to save and who to leave to die? I think we should at least allow the other creatures to escape."

"They'll cause some chaos, which should help us," added Oliver. "Then I think it should be up to them to see if they can get free of the sanctuary. Our focus is on the school group."

Colin looked into the sky as he was thinking. It was a blue, cloudless sky, and Colin could feel the sun's warmth on his skin.

He spotted a buzzard drifting on currents of air, looking for prey. Colin wondered what it was like to use the Wings of Icarus.

Lily spotted Colin daydreaming, "Come on, Colin, let's focus. We're doing well here, but we're going to need to get moving. We can't afford to be late to Lelandis. Besides, you'll get a sore neck looking up like that for too long."

Oliver had a sudden realisation, "How easy do you think it would be to watch that bird without a neck?"

Colin and Lily looked at Oliver, slightly confused.

Oliver hunched his shoulder and tried to look at the buzzard, only moving from his waist. "It's very difficult," he said. "You both try."

Colin and Lily copied Oliver.

"Yes, it's difficult," said Lily. "So Blemmies are probably bad at bird spotting. What's your point?"

"We need to exploit their weaknesses, remember?" said Oliver excitedly. "How about a distraction? You know, like magicians use to fool audiences. Lily, you could use the Wings of Icarus to fly around the stadium throwing stuff at the Blemmies. You were pretty accurate with those crumpets this morning, and I'm also sure I spotted some Legends with wings. What if there is a dragon or something? That would be a pretty big distraction, wouldn't it? They could join you in being a mischief."

"And then I'd get shot with lots of arrows," said Lily. "Thank you, Oliver."

"If the Blemmies can't look upwards, they can't shoot upwards," explained Oliver. "When they were practising their archery, they were firing at a target in front of them, not above them."

"I think that's a great idea," replied Colin, turning to speak to Lily. "We'd give you Woden's Eye too, and you could search for the waterfall passage."

Lily was coming round to the idea. "Okay, so we need a strong Legend, a flying Legend and a sneaky Legend, but we're only allowed two."

"I can be pretty floomin' sneaky," said Mistletoe. "Perhaps I could sneak into the prison? I'm not the best climber, but I might be able to squeeze through a few gaps to get in. *Where there's a will, there's a watermelon.*"

"That's very brave of you, Mistletoe," replied Lily. "You certainly have a good sense of smell which would help you. My only concern is if you can't get into the prison, our plan will be off to a dreadful start. It seems a bit risky."

"He'd attract a lot less attention than us," pointed out Colin. "It's not the worst idea ever."

"What if Lily dropped you in from a height, Mistletoe?" suggested Oliver.

"Excuse me!" replied Mistletoe. "I'm not being parachuted in if that's what you floomin' mean. I'm excellent at sniffing, not bad at sneaking, pretty bad at climbing and terrible at flying. I go in on foot or not at all, thank you very much."

"Okay, so an idea worth considering," said Lily. "Thank you, Mistletoe. Let's mull it over while we check out some Legends."

The friends had eaten their lunch, and they felt optimistic about their planning. Arto had been listening the whole time without making a sound. She followed them as they walked out of the amphitheatre and back to the Avenue of Legends.

CHAPTER TWENTY-ONE

Emerald Eyes

"When it comes to strength," Arto began, "there are Giants and knights, but for what you have described, I recommend Geryon. I have three suggestions for flying Legends to assist you: the Banshee, Brunhilda the Valkyrie and the Thunder Dragon. Come with me, and I'll show you their statues. We can look for stealthy Legends afterwards."

Arto walked lazily along the Avenue of Legends. Her long stride meant the friends had to jog to keep up with her. The first statue they reached was that of the Banshee. She was a short lady wearing a scruffy cloak with a hood covering her head. Her bony feet could be seen poking out from beneath her cloak. Her face was gaunt, and she had bony fingers with unpleasant looking nails. Oliver picked up one of the Banshee's figurines unenthusiastically. He was hoping for something much more exciting.

The friends carried on to another statue of a broad-shouldered, strong-jawed woman with long hair that flowed down past her shoulders onto a decorated breastplate. She wore a long patterned skirt and a top that exposed her powerful arms. In one hand, she held a long, rectangular shield with a large boss in the middle. In her other hand, she held a spear as if she was about to throw it. The woman also had large wings, like the Wings of Icarus, and the expression on her face was fearsome. This was Brunhilda the Valkyrie, and Lily liked the idea of flying around the Blemmy stadium with her. Lily picked up one of

Brunhilda's figurines.

A moment later, the friends were in front of a statue of a long, serpentine dragon that stood on its short back legs. The dragon's scaly body snaked into the sky. The Thunder Dragon had large wings that were spread above the heads of the statues beside it. Its head was bent forward, and its neck was straining as if it were breathing fire. Colin stepped forward and picked up her figurine. Oliver looked envious; the Thunder Dragon was far cooler than the Banshee.

Lily looked at her watch. "How long did it take us to get here?" she asked.

"I reckon about half an hour," answered Oliver, "although I was rather preoccupied with keeping a hold of the tandem after Thunder-Thighs started pedalling. Maybe Colin could become one of the Legends. Colin Thunder-Thighs; the Legend who can cycle at twice the speed of a normal book worm."

Colin started laughing. "You've started something now! If you were a Legend, what would your attributes be then?"

"Oliver the Armourer!" announced Lily. "He can forge armour out of any household item. Your statue would have you with a colander on your head, a bathmat over your chest and a cape of floral curtain."

"Don't forget the mop," added Colin.

"Okay then!" replied Oliver, enjoying the good-natured teasing. "Don't think you're getting away without a statue, Lily. How about Lily Honky-Toes? Defeat your enemy with the cheesy pong that wafts from her feet. Your statue would have you elegantly chewing your toenails."

"Disgusting habit!" Mistletoe exclaimed. "Floomin' revolting."

The three friends all laughed.

"Back to the original question," Lily said. "It took us half an hour to cycle here, it's already 2.30pm, and we want to be back at the Old Rectory by 4pm, although closer to 3pm would be better. We need to move if we want to meet up with Titus and communicate with the school group before the rescue. Let's check out these Legends in the arena quickly. We still need to consider some Legends who could sneak into the prison without being spotted."

The friends walked quickly back to the amphitheatre. They were conscious of the time and excited at the prospect of watching these Legends display their unique talents in the arena. When they reached the amphitheatre, they walked up the steps to the first row of seats and sat overlooking the arena. Arto had silently followed them.

"Right, here goes then!" said Lily, leaning over the arena wall. She dropped the figurine of Brunhilda the Valkyrie, and it smashed on the dusty arena floor. Instantly, Brunhilda appeared. She looked exactly like her statue, except now the friends could see she had startling red hair, bright blue eyes and bronze armour. Her wings were white and feathery, and she had a patterned skirt. Her shield was also surprisingly colourful with red and white quarters.

Brunhilda flapped her wings and rose into the air. "I am at your service, marble holder," she said in a deep voice with an accent that sounded slightly German. "Would you like to see what I can do?"

"Oh yes," Lily replied. "Please go ahead!"

Brunhilda flew down into the amphitheatre with her red hair and skirt rippling behind her. She picked up three spears from the tunnel and shot high into the sky. She paused briefly in the air and then darted towards one of the circular targets. When Brunhilda was at the friends' height, she released all three of her spears in quick succession. They shot into the middle of the target. The last spear hit with such force that the target was knocked over backwards.

Brunhilda then landed on the arena floor and gestured for Arto to join her. Arto disappeared down the stone steps and reappeared through the tunnel entrance pushing a ballista, a weapon that looks like a giant crossbow. Arto picked up a large projectile, called a bolt, and loaded it into the ballista with her mouth. The bolt was about the size of a fence post with a sharpened end. One of Arto's front paws held the ballista still while her other pulled back a winch. Suddenly, she released the bolt in the direction of Brunhilda, who was flying around inside the arena. Brunhilda deftly avoided the bolt before it went smashing into the amphitheatre seating. Shards of wood and chunks of stone flew everywhere. Lily, Oliver, Colin and Mistletoe quickly ducked behind the low arena wall in front of them.

"Wow!" Oliver exclaimed. "A warning would have been nice. They don't do health and safety here, do they?"

"I know," agreed Colin, "but it's pretty cool, isn't it? At least Arto is aiming away from us. I think we're alright."

Just as Colin finished speaking, Arto began releasing bolt after bolt. She reloaded the ballista remarkably quickly. Brunhilda was now working a lot harder. She dodged the projectiles wonderfully with her shield beside her and determination on her face. Shards of wood and chunks of stone were flying everywhere. Then Brunhilda began to tire, and her flying slowed. The three friends held their breath as they watched a bolt heading straight for her. Brunhilda realised she could not dodge the projectile, so she braced herself in the air behind her bronze shield. The bolt smashed straight into the shield and shattered completely. Brunhilda was pushed back in the air only a few metres. Once the projectile's remains had fallen to the ground, the friends could see that Brunhilda's shield had not even been marked. Brunhilda gestured for Arto to stop firing.

"My demonstration is complete," Brunhilda said to the friends. She was short of breath, and sweat was dripping down her cheeks. "I will be happy to serve you."

"Thank you very much, Brunhilda," replied Lily with a big smile. "Erm... we will now consider your application. You may return to your figurine."

"It's weird, isn't it?" said Colin after Brunhilda had disappeared, "I didn't know what to say to Geryon when he'd finished."

"Oh, but she is great!" exclaimed Lily. "She'd teach that horrible Agon Agathon a lesson or two. Did you see how she destroyed that big arrow with her shield?"

"It was hard to miss," replied Oliver, lifting a sharp shard of wood that had landed beside him. "Right, so do you want to go next, Colin? I'm looking forward to seeing what your Thunder Dragon does."

Colin stood up from his crouched position, leaned over the arena wall and threw the figurine of the Thunder Dragon against the floor of the arena. The real Thunder Dragon appeared from out of nowhere. She flapped her blue, leathery wings and flew up to the level of the friends. She had a slender and scaly body with a long tail. Along her back, from the top of her head to the point of her tail, there was a ridge of turquoise spikes. She had four legs, clawed feet and large blue whiskers that emerged from her snout.

"Thank you for chooosssing me," the Thunder Dragon hissed, "may I ssshow you my ssskillsss?"

"Yes, please," responded Colin enthusiastically.

The Thunder Dragon bowed to Colin before gracefully weaving high into the sky like a ribbon on a stick. She paused for a moment and looked as if she was taking a deep breath. Then suddenly, she dived towards the arena at great speed. From deep within her body emerged a thunderous roar that shook the amphitheatre. This was quickly followed by a jet of fire from her mouth and nostrils that set alight to the arena equipment. The Thunder Dragon swooped back up into the sky after her dive. The amphitheatre was now filled with smoke and the flickering flames of the burning equipment. The clouds of smoke forced the friends to move away from the arena to the higher seats. They briefly caught a glimpse of the elderly man walking his dog and the two young men sitting on the bench. The locals were still utterly oblivious to the amphitheatre and everything going on inside it.

The Thunder Dragon flew down to the friends. "I am at your ssservice marble holdersss," she said against the background of smoke.

"Thank you," said Colin, "Your demonstration was short and... erm... fiery. You may return to your statue now."

The Thunder Dragon vanished immediately.

"So that just leaves your Legend," Lily said to Oliver.

"I'm not sure she'll beat either of those," replied Oliver. "How come I get the boring one? You get a fire-breathing Dragon and a woman who looks like she could beat an entire rugby team in a tug-of-war. Meanwhile, I get a sullen hag who looks like she needs a manicure. Right, here goes."

Oliver threw the Banshee's figurine against the floor, and the Banshee immediately appeared in front of the friends. She wore a dull cloak with a hood over her head. Beneath her hood, the friends could see her skin was pale and gaunt, and her hair was greasy and streaked with grey. She was remarkably unremarkable. The Banshee stared expressionless at Oliver without saying a word.

"Erm, will you show us what you can do then?" said Oliver to break the creepy silence. The Banshee nodded and then disappeared. The friends looked around, confused.

"I thought they were supposed to wait until we dismissed them before turning back into their figurines," Oliver said.

"I can't see her figurine anywhere," responded Lily.

"There she is," exclaimed Colin, pointing to the middle of the arena. The Banshee was floating in the smoky air, completely motionless, and then she disappeared again.

"Where's she gone now?" asked Oliver. "Can either of you see her?"

The friends scanned the amphitheatre looking for the Banshee. Then Lily got a shock; the Banshee was standing right behind them. "Goodness me!" exclaimed Lily. "You frightened the life out of me." Lily had barely finished her sentence when the Banshee disappeared once more and reappeared high above the arena.

"Well, it's a cool trick," said Oliver, "but the other two were far more destructive. The Banshee just freaks people out."

"Wait a moment," replied Colin, "I think she's about to do something."

Colin was right. The Banshee's eyes turned emerald green as she opened her mouth and began screaming. At first, it was not very loud, but it quickly became louder and louder and louder. Within a few seconds, the Banshee's scream was unbearable. The sound filled the companions' minds and made it impossible to think about anything else. They pressed their hands hard against their ears and hoped the sound would disappear. Mistletoe began jumping around, barking madly. The Banshee's scream was one of the most unpleasant things any of the friends had ever experienced. Then it stopped, and the Banshee reappeared in front of them. Her eyes were no longer emerald green, but the sound of her scream continued to ring in the ears of the friends. It took them a moment to adjust to the sound of the birds tweeting, grasshoppers buzzing and the background hum of the motorway.

"Wow," said Oliver to the Banshee, "that's a truly horrible thing you can do."

The Banshee did not move or say anything.

"Can we trust you to do as we ask?" questioned Colin, concerned with the Banshee's lack of communication.

The Banshee stared back at Colin and nodded once.

"Well, thank you for the demonstration," Oliver said, "You may now return to your little statue."

In an instant, the Banshee disappeared.

"I suppose we'd better choose which one we want then," said Lily, wiggling a finger in one ear, hoping it would stop the ringing that remained from the Banshee's scream. "I'm not going to hide the fact that I thought Brunhilda was awesome."

"Yes, but it's not about which Legend you think is coolest. It's about which one fits best with our plan," said Colin.

"Colin is right," replied Oliver. "We need to be sensible here. We can come back after we've rescued the school group and have a picnic with Brunhilda if you like."

"Why are you both dismissing her?" Lily asked, slightly annoyed.

"Well, I think she was really good, but she was the least suitable for the role," explained Colin. "They'll be tens of thousands of Blemmies in the stadium tonight, and Brunhilda can't kill them all. I'd love to watch her beat up Agon Agathon, but unfortunately, we need a distraction, not a pitched battle. The Thunder Dragon or the Banshee will do a better job of distracting the Blemmies so Geryon can smash down the gate to the arena and let the teachers out."

Lily was annoyed but understood what Oliver and Colin were saying. "Well, if we're not having Brunhilda, can I suggest the Banshee? Imagine her disappearing and reappearing all around the stadium with that scream. The Blemmies won't be able to do anything. And have either of you thought that maybe she's the perfect person to sneak into the prison to communicate with the school group? She can materialise anywhere she likes, so we don't have to worry about her getting caught."

"I hadn't thought about that!" replied Colin. "Unfortunately, she's not very talkative, so we might have to write notes and get her to carry them to the school group."

"Another bonus of choosing the Banshee is we can get moving quickly," said Lily looking at her watch. "Time is running out."

"Well, I'm happy if you two are," said Oliver. "Who'd have thought it? The best Legend for the task has the most boring statue. Don't tell a book by the cover and all that."

"I'm feeling good about this plan," exclaimed Colin, who had put the figurine of the Banshee in his bag alongside Geryon. "Let's get moving. The sooner we get to Lelandis, the better."

Lily and Oliver also felt positive. The three friends had woken up that morning with no idea where to start with making a rescue plan. By showing initiative, following clues and using their brains, they now had a plan that might just work.

CHAPTER TWENTY-TWO

The Best Laid Plans of Potato Salad

The companions were about to descend the amphitheatre stairs when they heard shouting. They turned away from the arena and looked over the edge of the amphitheatre. The shouting was coming from the elderly man the friends had seen walking his dog. He was shouting at the two young men who had surrounded him. The eyes of the young men were focused on the dog. The dog was skipping around barking, and the elderly man looked scared and intimidated. He was hobbling backwards, placating the assailants with one hand and pulling on the dog's lead with the other.

Suddenly, one of the young men attempted to snatch the elderly man's dog. In an instant, the old man stopped retreating and took a firm step forward. His expression became pugnacious and determined. He curled his hands into fists, raised them to his jaw and tucked his elbows into his body. It was clear that this old man was familiar with a boxing stance. *WHACK!* In one fluid movement that belied his age, the man punched one of the assailants square on the nose, knocking him backwards over his bike. The other assailant, who had bent down to grab the dog, looked up to see the elderly man's other fist heading straight for his nose. *SMACK!* He flew backwards onto the grass. The old man grabbed his dog and followed up his punches with a growl and a grimace. The two yobs scuttled away, holding their bleeding noses and mumbling incoherently. They picked up their bikes and disappeared as quickly as they could.

This all happened very quickly. Lily, Oliver, Colin and Mistletoe ran down the amphitheatre steps and across the grass towards the man, who had staggered to a nearby park bench clutching his chest.

"Are you okay?" shouted Oliver, who was first to arrive.

"Just a little... flustered," said the man. He was still clutching his chest.

"Would you like us to call an ambulance?" Oliver continued.

"No, no, no... I just... need a minute."

"Don't be silly," exclaimed Lily, who was the next to arrive. "Call the police, Oliver! They'll bring an ambulance too." Lily sat down next to the elderly man and placed a hand on his knee to comfort him.

"You gave them a good boshing!" said Colin a moment later. "Would you like a drink of water?"

The man shook his head.

"The police are on their way," explained Oliver, putting his phone back in his pocket, "and so is an ambulance. They won't be long."

"Are you sure you're okay?" asked Lily, who was concerned that the man was downplaying how he felt for fear of causing an inconvenience. "Is there anything you need?"

"No, thank you... I just need a few minutes. The old ticker got a surprise... I felt the pacemaker kick in."

"What were those two idiots trying to do?" Oliver said to Lily and Colin.

"Floomin' dog snatchers!" replied Mistletoe. The man was too shocked to notice the beagle speaking. "Horrible people – gang members – they steal people's dogs and use them for training their fighting dogs. This poor thing would have been thrown into a pit and ripped to shreds."

Lily, Oliver and Colin could not believe people could be so cruel.

"Well, I'm glad you boshed 'em both," exclaimed Colin.

"You certainly gave them a good whack," added Oliver.

In the distance, the sirens of a police car and an ambulance could be heard. The elderly man was feeling calmer now and had stopped clutching his chest. His dog had jumped onto his lap to comfort him.

"It's been a long time since I've boxed, but you don't forget," said the man. He lifted his head, and the friends noticed his squashed nose. "Let me give you lot a bit of advice: don't go looking for a fight because you never know who you're facing. They could be a complete wimp or a retired boxer. They could also be a nutcase with a knife. Fighting is a last resort, but if you're backed into a corner and decide it's your only option, commit fully and give it all you've got. Attack hard and fast, and don't doubt yourself. Show courage."

Lily, Oliver and Colin talked to the elderly man until the police and ambulance arrived. The police wanted the friends to give statements, so they described what they had seen as quickly as possible, leaving out the bit about a mysterious Roman amphitheatre with a talking bear and some very destructive Legends. When they were finished, they hurried back to the amphitheatre, found their tandem bike and the roller skates, and set off as fast as possible.

The mid-afternoon sun shone, birds flew between the trees, and a gentle breeze was blowing towards the friends. The Hide of Courage slowly disappeared, and in half an hour, they would be back at the Old Rectory. The friends had lost time helping the elderly man, but they would still be on schedule to meet Titus if they cycled fast. Lily steered the tandem along a quiet country road lined with hedgerows. Behind her, Colin was pedalling hard, and Oliver was gripping tightly to the luggage rack. Mistletoe's head poked out of Oliver's bag, and his ears flapped in the breeze. Oliver began thinking about what might happen that evening. He visualised the rescue going perfectly to plan: the students escaping from the prison, the teachers being rescued from the Death Match, and Lily, Oliver and Colin leading them back to Earth. He imagined the newspaper headlines about the miraculous reappearance of the school group.

SCREECH!

Lily slammed on the brakes. The front wheel jerked suddenly, and the back of the tandem flew out to one side. Lily tried to correct the balance and turned the handlebars sharply the other way. Oliver was thrown in the other direction. Colin panicked but did not stop pedalling. The tandem's wheels skidded, tilted and lost grip on the road. Oliver let go, narrowly avoided the crashing bicycle and flew off the road into a hedge. Meanwhile, Lily and Colin landed heavily on the grass verge beside the road. There was a moment of silence as everyone processed what had just happened.

"Is everyone okay?" exclaimed Oliver as he clambered out of a bramble bush. Mistletoe was still in his bag, looking rather unimpressed.

"Yep, I'm fine," replied Lily as she picked herself up off the floor. "Just a few bumps."

"Likewise," added Colin, examining his bag. It had ripped badly in the crash. "It's lucky we fell on the grass bank and not the road. What just happened?"

"I think the front tyre punctured," explained Lily. "It blew, and I lost control of the bike."

"Is it completely flat?" asked Oliver, picking bramble thorns out of his arms.

"Yes," replied Lily. "I don't believe this. Everything seems against us! We need to get to Lelandis. We're already late, and now this!"

"The best-laid plans of potato salad," said Mistletoe.

"This is terrible luck," exclaimed Colin. "It's still a long way to walk. I reckon it will take three times as long to walk back to the Old Rectory."

"I'm guessing no one has a spare tyre or a repair kit then?" asked Oliver.

"Even if we did," began Lily, "do any of us know how to change a tyre?"

"Do buses run this way, Colin?" asked Oliver.

"Not very frequently. I'd call my parents, but they never pick up because they're always in meetings."

"Right, well, we're already losing time," exclaimed Lily as she picked up the tandem and began marching along the road. Colin ran over and held on to the bike's rear saddle to help her. Oliver quickly took off his roller skates and put on his shoes. He then joined the others marching down the country road towards the town.

The friends were soon walking through the suburbs of Bridgeward, and they began to hear music in the distance. They continued to stride along the path, and the music grew louder. Then, on a straight section of the road, they spotted a familiar figure in the distance. It was Boom-Box Bert.

"I'm not in the mood for that wally," said Lily. "Let's cross the road."

Oliver and Colin followed Lily to the other side of the road.

"That idiot has crossed the road too," exclaimed Lily. "Let's cross back over."

Boom-Box Bert also crossed the road again.

Lily was becoming very annoyed but decided that rather than cross the road a third time, she would give Boom-Box Bert a piece of her mind when they reached him. Colin was now hugging his torn bag to stop all of his books from falling out. With every second that passed, the friends became more anxious about the time, and the cheesy music got louder.

As Boom-Box Bert neared the friends, he pointed his index fingers and fired imaginary guns. Lily stared right into his eyes and was about to berate him when he turned down his music and spoke, "do you want me to fix that tyre, chicken?"

"I am not a chicken!" Lily replied sharply, "and... and... well yes, actually, could you fix it?" Lily's tone changed very quickly when she realised there was an opportunity to get back to the Old Rectory quicker.

"No problemo!" Bert responded. He began rummaging around in a small, faded bag he carried around his waist like a belt. "Aha, perfectomundo! You never know when you might need to fix a tyre."

Bert pulled out a puncture repair kit and a small pump. He then flipped the tandem upside down so that it was on its saddles and handlebars. Bert took off the front wheel and sat down on the curb to remove the tyre. The friends were pleased to discover they quickly got used to Bert's cheesy body odour. He bobbed and weaved in time with his music as he pulled out the tyre's inner tube and began patching up the hole. Their bike was being repaired as quickly as it got damaged. A sense of relief came over the friends when Bert flipped the tandem bike back onto its wheels and handed it back to Lily.

"How about you, big guy?" Bert said to Colin, who was rearranging the contents of his bag to stop his books from falling out. "I've got a needle and thread too."

"Oh, well, if you wouldn't mind... that would be great," replied Colin. He handed the bag to Bert, who began sewing it up. Bert noticed the old books and the figurine of the Banshee.

"It's lucky your little model didn't fall out," Bert said. "It would be a shame for it to break."

The friends gave each other wry smiles. It was indeed lucky the Banshee had not fallen out and broken. Bert might have had the fright of his life.

"These books are fantasimo! I love the Odyssey. My favourite bit is when Odysseus meets the Sirens. Beeswax – what a clever idea!"

"Oh yeah, it's good, isn't it," replied Colin. He had read the Odyssey, but he could not remember the details.

"So that's the bag sewn up and the tyre fixed. That'll be five big ones, please!" Bert held his hand out.

"Oh," exclaimed Lily, unimpressed. "You expect payment—"

"No, no, no," replied Bert with a smile, "gimme five big ones!"

Bert slapped Lily's hand and then pulled his hand back theatrically while making a noise like a firework fizzing. He then offered his hand to Oliver and Colin, who were all too willing to exchange high fives for a fixed bike and a sewn-up bag.

"Okay, cats, have a good one and look after each other. I'm off to see some old friends. Hasta la vista!" Boom-Box Bert then placed his boom-box on his shoulder and boogied on down the street.

CHAPTER TWENTY-THREE

A Man Called Montgomery

"Back on the bike, and let's get going," said Lily. "It's now past 4pm, and we're going to be late!"

"We've lost that much time?" asked Oliver. "We've now got less than an hour to get to Lelandis. We said 5pm was midway between noon and sunset, didn't we?"

"Yes," replied Colin, hurriedly getting back onto the bike. "We estimated 5pm. Come on, let's get going. All our planning will be for nothing if we're late."

"Just a thought," said Oliver as he sat on the pavement putting on the roller skates, "how do we know the days are the same length in the sanctuary? And how do we know Lelandis is the same as Earth?"

There was a moment of silence, and then Colin put his face in his hands. "Oh no!" he exclaimed. "It might not be the same time of year in Lelandis! In fact, the sanctuary might be at a different latitude. We don't even know if Lelandis is the same size as Earth!"

"Damn it!" cried Lily. "Our timings could be completely wrong! Maybe that's why the Blemmies were still training in Lelandis last night."

"We could have stuffed everything up," exclaimed Colin hopelessly. "The Death Match could have already taken place, and the students could have already been sold into slavery."

"Okay, let's stay calm," replied Oliver. "The truth is we just don't know. We're going to have to get to Lelandis as quickly as possible and hope for the best."

The friends resumed cycling with even more urgency than before. They desperately wanted to know if they were on time, but they would only find out when they reached Lelandis. Lily and Colin pedalled as hard as they could, imploring their legs to push through the burning fatigue. Oliver hung on to the back and desperately willed the tandem to move faster.

The friends were now cycling through the suburbs of Bridgeward. They whizzed past pubs, schools and corner shops. Shadows stretched across the road in front of them. Before long, the friends were cycling down a long, straight road past Bridgeward Estate. The estate lay behind a high brick wall that ran parallel to the road and stretched far into the distance. The friends were almost back at the Old Rectory.

Lily spotted a man with a stop sign on the road ahead. Behind him, other workmen were standing by a truck and a crane. Lily's heart sank. She could see they were going to be delayed again. With her focus on the road ahead, Lily did not notice they were cycling past the main entrance to Bridgeward Estate with its elegant gates guarded by two stone lions. Lily also failed to notice the expensive car pulling out of the gates directly in front of the friends.

SCREECH!

Lily slammed on the brakes and turned the bike abruptly to avoid crashing into the car. Oliver was almost thrown off the back of the bike for the second time. The car immediately began to slow down for the stop sign. Lily guided the tandem beside the vehicle, intending to give the driver a stern stare through the window. As she did this, she overheard the end of a conversation through a lowered window.

"You mustn't give up hope, Montgomery," said the driver to the passenger. "It has been a long time, but you mustn't give up hope." The tinted window rose as Lily reached the passenger side door. She could only see the silhouette of this man called Montgomery.

The driver stepped out of the car. "I'm terribly sorry," she said. "I was distracted and didn't spot you cycling along. That's a great bike you have there."

The lady walked around the back of the car to look at the tandem. She was a smart lady in her fifties with tidy, grey hair and black-rimmed glasses. She wore a tailored suit, shiny black shoes and a silver watch on her wrist.

"You... you... almost hit us back there," asserted Lily nervously.

"I know, I know, it was my fault entirely. I don't deny it. I am terribly sorry." The lady was now examining the tandem bike. "Wonderful Italian racer. These are very rare."

The friends did not know what to say. The shock of almost being knocked off their bike had passed, and Lily's anger had been abated by the lady apologising straight away.

"You look like you've been working hard," said the lady once she had taken her eyes off the bike. "Do you ride much?"

"Not really," replied Colin, with sweat dripping down his face.

"Take this advice from a keen cyclist; you must eat and drink regularly." The lady opened the boot of her car and pulled out three bottles of energy drink. "I see you have no water bottles. Here, have a drink each. We're going to be here for a while by the look of it."

The friends were slightly surprised by this generosity and glugged down the refreshing drinks. They watched the activity on the road ahead impatiently between gulps.

"Are you in a rush?" the lady asked.

"Yes, we are," answered Oliver.

"Where do you need to get to?"

"We're not far away," replied Colin. "We just need to get back to the Old Rectory on the other side of the estate."

"Really? That's a lovely building. I was the one who sold it. Listen, we're in a bit of a rush too, so I'm going to turn around and go a different way. Meet us at the entrance to the estate, and I'll let you in. Follow the driveway, but before you reach the manor, head down the avenue towards the woods where the rescue team is working. Unfortunately, they're not having any luck finding the school group, but anyway, you should be able to see the Old Rectory as you get closer to the woods. Have you finished your drinks? Pass the bottles to me. I'll take care of them. If someone is in a spot of bother, you should always try to help. They often return the favour when you least expect it, but most require it." The lady then got back into the car and began manoeuvring it round onto the other side of the road.

The friends were relieved to be on their way again. They cycled back to the entrance to Bridgeward Estate, where the lady had parked her car beside a keypad on a post. She reached her arm out of the window and entered a code. As the iron gates began to open, she wished the friends good luck and drove off. The friends shot through the gates as soon as the gap was wide enough.

The manor was slowly revealed as the friends shot past manicured lawns bordered with colourful, flowering bushes that attracted busy bumblebees. The building had countless windows looking out over a fountain that marked the end of the driveway. A grass avenue lined with trees stretched beyond the fountain and down a gentle hill towards the woods where the school group went missing. Lily turned the tandem onto the grass. Before long, the friends reached the avenue's end and were into the woods. Lily and Colin got off the bicycle, and Oliver was pleased to take off his roller skates. Colin broke into an awkward jog and led the twins through the woods towards the Old Rectory.

"I'm not... going to be able... to run all the way... through the passage," puffed Colin as the friends squeezed through a hedge. "Do you think... we could get... the tandem through the hole... in the fireplace?"

"It's worth... a try, isn't it?" answered Lily, who was also short of breath. "If we can... get it down the spiral staircase... it will be much quicker... than running along the passage. Although it would be a leap... of trust for you both... because I'd be the only one who could see... down there."

"My feet are going... to love me tomorrow," added Oliver. "I've already got blisters... from these dreadful roller skates. It's worth a try though... I watched Bert take off the wheels... and I reckon I can do it easily enough. Before that... someone needs to distract Auntie Dot if she's home."

"Leave it with me," said Mistletoe, who was pleased to be out of Oliver's bag and on his own four paws. "You lot go in the back, and I'll cause a floomin' scene at the front door. I'll meet you in the Priest Hole."

Mistletoe ran off along the pavement and down the path to the front door of the Old Rectory. He barked loudly before squatting unattractively on the front step and emptying his bowels.

"Oh, Mistletoe," exclaimed Lily to herself, "that's disgusting."

"Rather a genius idea, though," added Oliver, giggling. "He just better not push out the marble. He'll be no use to us without it. Now quick, let's move."

The friends crept around the rear of the house and entered through the back door. They snuck into the living room as Auntie Dot expressed her disgust at Mistletoe's gift. Together the friends flipped the bicycle upside down as Boom-Box Bert had done. Oliver took the wheels off, handed them to Colin and crawled backwards into the passage with the front of the bicycle frame in his hands. Lily held the back of the frame and followed.

With a little bit of thought and quite a lot of wiggling, the twins succeeded in getting the tandem's frame into the Priest Hole. Colin remained by the fireplace with the wheels in his hands. Something had caught his attention on the mantelpiece; it was the candles the friends had lit during the storm. Long drips of creamy yellow wax had formed on the honeycomb-patterned candles.

Colin remembered that Boom-Box Bert had said something about beeswax; it was to do with the Odyssey. Colin tried to recall the Ancient Greek story of Odysseus returning from the Trojan War. Then it struck him. "The sirens!" he exclaimed to himself. "Odysseus and the Sirens! What a brilliant idea." Colin took the beeswax candles, put them in his bag and headed down to the Priest Hole with the wheels.

"Well, that's the first bit of luck we've had for a while," exclaimed Lily, brushing cobwebs from her hair. "I can't believe we've managed to get the tandem down here. This will make the trip through the passage so much quicker."

"I've also just had a stroke of luck," announced Colin proudly. "I found beeswax candles."

The twins did not understand why Colin was so pleased with himself.

"It will make our lives much easier when we try to rescue the school group," continued Colin. "In the Odyssey, there are these creatures called Sirens. They live by the sea and sing to passing sailors to lure them and their ships onto the rocks. Odysseus tells his crew to put beeswax in their ears so they don't hear the Sirens' song. Beeswax is just what we need to block out the Banshee's scream!"

"I hadn't thought about that," replied Lily. "Her scream is horrible."

"Nice one, Colin," said Oliver as he shined his torch at the upturned altar. "Now, let's shift this stuff. Hopefully, there isn't a Blemmy waiting for us."

The friends set to work shifting the items that were blockading the hole. When only the upturned altar was left, Mistletoe emerged in the Priest Hole. "It's only me," he barked, "don't floomin' panic!"

"Perfect timing," replied Colin. "We need your nose, Mistletoe. Can you have a sniff around the hole, please? Tell us if you smell anything, well... Blemmy."

Mistletoe put his nose to the ground and began sniffing around the altar. "I can't smell any of those floomin' Blemmies," he said. "Lift it, and let's get going. I'll keep sniffing."

The friends lifted the altar, and the spiral staircase emerged. Oliver put on Woden's Eye and led the way down. The friends moved slowly and cautiously when they first explored the passage to Lelandis. They had not known what to expect, and every detail was observed. On this occasion, the friends did not have the time to contemplate their surroundings. They rushed down the spiral staircase like commuters late for a train. When they reached the bottom, the bike was reassembled, Oliver put on the roller skates and Colin jumped on the rear saddle. Lily put on Woden's Eye and then noticed the tandem had a front light which she switched on. They then set off.

Lily could see everything in the cavern, but the others could only see what was lit by the tandem's light. The path rolled under them like an endless conveyer belt. Around it, the stalactites and stalagmites cast long shadows that perpetually fanned around the bike as they peddled through this subterranean world.

The friends soon reached the Bridge over the Infinite Void. Lily and Colin dismounted the bike, Oliver took off his skates, and Mistletoe jumped out of the bag. Marius let them pass, and they ran over the bridge, leaving the tandem and the skates on the ledge where the Legionaries slept. Minutes later, they were at the base of the second spiral staircase. They began ascending as fast as they could. They would soon discover if they were too late.

CHAPTER TWENTY-FOUR

The Prison Complex

Agon Agathon stood at the entrance to the prison complex with Lime Fox by his side. In the distance, the area surrounding the stadium was buzzing with Blemmies. Many had participated in the Games and bore the bumps, bruises and breaks of competition. It was a colourful scene with everyone wearing stripy trousers in colours that matched the hair between their shoulders. In Blemmy custom, those without hair were free to choose whatever colour they liked, apart from purple; this was reserved for only the most important individuals, like Agon Agathon.

Amid the crowd were bookmakers who stood on boxes beside large chalkboards that displayed odds for the combatants in the Death Match. These bookmakers were being kept busy by rowdy crowds of Blemmies waving their hands and shouting their bets. Flickering flames rose from hundreds of fire pits that surrounded the stadium. Some of these fire pits were being used to cook snacks that were being sold to hungry spectators, and others were being used to light objects that Blemmy performers were juggling, swinging and twirling to onlookers. The Death Match was imminent, and excitement was growing.

"Agon Agathon! It has been too long! How are you?"

Agon Agathon turned to see a short Blemmy wearing yellow and white striped trousers coming towards him. He had spikey blond hair above his shoulders, and like Agon Agathon, he was considerably older than any of the Blemmies competing in the

Games. Beside this Blemmy, there stood a Blemmy slave child. A loose chain connected her wrists and ankles to make it difficult to run away. She was carrying a beaker of water on a tray.

"It's good to see you again," replied Agon Agathon, shaking the Blemmy's hand. "How are the Blemmies of the Southern Lands? It's been a successful Games for you."

"It has indeed been an excellent Games. You have done a wonderful job this year, and I hear there is more to come – humans in the Death Match! I cannot wait."

"Yes, word has spread fast," responded Agon Agathon. "It will be a full house in the stadium. The spectators are already beginning to take their seats. Ah, here comes Doria."

Doria, who was so grotesquely fat that she could barely carry her weight, was hobbling slowly towards Agon Agathon. She was accompanied by her Blemmy slave child, who was holding a parasol. Doria wore red and white striped trousers, excessive jewellery and enough perfume to knock out a Troll.

"Did you find out who was on your roof last night?" Doria asked with sweat dripping down her puffy red face.

"It wasn't anything to worry about," Agon Agathon replied, "just birds. Lime Fox chased them off. Now, where are the others, Doria? I need to be moving along with final preparations for the Death Match."

"They will be here soon," replied Doria with the usual gunky spittle collecting in the sides of her mouth.

A short time later, four more Blemmies with slave children joined Agon Agathon. They were nobles from different regions of the Blemmy lands who were looking forward to gambling huge sums of money on the outcome of the Death Match. Agon Agathon had invited them to see how the combatants were fairing so close to the event. They were also hoping to assess the human children before the auction.

Agon Agathon gestured for a Blemmy guard to unlock the door into the prison complex. The heavy door creaked open on its iron hinges, and Agon Agathon led the other Blemmies into a corridor between two high walls. These walls were not like the wonky walls of the smaller buildings in the sanctuary, nor were they built precisely like the important civic buildings. Instead, they had been created from stone not needed in the stadium's construction; a haphazard mix of large, well-cut stone and small irregular pieces. Spiders, centipedes and countless other insects made their homes in the many crevices in these walls. Resilient weeds also grew, and there were patches of grey-green and orange lichen. As the Blemmies walked along this corridor, they noticed how cold, damp and dim this environment was. The summer sun barely penetrated this space, and it was silent apart from the distant buzzing of wasps that had made a hive high above them.

The Blemmies walked around a corner to a tall and heavy portcullis. Looking between the gaps in the iron lattice, they could see the Giant sitting in the corner of his enclosure with his head in his hands. Doria's slave child gasped with shock and was promptly hit with the back of Doria's podgy, bejewelled hand.

"This is the Giant we caught last year," Agon Agathon announced proudly with a grin on his deformed face. "He was found washed up on a beach; probably a shipwrecked fisherman. He's shown good fight in training – powerful and moves well. In the past, Giants have fought better when hungry because it makes them foul-tempered. I halved his rations a few days ago, and it seems to be working."

The Giant heard Agon Agathon speaking and lifted his head from his hands. He stared angrily at the group of Blemmies and bellowed something loud and unpleasant in Giantish. His voice echoed through the prison complex. He then threw one of his big leather boots at the Blemmies. The onlookers staggered backwards as the boot hit the portcullis. Only Agon Agathon stood his ground. "Yes," he said to himself, "the halved rations are working excellently."

When their shock had subsided, the Blemmies began talking excitedly about the imminent Death Match and the prospects of the Giant. The Blemmies approached the portcullis again and peered through, eager to assess the Giant in more detail. When the Blemmies were satisfied, Agon Agathon led them further down the corridor to another portcullis that guarded the entrance to the Trolls' enclosure. Both Trolls were pacing around, looking very angry. One of them was muttering to himself and occasionally pounding his green chest. The other was slapping herself around the face like a boxer before a bout.

"Trolls are always reliable fighters," Agon Agathon explained. "The challenge is keeping them calm. They can get too excited too soon, and by the time it gets to the Death Match, they just want a nap. These two will fight well together – a mother and her son – family ties always encourage fierce fighting!"

The Blemmy nobles listened carefully and considered the wagers they would make. The Trolls did not notice them.

Next, the Blemmies were taken to the long central corridor lined with cages. Agon Agathon stopped beside the first cage containing the Dwarves. Some were sitting, a few were pacing around, and one was lying on his back with his eyes closed. The Dwarves became more animated when the Blemmies appeared. They recognised that they were important and not just guards. A few of the Dwarves came to the front of the cage, and one of them, who spoke a little Blemmish, began pleading to be let free. The prisoner was trying hard to think of what the Dwarves had to offer the Blemmies in exchange for being kept alive. They were excellent miners and could help the Blemmies find precious metals and jewels. They could also help excavate rocks to repair the buildings of the sanctuary. Maybe they could work as translators when ambassadors visited from the Dwarf kingdoms. But Agon Agathon was not interested. He only wanted one thing: a violent and memorable Death Match.

The lack of hostility and aggression being shown by the Dwarves had disappointed Agon Agathon. "These Dwarves are not quite ready for the Death Match," he explained to the other Blemmies. "Do not worry though. I will speak to the guards. I have a few tricks up my sleeve to ensure they are in the right frame of mind for the fight. You will not be disappointed. Dwarves are always fun to watch when they fight together. I remember watching my first Death Match. A group of Dwarves managed to kill all the other combatants. It was a wonderful moment when they realised there could be only one winner. The crowd went wild when they turned on each other. Now follow me. I'd like to introduce you to the King of the Monopods – the stupid old fool."

The King of the Monopods was sitting in the corner of his cage, looking frail and weak. Agon Agathon walked up to the bars of his cage and began toying with him. "Wake up, you old fool. How does it feel sitting in this dirty, damp and cold little cage?" The King of the Monopods lifted his head but did not respond. "Once the King of the Monopods, weren't you? You once sat on a golden throne, dressed in the most expensive clothes and eating the finest food in your kingdom. Now look at you. You're pathetic!" Agon Agathon swung one of his little legs through the cage bars and kicked the King of the Monopod's water bowl. It flew across the cage and hit the King. "The worst thing about you is that you've never once shown any fight. You're a coward!" The King of the Monopods rubbed his arm where the bowl hit him and remained quiet.

Agon Agathon turned to the other Blemmies, who had been grinning and sniggering as they watched the helpless Monopod being taunted. "I wouldn't bet on him lasting very long tonight. He'll probably just hop about avoiding the fighting until he gets tired, then some of the other combatants will finish him off. There isn't a death tonight that I'm looking forward to more. Now, from an old fool to some younger ones. Let's see the only Blemmies who will be fighting this year. They are late additions to the Death Match."

In a cage beside the King of the Monopods, there lay the two hungover Blemmies. They still looked as desperate and hopeless as when Lily had seen them from the sky.

"Not much to say about these morons," explained Agon Agathon. "Yesterday, they were competitors at the Games, but they desecrated the sanctuary with their drunken behaviour. Now they have an opportunity to redeem themselves in front of the gods by fighting bravely in the Death Match."

Agon Agathon turned to the two Blemmies in the cage, "I have some good news for you," he said. The two Blemmies sat up and looked hopeful. "We found your families. After you die in the Death Match tonight, your children and wives will be sold into slavery." Agon Agathon laughed at his cruelty, and the other Blemmies joined him. The Blemmy prisoners fell backwards, distraught with the news.

"Now I have left the best to last," Agon Agathon declared, eagerly rubbing his hands. "Let's see the combatants we are all most excited about. There is not a Blemmy alive who remembers the last time we had humans fighting in the Death Match, and they are quite a pair. The male has been a disappointment, but the female is quite something. The trainers have never seen such combat techniques. Our gladiators have refused to spar with her because she has knocked so many of them out."

The Blemmy nobles walked back along the central corridor before turning into a narrower corridor that led to Mr Montero and Miss Wilson's enclosure. Agon Agathon walked up to the portcullis, closely followed by the excited Blemmies, none of whom had seen a human before. When they spotted Mr Montero and Miss Wilson, they gawped and stared, fascinated by how they looked.

"They're like tiny Giants!" one of the Blemmies exclaimed.

"But not quite as small as the Dwarves."

"They're just like Monopods, but with two legs!"

"And what strange, long legs they have!"

"These humans were discovered a few weeks ago in the woods east of the sanctuary," Agon Agathon explained. "They were found by a shepherd who was hunting wolves that had been killing his sheep. We don't know why they were so far from human lands. They speak a human language our translators don't recognise. The gods must have sent them, and soon we will show our gratitude to the gods by watching them die in the Death Match."

CHAPTER TWENTY-FIVE

Waste Disposal

Moments before the school group were captured, Miss Wilson had reached her limit with Mr Montero's arrogance and stupidity. His fragile bravado was shattered when she confronted him, and he became docile and subservient. His concussion disappeared within a few days, and his memory returned. With it came the realisation that he had pulled everyone down into the cavern. Much to his embarrassment, he also recalled asking Miss Wilson out on a date.

Miss Wilson quickly took control of the school group as they stood in the cave with a strange headless figure pointing an arrow at them. Miss Wilson told the students to put their hands in the air and make no sudden moves. The Blemmy shepherd sent his sheepdog to get assistance, and by the time morning came, the school group were surrounded by armed Blemmies with Agon Agathon at their helm. Miss Wilson told Mr Montero and the students to cooperate. She reasoned that it had not been hard to reach this strange land, so a rescue party would soon find them.

The school group was marched to a watermill that sat on the bank of the river. From there, they were walked to a nearby village. After a few days in a makeshift cell, the school group were taken downriver to the sanctuary and separated. Agon Agathon visited regularly and seemed unsure about what to do with them. Miss Wilson's last instructions to the students were to remain positive, act smart and look for opportunities to escape. A rescue was feeling increasingly unlikely.

As the days passed, it became clear to Miss Wilson and Mr Montero that they would be made to fight in some sort of gladiatorial combat, and if they fought well, they might earn their freedom. This had been communicated to them by a Blemmy guard with a chalkboard. Trainers entered their enclosure the next day, followed by gladiators brandishing weapons. The humans were expected to train. At first, Miss Wilson refused, and Mr Montero followed suit. The Blemmy gladiators then attacked the teachers. Miss Wilson and Mr Montero reacted in very different ways.

Despite her small stature and quiet demeanour, it turned out Miss Wilson was exceptionally good at Taekwondo. She knocked out every gladiator she encountered, and by lunchtime, the gladiators were refusing to fight her. Miss Wilson had also knocked out the gladiators sent to prepare Mr Montero for the Death Match, although not before he had received some heavy blows. Despite her annoyance with him, Miss Wilson would not let Mr Montero get seriously hurt or killed. Agon Agathon told the Blemmy trainers that no more training was necessary. He was worried no gladiators would be left to warm up the crowds before the Death Match.

Miss Wilson and Mr Montero became aware of Agon Agathon and the Blemmy nobles gawking and pointing at them.

"Just carry on with what you're doing, Fred," Miss Wilson said calmly. "Let's not give them the satisfaction of seeing us angry. Besides, I don't want them to suspect we will attempt an escape when they move us to the stadium. Whatever happens, I'm not degrading myself by fighting in a stadium filled with those chest-faced flunking berks."

"There's still time for a rescue," Mr Montero said. "Surely someone has found the passage by now? They can't leave us here to die, can they?" Mr Montero put his head in his hands.

"I don't think help will arrive," replied Miss Wilson. "So it's either we die in the stadium, or we die trying to break free to rescue the students. When we're moved, which is probably soon, be prepared to run for it. Listen for my command and follow my instructions."

"How are we ever going to find the students?" responded Mr

Montero. "We haven't seen them for over a week."

"Let's be alert to the smallest opportunities and work things out as we go. Just do as I tell you."

The Blemmies could not hear Miss Wilson and Mr Montero speaking from where they stood. Even if they could, none of them understood English. On the contrary, Lime Fox had excellent hearing. She also still had a marble in her stomach, and it was very cold.

"Excuse me, Agon Agathon," said Lime Fox quietly. "May I have a word with you away from the others?"

"Of course," replied Agon Agathon as he moved away from the other Blemmies.

"The humans were speaking," Lime Fox whispered. "They are planning to escape when they are moved to the stadium. The female would rather die trying to escape than die in the Death Match."

"Excellent work, Lime Fox," replied Agon Agathon, deep in thought. "How is the male?"

"He is weak and has lost hope," Lime Fox explained. "The female is very much in charge."

"The male has been a disappointment," said Agon Agathon after a pause. "He better not let me down tonight,"

Agon Agathon returned to the other Blemmies. "Come," he said. "Let us see the young humans. I warn you; they will not sell cheap. I am confident they will make outstanding slaves."

The students, like the teachers, had a good idea of what was going on. One of the Blemmy guards, with a moronic and toothless grin on his face, had taken pleasure in explaining the situation with bad drawings on a small chalkboard. The students deciphered his doodles, and the more upset they looked, the more the Blemmy chuckled and grinned. He particularly enjoyed drawing a Giant squashing two humans with a big club and four smaller humans cleaning toilets.

The students were deep in conversation as Agon Agathon led the Blemmy nobles through the prison complex towards their cage.

"It can't be long now before the teachers are made to fight," said Sam, standing beside the cage bars and peering up and down the corridor. His football shirt was ripped and filthy. "Those Chest-Faces were being led around by the one with the squashed nose – the one we think is in charge."

"How much I'd love to whack him right on that big nose," Mia exclaimed, punching one hand into her other hand.

"We're running out of time," exclaimed Joe, looking at his digital watch. "If the teachers are being made to fight at sunset, they've only got an hour to wait. I don't want to be sold as a slave to one of these horrible Chest-Faces! Why hasn't anyone found the passage beneath the apple tree yet? How hard can it be?"

"Let's not give up hope," said Jay softly. She swept her curly hair from her face. "I thought I saw an angel in the sky last night, and I felt like it was watching over us."

"I hope you're right," replied Mia, "but it's too late now to rely on help. We're going to have to commit to our plan." Mia gestured at the jacket in the corner of the cage covering the hole.

"How long have we got, Joe?" asked Sam.

Joe took off his glasses and tried to find a dirt-free patch of clothing to clean them. He put them back on and looked at a series of markings scratched on the bars of the cage, "The evening patrol will start in 30 minutes. It's probably the taller guard with enormous ears and dark hair. The food will be distributed in the next 5 minutes. *Waste disposal* will take place in around 40 minutes, probably after the combatants have been moved to the stadium. This is also when the archers on the walls change shifts."

"*Waste disposal*," said Jay with a look of disgust on her face. "That's a nice way of putting it."

The students knew a Giant and two Trolls were imprisoned nearby. They had heard their loud grunts and roars. They had also seen Blemmies going in and out of their enclosures with carts full of food and barrels of water. What goes in must come out, and so for every cartful of food taken into these enclosures, a cartful of excrement was removed. It seemed to be a task none of the guards wanted.

"Let's recap the plan one more time," said Sam, beginning to draw a map with his index finger in the dust on the floor. "We make our move when the patrolling guard passes this corner. The archers on the walls should also be changing shift at this point. We sneak through the hole we've dug and move quickly to this door."

Mia bent down and took over explaining the plan, "This door is where the food comes in, and the poo goes out. Now nobody likes this part of the plan, but that's why it might just work. Keep telling yourselves, what's worse, being sold into slavery in a weird world and never getting back to Earth? Or spending a few minutes in a wheelbarrow used to move Troll and Giant poo?"

Sam, Joe and Jay cringed at the thought.

"The wheelbarrows are taken to the back entrance," Mia explained. "The Blemmies then go through the door and do whatever they do."

"They probably throw up because of the smell," interrupted Jay.

"This is our moment to move," continued Mia. "We take the covers off the wheelbarrows and empty them around the corner. We then return to the original spot, jump in and pull the covers over ourselves."

"Once we're through the doors, we need to think quickly," added Sam. "We don't know what's back there, so we need to work together."

"As Miss Wilson told us," added Jay, "we must act smart and keep positive."

Joe looked at his watch again and sighed. "I think this is our only hope. We've been here for over a week, and there's been no sign of rescue. It's all down to us. Let's keep our fingers crossed that Mr Montero and Miss Wilson manage to find a way of escaping too."

"I don't know how I will feel if we manage to escape, but the teachers don't," said Jay. "Will we risk our lives trying to save them? And what about the Chest-Face children next to us? Are we going to leave them to be sold into slavery?"

There was a moment of silence as the students considered the dire decisions they might have to make.

Since Lily had spotted the students the night before, another cage had been placed next to the students. It contained the four children of the two Blemmy combatants. Even the eldest of the children looked much younger than Mia, Jay, Sam and Joe. The Blemmy children sat huddled together, with the oldest child holding the other three tightly. The tracks of dried tears could be seen on their dirty faces. The students had tried to comfort the children, but this seemed to frighten them even more.

"But… but… we don't like the Chest-Faces do we?" Sam said, feeling conflicted. "They've imprisoned us and are planning to make the teachers fight to the death."

"Yes, but they are just children," replied Jay. "You cannot blame them for the brutality of the adults. Look at them. They're scared out of their wits. If I get the chance, I'm taking them with us."

At that moment, Agon Agathon led the Blemmy nobles around the corner. Lime Fox had arrived a few minutes earlier and had stood in the shadows listening to the children with a cold sensation in her stomach. She skipped over to Agon Agathon, who bent down low so Lime Fox could whisper in his ear. When Lime Fox had finished whispering, Agon Agathon smiled and then gave Lime Fox orders. She skipped off, and Agon Agathon carried on with the Blemmy nobles in tow. Their greedy, ugly faces were full of excitement. Each of them was willing to pay enormous sums for a human slave.

"So here are the human children," announced Agon Agathon. "They're very healthy. No signs of malnourishment, disease or disability. The guards tell me they're still quite spirited, but you'll soon beat that out of them."

The Blemmies grunted their approval without taking their eyes off the students. They were eyeing them from head to toe, deciding which ones would make the best slaves.

"I don't know what I'm looking forward to most," exclaimed Doria with the usual splatter of spittle, "the Death Match or buying one of these afterwards. You say they are *spirited*. May I suggest extra guards to surround their cage during the Death Match? It would be most disappointing if any of them were to escape."

"You read my mind, Doria," replied Agon Agathon. "Lime Fox has been sent to fetch two guards. They will stand by the back door until we return after the Death Match. They will ensure there is no attempt to escape. I do not want any embarrassing situations."

As Agon Agathon finished speaking, two guards carrying spears ran down the corridor and stationed themselves on either side of the back door. The students watched on in horror. One of them was by far the biggest Blemmy the students had seen. He was so big that his shoulders were higher than the door he was sent to guard. His face had a mottled complexion, and one of his ears was missing. There was no hair on his head, but his forearms were like those of a gorilla.

The possibility of escape had prevented the students from losing their morale, and the effort of preparing for an escape had kept them occupied. The students' plan was now scuppered. Their hearts sank, their chins dropped, and tears began to well up in their eyes. All of their efforts had been in vain. At that moment, the walls of the prison complex seemed taller, the bars of the cage seemed stronger, and the air felt colder. A life of cruel servitude awaited the students in this terrible land so close to Earth and yet so far away. The Blemmy nobles walked off cheerfully, leaving the students feeling completely hopeless for the first time since they had reached Lelandis.

Suddenly, a strange figure appeared in the students' cage. It was a woman with a gaunt face wearing a grey cloak. She was carrying a note and a lump of beeswax.

CHAPTER TWENTY-SIX

The Rescue

Lily, Oliver, Colin and Mistletoe had emerged from the spiral staircase breathless and flustered just moments before the Banshee appeared to the students. Mistletoe had immediately run out of the chamber to search for Titus. It was Titus who spotted Mistletoe, and together they sprinted to the chamber. Lily's hand emerged from the stone wall holding the spare marble Colin had discovered the night before. Titus took the marble, and the chamber beneath the Statue of Apollon appeared to him.

"I had given up hope of you returning," Titus said. "We don't have much time; the Death Match is imminent."

"Thank goodness!" exclaimed Lily as the nervous tension in her body eased.

Oliver and Colin felt the same. The relief quickly turned to excitement and apprehension. It was now time to put the plan into action.

"How long do we have before the combatants are moved?" asked Colin.

"Preparations are probably being made right now," Titus replied. "We need to move fast. I would much prefer to be in a position to observe the prison complex and the stadium. What is your plan?"

"Before we explain," replied Oliver, "we have a few things we need to do straight away."

Colin found the figurine of the Banshee and threw it against the floor. Titus stepped back with surprise as the pale and inexpressive figure of the Banshee appeared. Meanwhile, Lily scribbled a note on a piece of scrap paper she had pulled from Oliver's backpack. It was for the students:

Help from Earth has arrived! A rescue will be attempted just before the Death Match. It will begin when you hear a deafening scream. You must place this beeswax in your ears. We know you are also planning an escape. We will coordinate with you. Please write your plans on the paper and give them to the Banshee.

"What is this magic?" exclaimed Titus as the Banshee disappeared with the note and a lump of beeswax.

"If you think the Banshee is odd," said Oliver, "you wait until you see Geryon."

"It's the first stage of our plan," Colin explained. "The Banshee can disappear and reappear anywhere, and she will do as we ask. We will tell the students and the teachers to expect a rescue."

"Fingers crossed it works," said Lily.

The friends continued to explain the rescue plan to Titus while they waited for the Banshee to return, and Titus was impressed. Since the companions had parted company, Titus had reconnoitred the whole sanctuary by moonlight. He now had a detailed understanding of the routes into the sanctuary, the path of the river and the winding passageways between the stadium and the Statue of Apollon.

The Banshee reappeared. To the delight of the companions, she was carrying a reply:

We had given up hope! There is a back entrance to the prison complex where the food is brought in. We will be ready for you near this entrance. We don't have much time. The combatants are about to be moved. Good luck!"

"Great job, Banshee!" exclaimed Oliver as he patted her on the back. She did not look very impressed, and Oliver was taken aback by how bony and cold her shoulders were.

Lily hurriedly passed the next note to the Banshee. "This one needs to be delivered to the teachers. They are in the large enclosure opposite the Giant. Don't get spotted!"

The Banshee disappeared again with the note:

Help from Earth has arrived! Once you are in the stadium and have been unchained, you will hear a terrible screaming sound. Put this beeswax in your ears and be ready to escape through the main stadium entrance. We will meet you there. Please confirm you understand.

"Let's get ready to move," said Titus. "We need to take up a position closer to the stadium. It will take us a while to get there, and we could encounter obstacles."

The Banshee returned with a reply as Titus finished speaking. It was in Miss Wilson's handwriting:

We will be ready.

"Let's do this!" said Colin as he handed out chunks of beeswax to everyone. "You'll need to put this in your ears, Titus. The Banshee's scream is pretty unpleasant."

"Just like Ulysses," Titus muttered before heading out of the chamber with his shield in one hand and his sword in the other. Colin and Mistletoe followed close behind.

Oliver paused for a moment at the threshold of the chamber. "Don't forget to look for the waterfall passage, Lily," he said. "We need to know if Agon Agathon has it guarded and… be careful."

"You be careful too," replied Lily with a smile. "Let's get out of here alive."

Oliver returned the smile before running to join the others as they dodged down narrow alleyways, clambered over walls and scuttled across low rooftops. After a while, Titus stopped the companions in the shadows between two crumbling old buildings where wildflowers grew among shards of broken pottery, and a wild bramble reached out with its thorny shoots. The companions were beside the training fields that surrounded the stadium. They could see the stadium, the prison complex and the plaza that connected them. Fire pits burned everywhere, and the setting sun glowed red.

All of the Blemmies in the sanctuary had swarmed to the stadium. Those with tickets were now seated. Many more were hoping to buy tickets from touts outside the stadium. Others just wanted to be close enough to the action to hear the crowd roaring, sighing and chanting as the combatants were slowly killed one by one.

Ticketless Blemmies crowded around two parallel lines of guards standing shoulder to shoulder along the plaza's edge. These guards had cleared a wide avenue that led from the doors of the prison complex to the arena. The spectators seated above the arena entrance had turned to get a first glimpse of the combatants as they were transported to the stadium. The rest of the spectators were being warmed up by gladiatorial combat. These fights were violent and dramatic, but they were merely appetisers before the main course.

The gates of the prison complex began to open. The Blemmy onlookers murmured excitedly. Then one of the Trolls emerged, pulled forward by Blemmies holding ropes tied to iron shackles on the Troll's limbs and neck. Two columns of Blemmies prodded her forward with long tridents. Other Blemmies with bows and arrows monitored the Troll from a distance. The Troll had deep cuts all over her body from having struggled and fought with the guards in the prison complex.

The Troll reached the arena entrance. The iron portcullis began to creak and groan as Blemmies turned the mechanism that lifted it. Still, the Blemmy guards tugged and prodded the Troll forward. The spectators greeted the Troll with spitting, unpleasant gestures and abusive shouts. Some threw the leftovers of their stadium snacks at her, and there was raucous cheering when the projectiles hit their target. All this served to rile the Troll up even more. She looked up at the spectators, bared her teeth and released an angry roar that shook the stadium's foundations. When the Troll was finally in the arena, she was shackled by her neck to an anchor point on the floor. A signal was then given for the next Troll to be transported. The excitement in the crowd was incredible as the second Troll began its journey to the arena.

The gladiatorial combat in the arena had stopped, and fresh

Blemmy gladiators were being introduced to the crowd. The purpose of these gladiators was to make sure that the Death Match was memorable, and they did not fight each other, only the combatants. When one of the combatants became dominant, the gladiators would gang together and attack them. If one of the combatants was struggling, they might assist them. The gladiators were not allowed to kill the combatants; they just ensured that the Death Match was full of action and did not end too soon. It was a very prestigious job for a Blemmy, so only the best and most famous fighters were invited to take part.

Some gladiators were heavily armoured with large, cumbersome weapons like axes, broad swords and pikes. Others were lightly armoured with smaller weapons such as spears, maces and whips. The weapons were familiar to anyone from Earth, but the armour was strange on account of the Blemmies having faces in their chests. The more heavily armoured gladiators wore what looked like enormous helmets that covered their entire torsos but had holes for their arms. These pieces of armour were decorated in a variety of ways; some had colourful plumes of feathers, others had spikes all across the shoulders.

The Giant began his journey to the stadium as the second Troll was shackled in the arena. In the prison complex behind him, the other combatants had been chained up and led out of their cages. Miss Wilson and Mr Montero were going to be the last of the combatants into the arena. They stood with their hands and feet manacled together with just enough chain to allow them to shuffle forward.

When Titus, Oliver, Colin and Mistletoe had left the chamber beneath the Statue of Apollon, Lily had put on Woden's Eye and the Wings of Icarus. She then took a moment to remind herself of the role she needed to play in the rescue attempt. With a deep breath, Lily crept out of the chamber, darted across to the nearby buildings and collected as many stones as could be fitted in her pockets. She then flew into the sky.

The air was cool, and the sky was red as the sun set over the sea. Lily was too high for any Blemmies on the ground to see her, but she could watch events unfold far below. The imminence of the Death Match was making her very nervous, and it was the same for Oliver and Colin hiding in the shadows.

All day the friends had been racing to get to Lelandis in time for the Death Match. Their sense of urgency had distracted them from the reality of the rescue attempt. Now they were here, the enormity of their task became very clear, and they all separately began to doubt themselves. It was very different for Titus. He was an experienced soldier who knew how to control his emotions in dangerous situations. Lily, Oliver and Colin were just students who had started their summer holidays only a few days ago. The wait to commence the rescue was agonising. Every fibre in the friends' bodies urged them to do something; to either get on with the rescue or run away to safety. Their hearts were pumping, their adrenaline was rushing, but they just had to wait, with their doubts, concerns and fears slowly growing.

Titus became aware of how Oliver and Colin were feeling. "Do not weaken now," he whispered. "Everything has been building up to this moment. How you feel will not last, but if you run away, leaving the others to a terrible fate in this strange land, it will haunt you forever. You are not the first young men to have felt this way, and you will not be the last. Have courage, but not the reckless courage that will get you killed."

Nausea overcame Colin's stomach, and he was sick against the base of the crumbling wall. Oliver's stomach felt unpleasant too, like he desperately needed to go to the toilet.

"It's normal to feel sick," continued Titus. "The younger Legionaries are often sick when we form our ranks before battle, and some begin to panic. A cohort is not a pleasant place to be, but if every man sticks together and plays his part, you stand a chance of emerging alive and victorious. Look around you now. This is where we need to regroup once we've completed the first part of the rescue. Now focus on the task ahead."

Titus began putting the beeswax in his ears, and he gestured for the others to do the same before assisting Mistletoe.

The Dwarves, the Blemmies and the King of the Monopods were now being marched across the plaza to the stadium. The Blemmy spectators did not relent in their hostility. This was the cowardly, unfettered nastiness of individuals made anonymous by being in a large crowd. The Blemmies knew the objects of their scorn could not fight back. They spat, hurled insults and threw food. Then the spectators fell silent for the first time since they had taken their seats. Miss Wilson and Mr Montero emerged from the prison complex surrounded by Blemmy guards. Miss Wilson walked tall with her shoulders back and her face expressionless. She was determined not to show weakness, but at the same time, she did not want to show in her demeanour that a rescue attempt was imminent. Behind her steely eyes, she wondered who was coming to rescue them. Mr Montero was still anxious and afraid, but there was a change in how he held himself. The message delivered by the Banshee had given him hope, not only that they would be rescued, but that he might have an opportunity to redeem himself.

The eerie silence continued as the teachers were led into the stadium and onto the arena floor. From high in the sky, Lily watched as the gladiators stopped twirling their weapons and playing to the crowd. They stared at the teachers, the first humans in over a generation to fight in the Death Match.

All combatants were stationed around the arena and shackled to anchor points on the floor. Weapons and armour of different sizes were scattered around the arena among the grass and red flowers that presaged the blood that would soon be spilt. Lily fumbled in her pocket for the figurine of the Banshee. Her hands were sweating and shaking, and there was an unpleasant tightness in her chest. She breathed deeply and tried to remember what virtuous courage felt like by the Bridge over the Infinite Void. She needed to stay focused and control her emotions if the rescue was to succeed.

Lily saw Agon Agathon stand up from his seat far down below. All eyes were now focused on him. He raised his arms slowly into the silent air. The hundreds of thousands of Blemmies in the crowd held their breath. Then suddenly, Agon Agathon dropped his hands. From somewhere below the arena floor, a mechanism released all of the anchors shackling the combatants. The stadium shook as the crowd went wild. The Death Match had begun!

CHAPTER TWENTY-SEVEN

The Death Match

Lily immediately let go of the figurine of the Banshee and watched as it fell through the clouds towards the arena floor. The combatants were racing around, finding armour and weapons. The Giant grabbed a nearby club, and the Trolls ran across the arena floor to pick up two huge swords that were the size of a Blemmy. The Dwarves were working together. A few of them collected helmets and chest plates while the others focused on collecting weapons. The Blemmies had their eyes on a pile of spears. Meanwhile, the King of the Monopods had begun bouncing around, trying to avoid the gladiators who were looking to stir up the fighting. To the crowd's bemusement, Miss Wilson and Mr Montero had not moved. They had smuggled the lumps of beeswax into the arena, and they were now plugging their ears. Just as they finished doing so, the figurine of the Banshee smashed on the arena floor. The Banshee appeared, knowing precisely what she was expected to do. Her eyes turned emerald green, and she released her blood-curdling scream.

When Oliver heard the scream, he took a deep breath and threw the figurine of Geryon against the floor. Oliver's voice was shaking as he instructed the monstrous giant to smash down the entrance to the stadium arena. Geryon ran off across the training fields with his six arms swinging by his sides. Titus and Mistletoe chased after him as fast as they could.

The Blemmies were thrown into complete panic just as the friends had planned. They jostled for space to raise their elbows high enough to cover their ears with their hands. Some Blemmies twisted and leant back to look for the source of the terrible noise, which only added to the chaos.

Geryon reached the portcullis. He placed all six of his great hands on the iron lattice and was about to wrench the portcullis away when he stopped still. Geryon had noticed that Oliver and Colin had not moved. The two of them were rooted to the spot, overcome with fear. At the same time, Lily could not summon the courage to dive lower to join the Banshee. The Banshee was disappearing and reappearing all around the stadium with her emerald eyes glowing and her face and neck straining with the effort of her terrible scream. Then the screaming suddenly stopped. The Banshee had noticed that Lily was not helping her.

The Blemmy spectators removed their hands from their ears and regained their senses. Agon Agathon leant over the arena wall and commanded the gladiators to attack Geryon. The hundreds of prison guards around the stadium also began to organise themselves. Lily, Oliver and Colin watched in shock as their plan began to fall apart.

Titus and Mistletoe found themselves exposed on the plaza. Arrows were now being fired at them from high in the stadium. Titus pulled Mistletoe to his side and crouched down behind his shield. Arrows hit his shield like hailstones on a tin roof. Titus turned to see if Oliver and Colin were safe and realised they had not moved. Lily watched this all unfold from the sky and began to panic. She was puzzled by why the Banshee had stopped. Oliver and Colin were also confused. The friends felt a sudden urge to flee to the passage.

Then Colin understood. He spoke to Oliver, his voice trembling with fear, "Remember... what Arto the Bear... told us? The creatures... from the Avenue of Heroes... will only fight for us if we show courage... I will not be a coward!"

"You're right," replied Oliver, gulping, "and remember what that old man said... outside the Hide of Courage – commit fully... and give it all you've got. We mustn't doubt ourselves. Attack hard and fast!"

Summoning all the courage they could find within themselves, virtuous courage they had felt beside the Infinite Void, Oliver and Colin helped each other to their feet and then began sprinting towards the battle. Lily saw this, and it gave her strength. She too discovered virtuous courage deep within her, and she knew what needed to be done. Lily tucked her wings into her sides and dived down towards the stadium. She grabbed a handful of stones from her pockets and launched them into the crowd. The Banshee's eyes glowed again, and she resumed screaming with even more force than before. Geryon's muscles bulged as he tore the portcullis from the stadium and threw it aside. All three heads roared with pleasure, and he pounded his big, blue chest.

"Now we're talking!" Geryon bellowed.

"I thought you humans were leaving it all to me!"

"Let's smash stuff!!!"

Oliver and Colin quickly caught up with Titus and Mistletoe. "It's time to rescue the combatants!" shouted Oliver.

"*Better late than a ferret*," announced Mistletoe.

"Geryon!" Colin shouted. "Attack the Blemmies in the arena!"

One of Geryon's heads turned to Colin and winked. Geryon then approached the gladiators and began knocking them flying with multiple swinging fists. Clouds of dust and blades of grass rose into the air where the gladiators landed.

"Good job, Geryon!" shouted Oliver. "Now, come with me."

Oliver began running towards the prison complex. Geryon caught up with him in a few giant strides and scooped him up like a rugby ball. Behind them, Colin, Titus and Mistletoe were running into the arena to free the combatants.

"What's next?" Geryon asked Oliver.

"I want more!"

"More smashing things!"

"We need to go around the back of this building," shouted Oliver, finding his new position under one of Geryon's arms rather uncomfortable. "We're looking for a door into the prison."

"Do you want me to smash it?"

"Or tear down the walls?"

"Or both?"

"It looks like you'll need to do neither," shouted Oliver, spotting something that made his heart leap with joy. Mia, Jay, Sam and Joe were peering out from an open door awaiting their rescue. They were surprised to see a boy their age and a blue monster with six arms and three heads. Oliver told Geryon to put him down, and he ran over to the others.

"You must be the students then!" Oliver shouted with a beaming smile on his face. His voice was just audible despite the beeswax earplugs and the scream of the Banshee.

"And you must be the rescue party!" replied Mia, raring to go. "Although you're not quite what we were expecting."

Oliver noticed that the students were staring at Geryon. "Don't worry. He's on our side. Great job escaping! How did you manage to get out so easily?"

"The exit was guarded," Sam replied, "but the guards just disappeared when the screaming started. They also left the doors open."

"We crawled through a hole we dug under the cage," continued Joe, "and then just came straight through the back door without encountering any Chest-Faces."

"And do you know the best bit?" said Jay. "We didn't have to climb into wheelbarrows full of Troll and Giant poo!"

"What? I can't quite hear you," replied Oliver, putting a hand to an ear. "It sounded like you said something ridiculous about wheelbarrows and poo."

"We'll explain later," added Mia. "What's the plan then? Let's get out of here!"

"The teachers are being rescued as we speak," explained Oliver. "We need to meet up with the others and find the waterfall passage."

"Wait!" exclaimed Jay. "We can't leave those Chest-Face children in prison. Can we get this Geryon man… men… erm, thing… to break them free? It should only take a few minutes."

"What children?" Oliver replied.

"They are the children of the two Chest-Faces who are being made to fight in the stadium," Jay explained. "They are very young and very scared. We can't leave them to be sold as slaves."

"Only a few minutes?" said Oliver. "Let's not waste any more time. Show me where they are."

Meanwhile, in the arena, Miss Wilson and Mr Montero had run to the exit dodging the dazed gladiators Geryon had walloped. They barely noticed as Mistletoe ran past them with a beeswax candle in his mouth. Then they spotted the athletic figure of Titus in full armour and, running along next to him, the much less athletic figure of Colin.

"Colin!" shouted Miss Wilson with great surprise. "What on Earth are you doing here?"

"*Lelandis,* Miss," replied Colin with a smile, "not Earth, and I'm coming to rescue you! How are you both?"

"So you're the rescue party?" asked Mr Montero, looking from Colin to Titus. "Well, it wasn't what we were expecting."

"We're okay, Colin," Miss Wilson replied. "As much as I'd love to know why you and a battle re-enactment enthusiast are rescuing us, we need to get you to safety. What's the plan?"

"He's a proper Roman Legionary, Miss!" Colin replied. "The students are being rescued as we speak. Help us give beeswax to the other combatants so they can escape too. Mistletoe has already started." Colin pointed to the beagle with floppy ears that had just finished instructing the King of the Monopods.

"Hand out the beeswax, Colin," said Titus with urgency in his voice. "I'll take the Giant. Colin, you take the Blemmies, and your teachers can take the Dwarves. Mistletoe looks like he's taking care of the Trolls."

The teachers and rescuers ran back across the arena. As they did so, the King of the Monopods bounced out of the arena with an expression of surprise and delight. Colin persuaded the two Blemmies to take their hands away from their ears. He then poked the beeswax into their big lugholes. It was very odd seeing the Blemmies close up. Their ears were the same as human ears, just much larger and in a funny position beside their armpits. When Colin had finished, he pointed to freedom, and the Blemmies ran for their lives. The teachers had a similar experience with the Dwarves.

Titus was having a much harder time with the hangry Giant, who was coping well with the Banshee's scream because Giants are generally very loud. When approached by an armed human, his first impulse was to swing his enormous club. Titus dodged the swinging club multiple times with his usual agility. He then dropped his shield and sword and held his hands out to pacify the Giant. The Giant was confused; nobody had helped him since his capture. Titus offered the beeswax, gestured to his ears and pointed to the exit. The Giant understood and ran to freedom.

Mistletoe had the hardest task of all. Trolls are stupid and aggressive at the best of times, and they did not take kindly to a floppy-eared beagle telling them what to do in their native language with a perfect regional accent. After dodging kicks, ducking fists and side-stepping sword strokes, Mistletoe dropped the candle among the red flowers and ran for the exit, joining Colin, Titus and the teachers. Titus then led everyone across the plaza to the regrouping point between the crumbling buildings. The Banshee's scream was beginning to wane.

Lily had watched everything unfold from the skies. At that moment, she could see Geryon, the four students and Oliver running onto the plaza from the rear of the prison complex. Geryon was carrying the four Blemmy children under his arms. Meanwhile, the two Blemmy combatants were running out of the stadium. They spotted their children, and their children spotted them. Geryon put the children down, and they raced straight to their fathers with their arms open wide and tears in their eyes.

At this moment, the Banshee ran out of scream. Lily commanded her to return to her figurine as the Blemmies in the stadium were released from their suffering. They looked at the arena floor and realised the combatants had escaped. Even the Trolls had worked out what to do. The crowd began to murmur. The murmuring became louder and more impassioned. Individual voices shouted angrily. The Blemmies were enraged. Then Agon Agathon's furious voice boomed through the stadium, "CAPTURE THE PRISONERS!"

CHAPTER TWENTY-EIGHT

Miss Wilson's Combat Skills

The hundreds of thousands of Blemmies in the stadium rushed down the steps to the exits, where they formed haphazard, frenzied mobs. Agon Agathon led a group onto the arena floor and began shouting orders. The hunt for the escaped combatants had begun.

Lily swooped towards the plaza. She could see the two Blemmy fathers grabbing their children and running for their lives. The King of the Monopods had reached the outskirts of the sanctuary, the Giant was struggling to run through the winding streets, and the Dwarves had disappeared among the buildings. Oliver, Geryon and the students ran across the plaza towards the regrouping point. Colin, Titus, Mistletoe and the teachers were heading in the same direction from the stadium.

The Trolls had barely escaped from the arena when they were struck with a volley of arrows from Blemmies positioned in the arches of the stadium. The arrows peppered their tough hides, and the Trolls turned, ready to fight. They were met by more Blemmies led by Agon Agathon from the arena floor. The Blemmies attacked the Trolls, and the Trolls retaliated with crashing sword strokes and swinging kicks.

Meanwhile, Doria made her way out of the stadium with her retinue of loyal followers. She could deal with the disappointment of not watching the Death Match, but she had no intention of going home from the Games without human slaves. Four Blemmies appeared carrying a sedan chair on their shoulders. The chair was elaborately carved and upholstered with bright red velvet. Slaves helped Doria up onto the chair, where she flopped down inelegantly and shouted for her retinue to head to the docks. Doria had a plan to recapture the humans, and she did not want to waste any time. The four Blemmies groaned as they lifted her immense weight.

Oliver and the students reached the regrouping point first. Oliver had already told Geryon to return to his figurine. They crouched down behind the crumbling wall, removed the wax from their ears and watched as the others came running towards them.

"Is that Colin?" muttered Sam in shock. "Did he get captured too?"

"No," replied Oliver. "He came with me and my sister. The three of us discovered Lelandis and came to rescue you."

"Awesome!" replied Sam, "Colin has turned into a super nerd!"

"Who's the dude with the shield?" Mia asked.

"That's Titus," explained Oliver. "He's a real Roman soldier and was guarding one of the passages. After two thousand years, he'd become a bit bored and decided to help us."

"Of course," replied Jay sarcastically. "That makes total sense."

"Nothing here makes much sense, does it?" added Joe. "But yet it all seems so familiar. It's like Earth, but weirder."

"And more dangerous," exclaimed Jay. "The sooner we get back to Earth, the better."

"Oh, and here comes Lily," said Oliver. "She's my twin sister."

The students turned to see Lily gliding down and landing softly beside them.

"You don't look much alike," said Mia, staring at Lily's single eye.

"Our plan is working!" exclaimed Lily smiling. She spotted that the students were looking at her strangely. "Please don't be put off by the wings and the one eye thing. I'm a normal human, I promise."

At that moment, Titus, Colin and Mistletoe reached the

regrouping point with Miss Wilson and Mr Montero.

"Am I glad to see you all!" Miss Wilson exclaimed.

"Are you all okay?" added Mr Montero as he took the beeswax out of his ears. "We had no idea where you were or if you were alive."

It was immediately apparent to the students that there was less bravado in Mr Montero's demeanour. The students began telling the teachers what had happened to them.

Meanwhile, Titus spoke to Lily, Oliver and Colin, "You've done very well so far, but our mission isn't complete. We're still in a dangerous situation. We need to stay focused and not waste time. Is everyone present and correct?"

The friends nodded and were about to address the school group when they noticed their mood had changed.

"What's going on?" Oliver asked.

"The Blemmy prisoners we rescued are in trouble," replied Mia.

"Look!" Joe exclaimed, pointing. "The Trolls have been defeated. The Chest-Faces from the stadium are now chasing the ones you rescued and their children, but a group of guards has appeared on the other side of the plaza. They're trapped!"

"Those children are so young!" said Jay. "They can't be taken away from their fathers and sold as slaves. It's so cruel!"

Without a second thought, Miss Wilson began sprinting across the open ground towards the trapped Blemmies.

"Here we go again," sighed Mr Montero. "Honestly, she absolutely loves a fight. You lot wait and see what happens. This is a side of Miss Wilson you won't have seen before."

"What is the lady doing?" exclaimed Titus. "This is no place for a woman! There are twenty armed guards. She doesn't stand a chance."

"You're right," replied Mr Montero. "She can handle twelve of them of her own, maybe fifteen, but she'll struggle with twenty." Mr Montero took a deep breath. Every fibre in his body told him to stay clear of danger, but he knew Miss Wilson was outnumbered, and he owed her his life. "Right, here goes. You lot keep in the shadows. Oh, and I don't want any of you repeating what you're about to hear coming from Miss Wilson's mouth. She's very careful not to swear because she thinks it's rude, but I'm not sure her alternative is much better."

Mr Montero began sprinting over to help Miss Wilson. Titus followed closely after.

"What do you think Mr Montero meant about Miss Wilson being able to take on twelve Chest-Faces – or *Blemmies* as you call them – on her own?" asked Joe.

"She's only tiny, isn't she?" replied Jay. "She's also so polite."

"Remember those rumours about her going to the Olympics?" said Mia.

"But I always thought that was for gymnastics or horsey stuff," added Sam.

"Don't be so sexist," Mia replied. "Girls can fight too. Maybe she was a boxer or something?"

"Well, I think we're about to find out," said Colin. "She's reaching the Blemmies now."

The onlookers groaned and winced in unison. Without breaking her stride, Miss Wilson performed an amazing spinning kick that had made contact with the nose of one of the Blemmy guards. The sound of his nose breaking was like a firework going off.

"I think that explains it," announced Mia.

"Have that, you clonking, chest-faced snot-gobblers!" Miss Wilson roared. "Which of you turd-trumpets is next for a good flunking hiding?"

Lily, Oliver, Colin and the students turned to each other with their eyes wide open. Miss Wilson's language was certainly unexpected, and her fighting was remarkable.

Miss Wilson had her eyes set on the next Blemmy. She took her balance on one leg, raised her other leg high, and then began repeatedly kicking the guard in the face. He stumbled backwards, unable to mount a defence. The other guards became aware of Miss Wilson's presence, and three of them surrounded her, brandishing spears.

"Three of you sludge-buckets against one, huh? You bunch of flunking cowards!" Miss Wilson sprang into action. With a spin and a kick, she disarmed one of the Blemmies and delivered a painful blow to his crotch. As he keeled forward with his eyes watering, Miss Wilson's laces connected with his big nose. Miss Wilson quickly turned to the other two Blemmies, who were thrusting their spears at her. She grabbed both spears by her sides and used them to propel herself into a backflip. As she was twisting in the air, she kicked both Blemmies hard on their chins.

"You think you fart-biscuits can keep me in flunking prison, do you? I'm gonna flunking clonk you right up!" Miss Wilson followed up her kicks with a rapid combination of punches.

The students watched on with involuntary winces and exclamations of *ooof*, *owww* and *eeee* whenever Miss Wilson landed her blows. By now, Titus was close enough to launch his javelin. He hit his mark beautifully, and another guard hit the deck. Miss Wilson had finished off eight of the Blemmies.

"Where did you learn to fight like this?" shouted Titus as he reached Miss Wilson. "You must be a daughter of the gods! Watch your left side!"

Miss Wilson spun to her left and whacked a charging Blemmy with a flying heel. She grabbed his spear, twisted it around smoothly and struck him on the top of the shoulders with it. He fell to the ground, and Miss Wilson returned to her fighting stance. The ten remaining Blemmies now surrounded Miss Wilson and Titus. Mr Montero was still running across the plaza.

"On my command, let's finish these fish-belching, slug-gurgling FLUNKERS!"

"I'm ready when you are," replied Titus, taken aback by the language.

"NOW!" roared Miss Wilson.

There was a flurry of activity. Miss Wilson resumed her spinning, kicking and punching. Titus thrust his sword and parried attacks with his shield. The Blemmies lunged forward with their spears. One of the guards was felled, then another. Two more followed quickly after.

All the while, the Blemmies, who had defeated the Trolls, were getting closer, with Agon Agathon bellowing commands from their rear. The two Blemmy fathers saw them advancing, grabbed their children and ran for the shelter of the buildings. Mr Montero was finally closing in on the action when the advancing Blemmy archers came into range. There were now only three

Blemmy guards left.

Schoooooom!

An arrow flew past Miss Wilson's ear. Another hit Titus' shield as he ran his sword through a Blemmy. Miss Wilson felled another guard with a low, sweeping kick. Only one Blemmy was left, and it was the enormous Blemmy who had been sent to guard the prison complex door. He cracked his hairy knuckles and smiled as he approached Miss Wilson.

Suddenly Miss Wilson screamed. An arrow had gone straight through her shoulder. The students gasped as she fell to one knee. Titus was pinned down beneath his shield under a flurry of arrows. The students watched with their hearts in their mouths. A look of delight came across the face of the final Blemmy guard. He lifted a spear high over his shoulder, ready to finish Miss Wilson off.

SMASH!

Like a raging rhino, Mr Montero crashed his shoulder into the midriff of the enormous Blemmy. The sound of the impact was like a car crash. Mr Montero and the Blemmy flew through the air, landed and skidded across the stone plaza. Mr Montero was on his feet in a flash, pushing himself up with his hands on the Blemmy's face. He ran over to Miss Wilson under a hail of arrows, grabbed her and pulled her behind Titus' shield.

"Let's get to the buildings," Titus exclaimed. "Once we're there, we can skirt back around to the others."

Blood was pouring from Miss Wilson's shoulder, and the head of the arrow could be seen coming out of her upper back. Mr Montero heaved Miss Wilson onto his shoulders and ran the short distance to the buildings. Titus was close behind with his shield raised.

CHAPTER TWENTY-NINE

Doria

"That would've been so awesome if Miss Wilson hadn't been shot," said Sam, looking very worried.

"Do you think she's dead?" exclaimed Jay. "She wouldn't have been shot if I hadn't pointed out the Chest-Face children!"

"It's not your fault," said Mia quickly. "You didn't make her run over there."

"She looked alive to me," said Lily. "We can't hang around. The Blemmies are slow runners, but they'll soon be looking for us here. Miss Wilson will need medical attention, so we need to get her back to Earth quickly."

"Let's dodge through the buildings in the direction of the teachers," suggested Colin. "It shouldn't be hard to find them."

"But before we do that," Oliver began, "it's time for Geryon to make himself useful again." Oliver smashed Geryon's figurine against the floor.

"I'm back!" exclaimed Geryon's middle head.

"And ready to serve!"

"Just point, and I'll smash!"

"We need you to destroy everything behind us," instructed Oliver. "Topple walls, smash buildings and rip off rooves – anything to make it tough for the Blemmies to pursue us."

Geryon was very excited about his latest task and began straight away.

"Let's get moving," barked Mistletoe. "I'll floomin' sniff the others out. Follow me."

It was now dusk. The air was cool, and there was an eerie silence among the buildings. Occasionally the companions heard Geryon tearing the roof off a building or pushing over a wall. At one point, they thought they heard a brief disagreement between Geryon's heads over whose fault it was that Geryon had stubbed a toe. Only when the companions crossed wider streets could they hear the hubbub of the hundreds of thousands of Blemmies evacuating the stadium and searching for the escaped combatants. Mistletoe soon picked up the scent of humans, and within a few minutes, he had found Titus and the teachers. Sweat was pouring down Mr Montero's face from the effort of carrying Miss Wilson. She was alive and conscious but very pale. Mr Montero had taken off his shirt and wrapped it around the protruding arrow as a makeshift bandage.

"Nobody needs to see you naked, Mr Montero," said Mia.

"Now is not the time for silliness," Mr Montero replied, "or vanity for that matter. My vanity has caused us enough problems already."

"She's not looking very good," said Lily. "It will take too long to get her to the waterfall passage. We need to change the plan."

"I was thinking the same thing," said Titus. "She needs to be taken back through the passage beneath the Statue of Apollon; it will be much quicker." Titus turned to Mr Montero, "It's probably best if you go with your students to the waterfall. I can carry her from here."

"I'll come with you, Titus," said Lily quickly. "I've got Woden's Eye, and you'll need me to lead you through the passage."

"Well, in that case, you'll need an extra marble," added Colin. "Take mine so that you have one each. I won't need it to get through the waterfall passage."

"Thank you, Colin," replied Titus. "Take this in return. It will just be a burden to me now." Titus handed Colin his shield, and Colin's face lit up with excitement.

"Do you want the Wings of Icarus too?" said Lily. "You might need them to find the waterfall."

"You should keep them," replied Titus. "If we get caught, they will allow you to escape."

Mr Montero lifted Miss Wilson onto Titus' armoured shoulders. Titus was shorter than Mr Montero and much lighter, but he took the weight of Miss Wilson with ease.

"Head towards the setting sun," said Titus. "You'll soon reach the river. Then head upstream. Keep within the shadows of the buildings to avoid being spotted. Once you're out of the sanctuary, it should be easy to head along the riverbank. Then it's up to you to remember the way home. We'll see you on Earth."

"And be careful," added Lily. "I could see the waterfall from the sky, and there was a watermill not far from it. I couldn't see any Blemmies, but Agon Agathon will know you're heading there. I'm sure he'll be sending Blemmies there as we speak. You need to beat them!"

The companions parted ways. Mr Montero was now the only adult with Oliver, Colin, Mistletoe and the rescued students; Mia, Jay, Sam and Joe.

Mr Montero led the group as they dashed off towards the river through the winding streets of the sanctuary. Mia and Sam continued to revel in the adventure. They wanted to get back to the safety of Earth, but at the same time, they were having quite a lot of fun. Mia's brow was permanently furrowed on her elf-like face. She ran through the sanctuary peering down side passages with her fists clenched, ready to take on any Blemmy they encountered.

Sam thought the whole experience would be so much fun to tell his friends. He could not believe he had seen a real Giant, Trolls and that awesome blue monster with three heads and six arms. He also saw Miss Wilson destroy countless Blemmies and Mr Montero rugby tackle the biggest one.

In contrast, Jay was very worried about Miss Wilson. She was appalled that the barbaric Blemmies had put Miss Wilson in a position where she had needed to resort to violence. Jay just wanted to be back on Earth as soon as possible. She could then tell the Police about the sanctuary so they could send armed officers, or maybe the British Army, to put a stop to all the barbarism.

Last of all, there was Joe, whose inquisitiveness had started this whole adventure. Like Jay, he just wanted to be out of danger and back on Earth. As the group progressed towards the river, he wondered about this peculiar world. It seemed to exist in parallel to Earth. It could not be in the same universe because they had found their way here through a strange passageway and not on a spaceship. Joe remembered the images he had discovered on the boulders in the passage. They were like prehistoric cave paintings he had read about, artwork from thousands of years ago when humans were hunter-gatherers with no towns and cities. The images on these boulders seemed to suggest contact between Earth and Lelandis for tens of thousands of years. Then there was the Story of the Headless Archer. It was clear this story was based on the Blemmies. In the past, there must have been people from Bridgeward who had discovered Lelandis and Blemmies from Lelandis who had discovered Earth. The most peculiar thing of all, something Joe had noticed at night time when he stared up at the sky, was that the stars and the moon were the same as on Earth, just much brighter.

The sun had completely set, and the twilight was fading fast. The companions had made good progress and were running past run-down industrial buildings. There were coils of rope, rotten boat hulls, oars and fish traps leaning against walls and blocking alleys. Hundreds of thousands of Blemmies were in pursuit. They were slowly and irresistibly flooding through the buildings. Geryon was working hard to hinder them, but it was like using an umbrella to dam a river.

"We're almost floomin' there!" barked Mistletoe, who had returned from scoping out the way ahead. "The river is just beyond these buildings. We're well upstream of the docks and not far from the sanctuary's edge."

"Thank you, Mistletoe," called Oliver. "We must be well ahead of the Blemmies now. They won't be moving through the sanctuary as fast as us."

"And even if they are," replied Mia, "I'll give them a good bashing!"

"I admire your courage, Mia," said Mr Montero, "but you're outnumbered and out-sized. We are not in a position to stand and fight. We need to run."

"Which side of the river was the waterfall?" asked Colin, proudly carrying Titus' shield over his shoulder.

"The far side," replied Joe immediately. "I'm sure of it."

"Is there a bridge?" Oliver asked Mistletoe.

"I couldn't see any bridges," Mistletoe replied, "and it's a floomin' big river. You'll see it yourselves soon enough."

"Do you know how far behind us Geryon is?" Colin asked.

"He's not far at all. I can smell him," replied Mistletoe

"I think his job is done," exclaimed Oliver. "Can you find him and tell him to return to his figurine, please?"

Mistletoe nodded and ran off through the buildings. Moments later, the companions reached the banks of the river. In the distance, they could see the fire pits lighting up the main docks. The riverbank was much wilder where they stood. There were bushes, trees and wildflowers growing all around them. Mud tracks cut through the vegetation and connected the buildings to the pebbly banks of the wide river.

"We'll need to get across at some point," said Mr Montero. "It makes sense to try here where we should be able to find boats."

"Do we have permission to break into the buildings?" asked Sam.

"Yes, of course," replied Mr Montero. "Everyone start searching, and do whatever you have to do."

Oliver, Colin, Sam and Mia ran to the buildings and started trying to find a way to break in. They found a big stick and decided to lever open a double door at the front of one of the buildings. The door began to creak open. Then suddenly, the stick snapped, and the doors slammed shut again. Undeterred by the setback, Mia ran to the riverbank and found a large branch. Meanwhile, Mr Montero, Jay and Joe searched the narrow alleys and side streets at the back of the buildings. They found plenty of junk, but not one boat.

Mistletoe returned just as Oliver, Colin, Sam and Mia were trying to lever open the door with the branch.

"I got to him just in floomin' time," Mistletoe said as he dropped the figurine of Geryon at Oliver's feet. "He was leaning up against a building, completely floomin' exhausted."

"Damn," exclaimed Mia. "We could have done with his muscle right now."

"He's probably knackered," said Oliver. "He's done a lot for us already. Let's hope he doesn't take long to regain his energy."

"Come on, everyone," said Sam. "We can do this without him."

The team grabbed the branch and heaved. The door creaked open even further. Mistletoe peered into the warehouse as the door opened. Then the branch snapped loudly, and everyone fell to the floor.

"Well, there's a floomin' boat in there," Mistletoe announced. "I'll get the others. If we all put our floomin' weight into it, we should be able to break in."

Moments later, Mistletoe returned with Mr Montero, Jay and Joe. The others had found the trunk of a small uprooted tree on the pebbles. It had been washed smooth with the flowing water. Everyone joined in to drag it to the wooden doors and jam it into the gap. Unfortunately, the trunk was slightly too big. Another small stick was needed to widen the opening first.

Everyone was becoming impatient. They were being pursued by Blemmies and just needed to cross the river. All they wanted was a boat, and they were using up valuable time trying to break into a boathouse with doors that would not budge.

Colin and Joe wedged a smaller stick into the gap between the doors and pulled hard. The doors began to open, and everyone else wrestled the tree trunk into the gap. Colin and Joe dropped their smaller stick and joined the others on the trunk. The companions heaved with all their might. The wooden doors creaked and warped but still would not give way. Something was securing them very firmly from the inside.

"STEP ASIDE!"

A deep and booming voice made everyone jump. The companions turned around and saw the Giant striding along the riverbank, still holding his club from the Death Match. They dropped the tree trunk and staggered backwards in fear and awe. The Giant was the height of a two-storey building. It was on account of his size that he had taken so long to get through the winding streets of the sanctuary.

"Do not be afraid," the Giant continued, "I owe you my life. You didn't need to save me, but you did. I don't need to save you now, but I will."

The Giant bent down and heaved at the tree trunk like it was a giant crowbar. The door ripped openly instantly, and shards of timber flew everywhere.

"I guess you want this?" the Giant asked as he grabbed a rope attached to the boat's bow. He pulled it down the bank to the side of the river. "Get in – I'll pull you across."

Oliver translated the Giant's words to the others, who could not believe their luck. They clambered into the boat, and the Giant waded into the river. Within a few strides, he was up to his knees. After a few more, he was up to his waist. By the time the Giant had reached the middle of the river, he was up to his chest.

"The Blemmies are not far behind us," the Giant said as he pulled the boat across the river. "They have already reached the docks, but they have been much slower pursuing you through those damn buildings. I nearly twisted my knee so many times! There are lots of them, so your only hope is to run. They don't stand a chance of catching me on open ground with their tiny legs!" The Giant laughed, and waves spread from his billowing chest.

The Giant reached the far bank of the river and dragged the boat onto the pebbles with a big heave that almost threw the companions out. He emptied the water from his boots and ran off through the countryside. His enormous feet created footprints the size of manhole covers when they struck the ground.

"How come you can speak the Giant's language?" Joe asked Oliver as the companions hid the boat in the thick vegetation on the bank of the river.

"We found these marbles on Earth," replied Oliver. "If people speak a foreign language to us, the marbles translate what they say."

"And they translate what we say into their language," added Colin. "They also reveal passages to Lelandis and secret places on Earth. They are the reason we found you."

"Luckily, you did," replied Mr Montero. "Come on, let's

move."

The companions began marching upriver. The hills ahead were silhouetted against a starry sky. There were no buildings on this riverbank, just fields bordered by wild hedgerows and copses. There were muddy routes down to the water where livestock went to drink, and the companions occasionally saw the silhouettes of cattle standing under trees.

The companions moved swiftly through the open countryside, only slowing to get through hedgerows between fields. When the twilight finally disappeared, they continued by the light of the moon and stars, always making sure they moved parallel to the river. The agricultural land gave way to woodland as the terrain began to undulate. Mr Montero guided the group through a small field to avoid a dense wood that bordered the river. This took the companions out of sight of the river for the first time, but they could hear the river in the distance. The water rumbled and splashed loudly as if the river had become shallow and fast. The students could not remember a stretch of the river like this when they were transported to the sanctuary, but they thought nothing more of it.

Soon the companions were beyond the fields and trekking through woodland. There were areas of thick vegetation in the woods that could not be penetrated. In other areas, the vegetation was sparse, but the woodland floor was uneven, with fallen branches everywhere. To make things worse, the canopy blocked the light of the moon. Mistletoe ran to the front of the group to guide with his sense of smell, and Oliver and Colin still had torches. After making very slow progress, the companions eventually found themselves following a track that wild animals must have made. Their pace increased, and the companions soon found themselves following animal tracks that led them back towards the river.

"What can you remember about the waterfall?" Colin asked the others as they walked along the narrow track, ducking under branches and stepping over logs.

"It was very big," replied Sam. "I'm sure we'll hear it when we get closer."

"And it wasn't far from a watermill," added Jay.

"The mill was only 5-10 minutes downriver from the waterfall," said Joe. "We stopped there for a while before the Blemmies took us to the village."

"I wonder what Agon Agathon has planned for that passage," said Oliver. "Lily told us there weren't any Blemmies guarding the waterfall, but I don't trust Agon Agathon. I'm sure he'll have a surprise for us."

"Which one was Agon Agathon?" Jay asked.

"He's the Blemmy in charge with the big, squashed nose," replied Colin. "The green fox is his loyal servant."

"Well, we'll just have to keep alert," said Mia, brandishing a stick like a sword. "We might still encounter Blemmies before we reach the passage."

"I think I can see the watermill," interrupted Mr Montero. "Can you hear it? I think it's in the clearing ahead."

The companions stopped and listened. They could hear a slow and repetitive sloshing sound. Mr Montero led the group towards the clearing. As the companions stepped out of the darkness of the trees and into the light of the moon and the stars, they saw the watermill by the riverbank. Its wheel was turning slowly in the mill race that was channelling water away from the river. The mill looked very similar to the rustic buildings of the sanctuary, with exposed timbers and uneven walls. The companions also spotted bats darting to and from the building, hunting insects.

Mr Montero stopped and turned to the others, "We need to be very quiet. There could be Blemmies in the watermill. We'll skirt around the edge of the clearing, onto the bank of the river, and we should be at the passage in no time."

"Mistletoe," whispered Oliver, "can you smell Blemmies?"

"It's floomin' difficult to distinguish smells at the moment," Mistletoe replied quietly. "The tracks smelt of deer and wild boar. I also thought I caught a waft of Blemmies earlier, but it could have been a badger. As my mother used to say: *the burly twerp catches the slipper.*"

"That doesn't make any sense," whispered Mia.

"He keeps coming out with incorrect phrases," explained Colin. "I think he's trying to sound clever, but they never make sense."

"Just because you lot don't floomin' understand my phrases doesn't mean a dog doesn't," replied Mistletoe with his voice rising beyond a whisper. "This clearing also smells floomin' odd. There's something very sweet and floral, but underneath is the smell of something far more unpleasant. It's like when you humans finish in the toilet and spray air freshener. Maybe there's a flower garden nearby that's been freshly manured. It's floomin' strong—"

"Everyone be quiet and stay still!" exclaimed Mr Montero urgently. "I just saw movement in the trees."

Everyone followed Mr Montero's orders. The companions looked around to see what was happening. They now wished they were back in the darkness of the trees and not in this clearing under the bright moonlight.

"Stay where you are and do not move!"

The voice came from Doria. She was carried into the clearing on her sedan chair by four dripping wet Blemmies. At the same moment, the companions felt spears being prodded into their backs. They were surrounded.

CHAPTER THIRTY

Revelation and Redemption

Titus led Lily through the sanctuary with Miss Wilson across his shoulders. For the first time, Lily saw that Titus was at his physical limit. Beneath his helmet, sweat dripped down his gaunt cheekbones, and he was breathing heavily. His armour clinked and clanged as he became more fatigued, and his running became more laboured. Miss Wilson was still alive, but her eyes were now shut, and her breathing was faint. Above the buildings, Lily could see the Statue of Apollon.

Titus stopped suddenly in the shadow of a tree at the perimeter of a walled courtyard. He gestured to Lily to keep quiet, and they crouched down. There were four entrances to the courtyard and a dry fountain at its centre. It looked like someone had once cared for this place, but now it was neglected and overrun with weeds and sprawling vines. Voices and running feet could be heard growing louder beyond the walls. Moments later, a mob of Blemmies ran straight through the courtyard. Some were carrying blazing torches with flames that rolled and flickered behind them as they ran. None of them stopped to look in the shadows of the courtyard. Had they done so, they would have easily spotted what they were hunting.

"They have caught up with us more quickly than I expected," whispered Titus. "Stay close."

Titus and Lily shot across the courtyard and through a different archway to the one that the Blemmies had passed through. They then followed a winding backstreet that led to a wider avenue. Just as Titus was about to cross, Lily put a hand in front of him. At the far end of the avenue, in the direction of the statue, a horde of Blemmies was lit by their flaming torches. There must have been more than a hundred, and they were surrounding two individuals in the middle of a heated argument. The two adversaries were gesturing wildly with their brawny arms. The lights of the flaming torches cast every movement in shadows on the surrounding buildings, creating a devilish scene. More Blemmies leant forward and joined the quarrel. Others looked into the darkness impatiently. Eventually, the group split acrimoniously and disappeared among the buildings.

"That was the way I had planned to go," Titus whispered. "We must try another way."

Titus and Lily darted across the avenue, knowing there were Blemmies everywhere. They followed an alley until it opened into a wide yard. Large marble blocks were stacked along one side, and there stood in the middle an unfinished sculpture of a Blemmy. It was complete from the waist upwards but raw stone below this, and it was surrounded by chipped marble, pale dust and discarded tools. There was an open archway beyond the sculpture. Lily peered through it, and her heart leapt. "The statue," she whispered, "I can see the Statue of Apollon."

"This yard is open and exposed," replied Titus between deep breaths. "We'll be easy to spot. I don't like it, but we have no other choice. Let's move fast and pause behind the sculpture."

Titus scampered across the open yard with Lily close behind. They sheltered briefly behind the sculpture and then carried on to the archway. Titus stood on one side, and Lily stood on the other. They readied themselves to sprint over the open ground in front of Agon Agathon's residence to the chamber beneath the Statue of Apollon.

Lily looked back at the sculpture, and she was instantly filled with hate. It was a sculpture of Agon Agathon. He stood with his hands on his hips and his shoulders back. His grotesquely misshapen nose looked imperious as he gazed into the distance, smirking. Lily desperately wanted to run back to the sculpture and topple it. She looked at the hammers on the ground and thought about how much she would enjoy lashing out at Agon

Agathon's stone face.

At that moment, Titus and Lily heard the rumbling sound of hundreds of running Blemmies on the other side of the wall. They could feel the heat of their torches, smell their foul body odour and hear them panting. Titus pressed himself against the wall with Miss Wilson still on his shoulders. Her breathing was now barely perceptible. Lily held her breath, desperate not to move or make a sound.

"HALT!" bellowed Agon Agathon. "Search the area! They will be around here somewhere. I know it."

Lily was horrified. They were so close to the passage, but now escape seemed impossible. She could hear the sound of the Blemmies running off to explore every building, street and alley in the area.

Titus looked at Lily across the archway. "Put on the Wings of Icarus and be ready to fly," he whispered with his hand on the hilt of his sword. "I may not be able to save the lady or myself, but you can—"

"I know you are there," whispered Agon Agathon from only inches away on the other side of the wall. "Stay still, remain silent, and you will get back to Earth alive."

Lily and Titus could not believe what they were hearing.

"I think I have spotted them!" Agon Agathon roared. "Everyone, head to the marketplace and search every side street!"

Titus drew his short sword as the light from the flaming torches faded. Lily was trying to comprehend the situation. Was Agon Agathon helping them? Or was this a ruse?

"I'm going to step through the door now," Agon Agathon whispered. "You need to be prepared to listen to me, or the woman will die in minutes."

"Come then," Titus replied fiercely. "My sword is drawn, and I am prepared to run it through you."

Agon Agathon stepped through the doorway and held out a small bottle filled with a red liquid. "Give this to the woman," he said. "The arrow she was shot with was tipped with enough poison to kill a Troll. The red liquid is the antidote. You humans have caused me more problems than you could possibly imagine. Trying to save your lives without losing mine has been an unenviable task, and I still have to clear up the mess you have left me with. When I sent Lime Fox to get help from Earth, I wasn't expecting her to come back with children. Now listen to me very carefully; you have discovered something you cannot begin to understand. You must not tell anyone about Lelandis and the passages. I am most worried about the waterfall passage – anyone can get through it. You must keep it a secret on Earth, and I will continue to keep it a secret on Lelandis. One last thing, it is important that you find Montgomery. Tell him not to give up hope. I have news, and I need to see him urgently. Wait for me to be out of sight and then head for the passage."

And then Agon Agathon was gone.

Lily was perplexed. The creature she abhorred was now their saviour. She could not reconcile this with the cruel bully she had overheard boasting about the Death Match. Agon Agathon had been ready to watch innocent creatures fight to the death for entertainment. He may have saved their lives, but did he care about the other combatants who had escaped? Or even the Blemmy children he had planned to sell into slavery.

Lily's thoughts were interrupted by Titus. "It is time to go," he said. "We can give the lady the antidote when we are in the chamber."

"Do you trust him?" Lily asked.

"He could have easily captured us," Titus responded, "and besides, we have no option. The lady needs help. He will have his motives. They may be benevolent. They may be selfish. They're probably a combination of the two."

Titus and Lily sprinted through the archway and across the cobbled street to the Statue of Apollon. There were no Blemmies anywhere, and the marbles went cold as the chamber appeared. Titus put Miss Wilson down on the chamber floor, and Lily quickly poured the red liquid into her mouth. Miss Wilson swallowed it weakly with her eyes still closed. Lily could see the colour returning to her face immediately. Titus then lifted Miss Wilson back onto his shoulders, and Lily led the way down the spiral staircase.

*   *   *

"I knew you'd head in this direction," said Doria with more spittle than usual around her mouth; it was as if she was salivating with excitement. "You thought you could escape, didn't you? Well, now I've captured you all, I guess I'll have seven human slaves, and I won't have to pay a thing!" Doria laughed like a croaking toad. "I also managed to steal the wives of those Blemmy combatants in all the chaos you created in the sanctuary. It's turning out to be a wonderful day for me! Look at you all with your peculiar long legs. I bet you didn't think us Blemmies with our normal-sized legs would be able to catch up with you? Well! We may not be fast on land, but we are in the water! My retinue swam me upriver in a boat."

Only Oliver and Mistletoe understood Doria, and they now realised it was not water crashing over rocks they had heard earlier; it was Doria's retinue swimming at full speed. The surrounding Blemmies edged forward with their spears, forcing the companions into a tight group.

"What is the ugly, fat one saying?" Mia asked.

"They're floomin' capturing us," Mistletoe replied.

"I think we gathered that," said Sam.

"They swam upstream," Oliver explained. "That's how they managed to overtake us."

"Are you telling me she can swim?" Jay exclaimed.

"She came on a boat," replied Oliver. "The others towed her along."

"They must be knackered," Mia replied sharply.

"Have you still got that figurine of the blue bloke, Oliver?" said Mr Montero from the side of his mouth. A spear was pointing in his face. "If you do, now would be a great time to drop it."

No sooner had Mr Montero finished his sentence than Geryon appeared out of thin air. The Blemmies staggered back in shock.

"Attack the Blemmies!" Oliver shouted.

"A fight? I LOVE fighting!"

"I warn you, though, I'm pretty tired. You woke me up from a lovely sleep."

"What about the Dwarves?"

"Dwarves?" Oliver replied. "What are you talking ab—"

Oliver did not finish his sentence. The Dwarves from the Death Match rushed from the woods and attacked the Blemmies with the weapons they had picked up in the arena. Fighting broke out all around the companions. Oliver shouted at Geryon to only attack the Blemmies, and Geryon began swinging his enormous fists around with deadly consequences for anyone foolish enough to come into range. The air was filled with screams of pain, grunts of exertion and the clangs of weapons against armour.

"Get to the shelter of the trees!" shouted Mr Montero as a Blemmy flew overhead after a particularly good punch from Geryon.

The companions dodged through the mayhem that was all around them. They jumped over bodies, ducked swinging swords and side-stepped the fighting Blemmies and Dwarves. Oliver beckoned for everyone to crouch beneath Titus' shield when they reached the trees. They peered over the shield and saw that Mr Montero was still in the middle of the melee with his eyes focused on Doria. She was sitting on her sedan chair, looking exposed and worried. Mr Montero began charging towards her, and the companions watched with their breath held. They knew what was going to happen, and it did not disappoint. Mr Montero launched himself into Doria's fleshy stomach. The sedan chair smashed into pieces, and Doria squealed like a pig as she flew through the air and landed in a bush. Mr Montero pressed his hands awkwardly into her face and pushed himself back onto his feet. He stood up, raised his hands, and shouted, "I AM FRED BROCCOLI!!!"

"He's not got much variety with his combat technique, does he?" Mia said.

"No, but I think we can all agree his signature move is awesome!" exclaimed Sam.

Doria's retinue gave up the fight and scattered into the surrounding trees. Doria was left dazed and confused in a bush with only her wiggling legs visible. The only other Blemmies in the clearing were chained up by the watermill. They were the wives of the two Blemmy combatants in the Death Match.

One of the Dwarves put four fingers in his mouth and whistled loudly. From out of the woods emerged the two Blemmy combatants from the Death Match hand-in-hand with their children. When the children spotted their mothers, they ran across the clearing towards them without a concern for anything else. The fathers were close behind. In the chaos of the battle, the companions had not noticed the fathers fighting alongside the Dwarves. The Blemmy children had hidden in the trees.

Oliver, Colin, Mistletoe and the students returned to the clearing where Geryon had laid down to nap, and the Dwarves were regrouping.

"We couldn't leave without saying thank you!" announced one of the Dwarves when he saw the humans.

"You saved our lives," said another Dwarf with a battle axe resting on his shoulder. "We felt like we needed to repay you."

"You arrived just at the right floomin' time!" replied Mistletoe.

"How come you were nearby?" asked Oliver, who had just instructed Geryon to disappear for a well-earned sleep.

"We were heading to the hills," replied a Dwarf with a bushy red beard and big eyebrows. "Dwarves don't do well on open terrain. We need high ground to find out where we are. Like you, we were following the river when we came across those two Blemmies with their children. They warned us about a group of Blemmies swimming upstream. They were following the boat because they had spotted their wives shackled up. We all fancied getting a bit of revenge, so we decided to help them out. Not long after that, we spotted you in the woods."

"It's lucky you did," said Oliver.

"We should all be safe now," said one of the Dwarves. "We didn't spot any more Blemmies on the river, and they won't catch us on land. We mustn't be complacent, though. We need to keep moving. You are welcome to join us for the first part of your journey. I guess you are planning to head south to the human lands?"

"Yes, something like that," replied Oliver. "Thank you for your offer, but please carry on. We know our way home."

"As you will," replied the Dwarf.

With that, the Dwarves bowed their heads and left the clearing. They faced a long and dangerous journey back to the Dwarf kingdoms.

As Oliver related his conversation to the other companions, the two Blemmy families approached them to express their gratitude for being saved. They walked across the clearing with their long arms around each other. They were mentally and physically exhausted but still able to feel the joy of reunion and freedom. The Blemmy children, who had been so worried and scared in the prison complex, were full of smiles that warmed the companions' hearts. Then one of the youngest ran across to Jay and hugged her. Jay was taken by surprise but quickly returned the embrace. The other children followed, each one finding a human to hug. Laughter filled the air, and as the companions hugged these strange, human-like creatures, they realised how familiar they were.

A short time later, the Blemmies headed off into the woods. It was then the turn of the companions to head home. Mr Broccoli led the rest of the group with confidence along the riverbank towards the sounds of the waterfall. Mr Broccoli's confidence was different to the arrogance of Mr Montero. Mr Montero's fragile character had been shattered in the past few weeks, and Mr Broccoli was rebuilding it on a solid foundation of self-respect and self-awareness.

The companions felt safe for the first time during their escape. Their pace quickened, and they allowed themselves to become excited about returning home. The waterfall appeared in the distance, lit by the moon. Soon there were dragonflies everywhere; flashes of electric blue, neon yellow and bright red. The dragonflies guided the companions to the base of the waterfall and up the rocky track that climbed the cliff face beside the crashing water. Moments later, they stood on the rocky ledge behind the falling water.

"Can anyone remember where the passage appeared?" asked Oliver as the dragonflies zipped around, lighting up the space with their kaleidoscopic glow.

"I am not the right person to ask," replied Mr Broccoli, who had been concussed the last time he was here.

"It was along here somewhere," replied Joe. "There must be a carving in the rock we need to press. I opened the entrance beneath the apple tree by pressing a carving of the Headless Arch— I mean a Blemmy."

"That matches up with what Lime Fox told us," added Oliver. "She described a carving of a human partially hidden by moss."

"But she also betrayed us to Agon Agathon," replied Colin. "So we know she can't be trusted."

"Never trust a fox!" barked Mistletoe, sniffing around intently. "The treacherous floomin' bin-raider has been here recently. I can smell it in the air."

"What about Blemmies?" asked Mia.

"Not a floomin' scent," replied Mistletoe. "Over here, I've found something."

Mistletoe's nose had led him to a spot on the damp floor beside the moss-covered rock face. There were two objects: a figurine and a marble. Above these items, the moss and clambering vegetation had been pulled aside to reveal a carving of a human.

"The Banshee!" exclaimed Oliver as he picked up the figurine. "How did she get here?"

"And that must be Lime Fox's marble," said Colin, looking confused. "Are you sure Lime Fox isn't here, Mistletoe?"

"The scent is not fresh," Mistletoe replied. "She was here maybe an hour ago."

"Why would she put these here?" asked Oliver. "It's as if she wanted to return them to us."

"I wonder if she revealed the carving for us too," replied Colin.

"*Where there's a will, there's a wombat,*" said Mistletoe.

"Well, pick them up then," prompted Mr Broccoli. "Let's not dawdle. All of us want to get home."

"Yeah, pick it up, Colin," said Oliver, remembering Lime Fox had swallowed the marble. "Why don't you show the others that cool thing the marble does when you lick it?"

"Very funny," replied Colin, picking up the marble with only two fingers.

"What does it do when you lick it?" asked Joe.

"Yeah, show us," said Mia.

"I am not licking this marble," said Colin as he dropped the marble into his pocket as if it were radioactive. "It has only recently emerged from the backside of Lime Fox."

"Eurgh!" exclaimed Jay. "That's disgusting. What was it doing there?"

"It's one of many things we still need to explain," replied Oliver.

"But what does it do when you lick it?" asked Sam.

"For goodness' sake!" replied Colin as Oliver giggled. "It does nothing if you lick it. Oliver was being a git."

"Enough being silly," interrupted Mr Broccoli. He stepped forward and pressed the carving of the human.

The water immediately stopped crashing down beside them. The companions turned and discovered they could see out across Lelandis. The river still flowed beneath them, and the mill's waterwheel still turned. Beyond this, the companions could see the dim lights of the village where the school group were taken when first captured. Further down the river, and lit by thousands of fire pits, the Sanctuary of Games dominated the vista. Clouds drifted across the full moon, and a shower of shooting stars animated the night sky. The companions turned back to the rock face and discovered it had disappeared. Instead, they found the passage back to Earth and countless dragonflies waiting to lead them home.

CHAPTER THIRTY-ONE

Detective Inspector Cooper

"Lily! Oliver! Come and give me a hug. It sounds like the two of you have been having quite an adventure!"

"Hi, Mum!" Lily shouted with a smile from the doorway of the Old Rectory. A moment later, she was joined by Oliver, who bounded down the stairs using the bannisters to clear three steps at a time.

"Morning, Mum!" Oliver shouted. "Great timing. Auntie Dot has just made lunch."

"Excellent! Come and help me with my bags. I must say you both look healthy. I swear your posture has improved too; you're both standing very tall and proud."

Lily and Oliver put on their flip-flops and walked through the front garden to where their mum had parked on the road. She was standing beside the open boot of her car.

"It's so good to see you both," exclaimed the twins' mum as she gave Lily and Oliver a big hug. "Did you get to sleep at a sensible time last night? I hope you've not been on any more of your nighttime adventures. I can't believe you thought it would be a good idea to wander around in the woods at night, especially after the school group went missing. Anyway, you're minor celebrities now, aren't you? The story is all over the news!"

"It wasn't that dangerous, Mum," replied Lily. "As we told you on the phone, we just went to find Mistletoe in the woods because he was barking."

"We didn't get very close to where the rescue team was

working," added Oliver.

"Regardless," replied the twins' mum, "you were lucky not to get hurt. You two seem to have a habit of getting in the news. Remember that incident in London with the cheesecake and the Queen? Look, here comes Mistletoe. He's the true hero of this story – the dog that found the missing school group! I still find it strange that the teachers and students managed to find their own way out of the cave complex. The rescuers couldn't have been doing their jobs properly. They were searching for weeks and discovered nothing, and then suddenly the school group appears out of nowhere! There needs to be an inquiry into all of this."

Mistletoe ran up the garden path to join the twins and their mum. "I've pinched some more floomin' lunch," he barked. "When you lot go to the kitchen, I'll head down into the Priest Hole to give the food to Titus. Just make sure Dot and your mum don't leave the floomin' kitchen."

Lily and Oliver acknowledged Mistletoe with nods. Mistletoe's marble had recently completed its journey through his digestive system, and it was currently on the altar in the Priest Hole. This meant that now only marble holders could understand what he was saying. To everyone else, he was just barking.

"What do you want me to carry then?" Oliver asked. "I'm starving. Auntie Dot has laid out a feast as usual."

"This one's for you, Oliver," the twins' mum replied, handing Oliver a box. "You'll be excited to know it contains your games console as you requested. It was a bit too much effort to put a television in the car, but I thought you might take it over to your friend's house and connect it to his television. What's his name again? Carl? Kevin?"

"Colin," Lily answered. "He's coming over for lunch so you can meet him."

"Thanks, Mum," replied Oliver. "I'd completely forgotten about that. We've been having so much fun with other things. We were thinking about going to the hospital after lunch to check on the teachers and students."

"Good idea. How are they all? I heard on the news they were suffering from memory loss."

"We phoned yesterday, and a nurse told us they're doing

well," Lily replied, "but we haven't spoken directly to them since they were found."

This was a lie. Lily and Oliver had been messaging Miss Wilson regularly. She was the only one in the school group who was not suffering from memory loss, and she remembered everything that happened in Lelandis, although the flight back to the passage on the shoulders of Titus was a bit hazy. Mr Broccoli and the students lost all memory of what happened in Lelandis the moment they emerged from beneath the ancient apple tree.

Two nights ago, as Lily had led Titus through the passage from Lelandis to Earth, she had mulled over what Agon Agathon had said about not telling anyone about Lelandis. She was very uneasy about trusting Agon Agathon, but her instincts told her he was right; the passages needed to be kept a secret. Lily knew she needed to form a plan. Her first concern was getting medical help for Miss Wilson. Her second concern was the safety of the companions she had left to find the waterfall passage. If they had successfully found the passage, Lily needed to reach them the moment they returned to Earth. She could then tell them to keep Lelandis a secret before they encountered anyone. If the others had not successfully reached the waterfall passage, Lily needed to be prepared to find it herself and go looking for them with Titus.

With Miss Wilson on his shoulders, Lily and Titus had crept out of the Old Rectory without Auntie Dot noticing. It was close to midnight. They ran along the road and ducked through the bushes onto Bridgeward Estate, where Titus laid Miss Wilson by a tree. Lily phoned the Police and explained that she had found a lady with an arrow in her shoulder on Bridgeward Estate. Agon Agathon's red liquid had brought Miss Wilson back from the brink of death. She was now fully conscious but weak and in great pain. Lily explained the situation to her, and Miss Wilson agreed to keep Lelandis a secret. She also pointed out that Titus needed to be ready to hide when the police and ambulance arrived. Lily and Titus then ran off to the old orchard.

Lily and Titus hid behind trees a short distance from where the rescue team was working. Lily was worried. She could hear sirens in the distance, and she knew she would soon have to return to Miss Wilson. As the sirens grew louder and there was still no sign of the others, Lily returned to Miss Wilson, leaving Titus to wait. He did not have to wait very long. Mistletoe emerged first from beneath the apple tree. He was closely followed by Mr Broccoli. Next came Oliver and Colin, then Mia, Jay, Sam and Joe. They all looked tired and filthy but relieved to be back on Earth.

Titus whistled, and Oliver, Colin and Mistletoe ran over to where he was hiding. They were delighted to hear that Lily and Miss Wilson were safe. It was at this point Oliver and Colin noticed that Mr Broccoli and the students were wandering around with vacant and confused looks on their faces. It soon became apparent they had no recollection of their last few weeks in Lelandis. Oliver and Colin decided to head towards the flashing lights they could see through the dark woods. They found Lily and Miss Wilson surrounded by Police and paramedics. The emergency services were then alerted to the presence of the rest of the school group. Meanwhile, Mistletoe led Titus into the woods to find somewhere safe to hide.

Within an hour, the members of the lost school group were in a hospital, surrounded by their families. News spread quickly that the school group had been found, and the hospital car park was soon filled with television crews, reporters and journalists. In the early hours of the morning, Lily, Oliver and Colin finished giving statements to the Police and returned home. Mistletoe then ran into the woods and found Titus. The friends distracted Auntie Dot in the kitchen while Mistletoe led Titus into the Priest Hole. It was not the nicest place for Titus to stay, but it was safe.

"Catherine, my dear!" exclaimed Auntie Dot as Lily and Oliver led their mum into the kitchen. "It's so good to see you! What jolly good fun! Please, sit down. I've made lunch. You must be so hungry. How was your journey?"

"It's good to see you too, Dot," the twins' mum replied with a smile. "The journey was okay, thank you – the usual traffic in London. This kitchen is lovely! You've done a wonderful job."

The conversation was interrupted by a bicycle bell ringing outside. Lily and Oliver looked out of the kitchen window and spotted Colin. He waved and pointed at a dark green bicycle he had just dismounted. A few minutes later, Colin was sitting in the kitchen, tucking into the delicious lunch with the others.

"So I told my parents that I can ride a bike," began Colin. "They remembered that my dad's old bike was in the loft. My dad doesn't have the time to ride it anymore, so he said I could have it. It's still super-fast! This morning, I went on a ride over Wandalgan's Bridge to the Plague Town and back again. It was great fun!"

Lily and Oliver could not help but smile at Colin's joyful enthusiasm for cycling.

"Why don't you ride your bikes up and down the street this afternoon?" the twins' mum said. "I hear you've been riding a tandem."

"Well, the tandem was a lovely thing for Auntie Dot to get," replied Oliver, "but we rode it quite a lot over the weekend. I think we need a bit of rest."

"Maybe," the twin's mum began, "as you've both been so well behaved, I'll look into getting you one for your birthday."

"What a jolly good idea!" exclaimed Auntie Dot.

Lily and Oliver gave their mum a special look that she understood, but Auntie Dot did not. It was a look that said, 'don't you dare buy us a tandem for our birthday.'

"Oliver is right," said Lily, "we rode the tandem quite a lot over the weekend. Besides, we're going to the hospital, remember?"

"Is it far?" the twins' mum exclaimed. "I could drive you. Is it safe to walk around Bridgeward on your own?"

"Mum!" exclaimed Oliver. "What do you think is going to happen? Do you think we'll get captured by the Headless Archer or something?"

"The Headless who?"

"It's a local ghost story," explained Colin. "The Story of the Headless Archer started after the English Reformation when— oh, forget about it. It's just a ghost story."

"How very silly. His bow and arrow probably aren't much use if he hasn't got a head. Does he just wander around bumping into people?"

"Something like that," said Oliver.

When lunch was finished, the twins persuaded their mum to

let them walk to the hospital on their own. The three friends left the Old Rectory, and the conversation quickly turned to Lelandis.

"I still don't know what to think about Agon Agathon," said Lily.

"It sounds like he had every opportunity to capture or kill you," replied Oliver, "but he chose to help you."

"Yet only a few hours before, he had been ready to watch the teachers get killed in the Death Match," Colin pointed out. "That doesn't sound like someone desperate to save them. I also thought he sent Doria to capture us."

"Doria was acting alone," said Oliver. "She just wanted us all as slaves. A few things make me think Agon Agathon may have been helping us. Remember when he spotted us on the roof? Lime Fox knew about the chamber beneath the Statue of Apollon, but Agon Agathon didn't send any Blemmies to check it out. The students also managed to escape from the prison complex very easily. Apparently, the guards just disappeared the moment the Death Match began."

"Well, I think he is right about keeping the passage secret," said Colin. "There are many examples in history of one civilisation discovering another, and the less technologically advanced civilisation generally doesn't come out very well. Do you know what happened when the Spanish discovered South America? Or when the British decided to colonise Australia? Let's just say it didn't end well for the Aztecs or the Aboriginal Australians."

"You're such a nerd, Colin," replied Lily. "I reckon you've read more books than most adults."

Colin smiled. "Unfortunately, I don't think I'm going to find much in my books that will help us understand why Lelandis exists. Its existence turns our understanding of the Universe upside down."

"It certainly does," added Lily. "Think about the Infinite Void – is that like a space between universes?

"What about the Spirit of the Cave Titus told us about?" said Oliver. "Is that some sort of god? I also remember Arto the bear saying gods created the Hide of Courage."

"The marbles are pretty amazing too," said Colin. "Have you

spotted that everyone who came back to Earth *without* a marble has lost their memory? Yet everyone who returned *with* a marble can still remember what happened in Lelandis. Luckily, I picked up Lime Fox's marble, or I would have lost my memory too."

"It's all pretty mind-boggling," said Lily, "and I think there is one person who might be able to help us understand it more. We need to find this mysterious man called Montgomery."

"Lily, tell Colin what you told me earlier," prompted Oliver.

"So Agon Agathon instructed me to find a man called Montgomery. I need to tell this man 'not to give up hope'. Agon Agathon also wants to see him urgently. I thought I recognised the name, but I couldn't think where from. Then this morning I realised. It was when that lady helped us at the traffic lights. Do you remember her? She gave us the energy drinks. Well, I'm sure I overheard her telling a man called Montgomery 'not to give up hope!' I wish I'd seen the man's face."

"We need to find out who he is," exclaimed Oliver.

The friends continued to talk, and they soon reached the hospital. The reporters, camera crews and journalists were still in the car park waiting for updates on the condition of the members of the school group. Lily, Oliver and Colin made their way to the ward where Miss Wilson, Mr Broccoli, Mia, Jay, Sam and Joe were being looked after. They spotted the four students first. They were sitting together in a small common room with a television.

"Oh, hello," exclaimed Sam. The others students turned around and smiled.

"Hey, everyone," said Colin. "How are you feeling?"

"Very good," replied Mia, "although I don't know why we've been kept here for so long. We all feel fine and just want to go home."

"The nurse told us we will be allowed to leave tomorrow morning," said Jay. "It's probably for the best. None of us can remember anything that happened since we went missing."

"So your memories haven't returned yet?" asked Oliver.

"Nope," replied Joe. "It's really weird. I remember following some brightly-coloured dragonflies into the woods of Bridgeward Estate. I also remember falling into a hole, but nothing more."

"We're all the same," added Sam. "We remember Mr Montero bundling us all into a cavern, but nothing afterwards. It's just a blank. Apparently, we have lost over two weeks of memory."

"When does your memory restart?" asked Lily. "What can you remember about us finding you in the woods?"

"Not much, really," replied Mia. "I just remember being tired, hungry and confused."

"What's also weird is that we've all had really vivid dreams," said Joe. "I dreamt that all of us – you three included – were being dragged across a river in a boat by a Giant. It was such a realistic dream."

"And I dreamt about a big blue monster with six arms and three heads," added Mia. "He was breaking into a prison or something."

"I wish my dreams were as fun as yours," said Jay. "I just dreamt about two enormous wheelbarrows full of manure. I could even smell the manure in my sleep. It was disgusting!"

At that moment, a policeman appeared at the door. He was tall with a big, black moustache and bushy eyebrows. His police uniform was immaculate, his boots were polished to a crisp shine and he stood with perfect posture.

"Hello all and sundry," he announced. "What's going on here then? Having a chinwag, are we?"

The students and their rescuers looked at the policeman, and no one said a word.

"My name is Detective Inspector Cooper," continued the policeman, "but you may call me Detective Inspector Cooper." The policeman chuckled to himself. "Now then, it is my responsibility forthwith to investigate what happened to you here students. I would like it to be known that I will be making your acquaintance in the not too distant future so as to question you about what occurred in them there woods of Bridgeward Estate. Is this here understood?"

Everyone nodded.

"Excellent. I am particularly partial to English Breakfast tea and bourbon biscuits. You might want to make a note of that for when I visit. Good day." Detective Inspector Cooper nodded sharply and turned like a soldier on the parade square. He then walked over to speak to some of the nurses.

A short time later, Lily, Oliver and Colin headed to Miss Wilson's room. Colin knocked gently on her door.

"Come in," Miss Wilson called.

The three friends entered the room. Miss Wilson was lying in bed watching television with her arm in a sling. Her whole shoulder was wrapped in bandages. When she realised who was visiting, she turned down the volume on the television and gestured for them to shut the door.

"How are you all getting on?" Miss Wilson asked. "What about the others? Have they regained their memories yet?"

"We're good, thank you, Miss," replied Colin. "The others seem fine. They still can't remember anything."

"Probably for the best," replied Miss Wilson. "I'm pretending I've lost my memory too. It's going to make it a lot easier to keep everything secret. How's Titus?"

"He's safe," Lily replied. "Mistletoe is making sure he is getting fed. Yesterday Mistletoe deliberately got Auntie Dot lost on a walk so we could get Titus out of the Priest Hole and let him have a shower."

"He took ages in there," added Oliver. "He said it was the best thing he'd ever experienced."

"He also wanted us to give him olive oil to wash with," added Lily. "It must be a Roman thing."

"That's good to hear," replied Miss Wilson. "Let's keep him in your Priest Hole for now. We'll work out how to get him a normal life in Bridgeward once I'm discharged from the hospital."

At that moment, the door to Miss Wilson's room burst open, and in strode Mr Montero. "Hello Penny, my dear!" he exclaimed. "How are you getting on? The nurse just told me that we should all be discharged tomorrow morning. You might have to stay a little bit longer though." Without thinking, Mr Montero patted Miss Wilson on her injured shoulder.

"Hello, Fred," replied Miss Wilson with a wince and a sigh.

"Fred? Who's Fred?" responded Mr Montero. He looked around, pretending to search for someone called Fred. "No

Freds here I'm afraid, just me, the one and only Flex Montero!"

Lily, Oliver and Colin immediately spotted that Mr Montero's demeanour was not the same as during the escape from the sanctuary. His memory had disappeared, and with it went the lessons he had learnt in Lelandis.

"I have to tell you this, Penny," continued Mr Montero with a smirk. "I had the funniest dream last night. I dreamt you were in a fight outside a giant sports stadium. Ha! Imagine that! You in a fight! Did I ever tell you about the time I knocked out a heavyweight boxer? Anyway, you were getting beaten up, but luckily for you, I saved the day by rugby tackling your opponent. It was a beautiful tackle – technically perfect. There's a reason why the England Rugby coaches were desperate for me to train with the squad. Anyway, it's always nice to save a *damsel in distress*, even if it was just in a dream."

"Thank you, *Flex*," replied Miss Wilson through gritted teach. "I am eternally grateful."

Mr Montero then left the room as quickly as he entered it.

"What a complete flunking numbnut!" exclaimed Miss Wilson as the door shut. She then caught sight of something on the television. "Oh, what's this on the news? Look, it's about us."

Miss Wilson turned up the volume, and everyone looked at the television. A headline read: *mysterious figure spotted on the night school group found.* A pencil sketch was then shown of the figure. He was wearing a helmet, a tunic and armour over his chest and shoulders. There was a short sword around his waist, and he was carrying a woman over his shoulders. The sketch disappeared. In its place, there was the face of an elderly lady the three friends immediately recognised. It was Gertrude.

"…I was out walking my precious little Digbert at about midnight," explained Gertrude to the interviewer. "I sometimes struggle to get to sleep at my age, so I often go out for a little walk to stretch my legs. I always thought Bridgeward was a safe place, but I no longer feel safe after seeing this terrible figure in the darkness. I saw him running down the road. It was the same night the school group were found. He looked like he was carrying someone. Oh, it was terrible!"

The interview finished, and there was silence. Then there was a knock at the door. The individual who knocked did not wait to be invited in.

"Well, well, well!" exclaimed Detective Inspector Cooper. "I have just had the privilege of seeing a most intriguing interview conducted on the telebox news! An eyewitness account of a rather peculiar looking gentleman carrying a lady upon his shoulders, and at approximately the same time you lot discovered the school group. I have also just received reports on my telephonic device from our forensic team. The arrow what you were shot with is remarkably similar to the arrows used by English longbowmen during the Middle Ages. How very peculiar!" Detective Inspector Cooper paused and glared at the three friends from beneath his bushy eyebrows. His moustache twitched. "Something very fishy is going on here, and I don't like it one bit. I'm going to be watching you lot – I'm going to be watching you lot very closely."

To be continued.

Thank you for reading The Headless Archer.
Find out more about the author and his work at...

www.thomasberrybooks.com

Please recommend this story to your friends and
family if you enjoyed it.